"I owe allegiance to nothing and no one,"

Loo-Macklin told the Nuel softly. Soft and cold, so cold that even the alien who was not terribly well versed in human voice tones was conscious of it. "I owe responsibility only to myself. I have no more, no less fondness for the Great Families of the Nuel than I do for the Board of Operators or anyone else."

A tentacle toyed with an arm of the horseshoe-shaped chair. "You are fully aware, I am sure, of what the reaction would be among your own kind if your work for us were ever to be discovered."

"That's my problem," Loo-Macklin replied, "not yours."

"Quite truly." The lids half-closed over the vitreous orbs, sliding in from the sides until only the long pupil showed between them. "Of course, you realize that if we discover that you plan to function as double agent, we have numerous ways of dealing with such duplicity, and our methods are unpleasant in ways humanity has not imagined . . ."

"I never break my contracts." Loo-Macklin stood and approached the Nuel. Heedless of the slime oozing from the alien's tentacles, he extended a hand.

Books by
Alan Dean Foster

Alien
Outland
Clash of the Titans
The Man Who Used The Universe

Published by
WARNER BOOKS

THE MAN WHO USED THE UNIVERSE

ALAN DEAN FOSTER

WARNER BOOKS

A Warner Communications Company

WARNER BOOKS EDITION

**Copyright © 1983 by Alan Dean Foster
All rights reserved.**

Cover art by Barclay Shaw

Warner Books, Inc.,
666 Fifth Avenue,
New York, N.Y. 10103

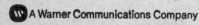 A Warner Communications Company

Printed in the United States of America

First Printing: August, 1983

10 9 8 7 6 5 4 3 2 1

THE
MAN
WHO
USED
THE
UNIVERSE

I

It's very old, the protection racket. So are murder, prostitution, graft and a number of other sordid frailties that technology cannot seem to cure. These faults are not exclusively human. They're found in other intelligent races. But it's in mankind that technological advancement has outpaced the social to a degree unmatched by any other sentient species.

Longevity institutionalizes vice as well as virtue. Sex has been for sale longer than salvation; stealing money has always been more popular than working for it. It was inevitable that a maturing society unable to eliminate such ills would learn to cope with them. Government was agreeable. Anything which can be coped with can be formalized, and anything which can be formalized can be taxed.

So it was that Kees vaan Loo-Macklin found himself outside the simple shop front in commercial corridor B of the hundred-kilometer long cylinder that was the city of Cluria and considered how to go about killing his first man.

There wasn't much of a crowd milling about the darkening street. It was late in the afternoon, almost evening, close to closing time for most shops and businesses. Feeble light fell through the transparent, arching roof of the city, dirty yellow after its fight with the pollutants trapped beneath the permanent inversion layer that covered most of the world.

Within the parallel enclosed tubes that comprised the cities the air was reasonably fresh. The builders of Evenwaith's great industries had long ago given up trying to prevent the poisoning of the atmosphere. It was simpler (and cheaper) to seal each city inside the long glass-and-steel worms the inhabitants called the tubes so that the factories could belch their sulfur dioxides and ozones and chemicals into the sky without harming the human population.

Unfortunately, the native flora and fauna of Evenwaith had no tubes to retreat to, no gas masks to don. Outside the tubes the surface was barren scrub and gravel desert, leaden skies dominating a land of weeds and weak animals. Even the insects choked.

None of which troubled the busy people of Cluria. Business was good and there was plenty of work. What did it matter that you couldn't go outside? There was enough to do inside.

None of the preoccupied pedestrians spared Loo-Macklin a glance. He was clad in a brown shirt that was puffed at the sleeves and V-necked, loose black coveralls with straps over his shoulders, and a black cap.

From a distance he was easy to overlook. He was less than average height. Up close, however, he became suddenly more impressive, particularly if he turned to face you and you received the full impact of his stare. You would also note that there was a hundred kilos of muscle on that squat frame, most of it concentrated in chest and unusually long, massive arms. He wore his blond hair cut short, for in his profession long hair could prove a fatal encumbrance. Sleepy blue eyes examined the world from beneath a high forehead and there was about him an air of lounging insouciance.

It was only an air, however. Loo-Macklin absorbed everything that went on around him. He just didn't want the world to know it was being absorbed.

He had a very small mouth, a nose that had been broken many times, and those exceedingly odd blue eyes that never seemed to open more than halfway. They were certainly a striking color, almost a turquoise, and all the more remarkable for the fact that there seemed to be nothing behind them.

A well-dressed man and woman, hand in hand, came strolling down his side of the street. They passed him as though he weren't there. It was a talent he'd refined, the ability to become part of the scenery.

He followed them as they passed, looked the other way up the street, then put his hands in his pockets and walked casually across the pavement. He was twenty-two years old and had been a registered illegal for five years.

There were a hundred classes of citizenship, both legal and illegal. Of course, you could hold both, depending on your profession and avocations. Loo-Macklin was an eighty-third-class illegal and had spent two years in that status. He was tired of it. Any twenty-two-year-old would have been. But Loo-Macklin was very patient, which the average citizen his age was not. Patience was a prerequisite in his chosen line of work.

He'd started making a name for himself in Volea, a small semi-agricultural city to the south of Cluria. A recommendation by the gang leader he'd worked for there brought him to the attention of powerful underworld figures in the metropolis. For two years he'd worked for one of the city's dozen criminal syndicates.

He'd learned the methodology of operating a large illegal concern. Learned it well, despite warnings from associates not to study beyond reasonable aspirations. He'd ignored them. Thus far it hadn't caused him any trouble. He wanted to be ready when the inevitable suggestion of promotion came along.

He punched in the code on the plastic buttons set into the security door. The code had been provided for him by the syndicate's computer. It slid aside and he entered.

There was a single aisle running the narrow length of the store. Each wall was a long, flat video screen. On them were displayed, elegantly lit and arranged, the store's wares.

Despite its somewhat seedy location, the store's stock was quite impressive. Some of the best citizens of Cluria, or their representatives, made purchases here. The real jewelry was kept locked in a securoom somewhere below street level and was brought up only when an actual purchase had been consummated and credit had cleared.

The system proved a very effective anti-theft arrangement, though it was not perfect. Loo-Macklin could have cared less. He was not there to steal.

The owner came out of a back room. It was five minutes to sunset time and he was clearly impatient to close up. He was quite tall, well-built and middle-aged. He'd chosen to let natural baldness develop.

As he watched Loo-Macklin he removed the contact jeweler's loupe from his left eye and slipped the sliver of plastic into the cleansing case he wore as a ring on one finger. Loo-Macklin stopped opposite a floor-mounted screen which simulated a display case. He still had his hands jammed in his pockets. The owner was on the other side.

"Hello." Loo-Macklin spoke quietly. He always spoke quietly, never yet having encountered a situation which required him to raise his voice. Nobody yet knew what he would sound like if he ever got really angry.

"Hello yourself, citizen." The owner's head nodded toward the doorway. "If you've come to make a selection today you'd better hurry. I'm closing in a couple of minutes." He eyed Loo-Macklin up and down, added, "The cheaper jewelry is in the third section, right-hand wall and in the middle of the screen."

"I'm not here to buy," Loo-Macklin informed him, "I'm here to collect."

The man's eyebrows rose and he appeared amused. He leaned forward, his hands resting on the top of the display screen.

"I'm not aware that I owe you anything. In fact, I don't even know you."

"That's not necessary. I'm here on behalf of someone you do know. Hyram Lal."

The man sighed and looked bored.

"Not again. Look," he said tiredly, "I've told Lal that I'm doing just fine on my own. There hasn't been an attempted break-in here or in my vault for nearly half a year. Maybe he can frighten some of the other merchants on the street into paying him protection money, but the police in this section of the tube are reasonably honest and efficient and I haven't had any trouble. I'd rather pay the police anyway." He smiled wickedly.

"No, that's not quite true, what I just said about trouble. I have had a few problems. About a month ago a couple of sickly looking ghits wandered in and threatened to smash my screens if I didn't succumb to your friend Lal's blandishments. It was really funny, like something out of a history tape. They brought alumin pipes and the first time they took a swing at one of my screens and intercepted the shieldfield I've got running over them they both lit up like a pair of mollywobbles. Took me an hour just to properly deodorize the store.'' His smile widened.

''I find it peculiar that Lal would send one ghit where two had failed.''

Loo-Macklin gave a barely perceptible shrug. ''I don't know about the two men you're talking about or anything else that's spizzed between you and Lal. I only know that I'm here to collect. One hundred credits for six months back insurance and another hundred for the rest of the year.''

The man laughed, shook his head in disbelief. ''That's another thing about your boss Lal; he's overpriced as well as stupid.''

''He's not my boss,'' said Loo-Macklin quietly. ''I work for him.''

''Doesn't that make him your boss?''

''Not necessarily,'' Loo-Macklin replied. ''It makes him my employer. 'Boss' has a different connotation.''

'' 'Connotation,' '' murmured the smiling owner. ''Oh, I get it. He sends along two idiots with alumin bars to try and beat me into submission and when that doesn't work, he decides to send a semanticist to try and talk me into it.'' He leaned forward over the screen, his expression turning nasty.

''Well, I'm not interested in your spiel, I'm not afraid of your *boss,* and I'm not worried about however many ghits he decides to have visit me! He can send along fools to talk or strike and it won't make me pay him a half-credit.

''The security arrangements for this shop are very elaborate, the best available in Cluria and the equal of anything that can be brought in from Terra itself. So I'll run my business, thank you, without your boss' 'protection.' Tell him to fibble off and go bully someone else. He doesn't frighten me. I've got friends, too. Legals. They buy a lot of merchandise from me and they'd be damned upset if anything happened to their source of supply."

Loo-Macklin waited until the owner had finished, then said patiently, as if speaking to a child, "You owe Hyram Lal one hundred credits back insurance and another hundred for the remainder of this year."

The owner shook his head slowly. "A deaf semanticist he sends, no less."

Loo-Macklin extended his right hand. "You can pay in cash or by transfer, but please pay now. You are overdue."

The joke seemed to be wearing thin on the other man. "Oh, come on, I've got to lock up. Why don't you just leave while you're still in one piece and go tell the ghit you work for it will be a hell of a lot cheaper for him to just leave me alone."

"If you don't pay me right now," Loo-Macklin told him, "I'm going to have to kill you." This declaration was made in such a calm, utterly emotionless tone that the shop owner's expression twisted. He lost half his smile, replaced it with half a frown, and ended up only looking baffled.

"Really?" His hands tensed ever so slightly. "You killed many people?"

Loo-Macklin shook his head. "I've never killed anyone . . . before now."

"Well, I have something to tell you, young man. Why I bother I don't know, except that you're obviously so unsuited to what you're here for I suppose I feel a smidgen of pity for you. You notice the position of my hands?"

Loo-Macklin's eyes didn't move from the other man's face. "I noticed them when I walked in. So?"

"So you cannot have a very large caliber explosive weapon in either of the pockets where your hands have been since you came in. For the last couple of minutes, both of my hands have been resting on specially keyed portions of the fake display screen that stands between us.

"This keyed screen runs directly into the power control which operates this store, which in turn is linked to Tube Power Central. If you're holding a ray weapon on me, it won't have sufficient power to knock me aside, either. Should I fall forward and my hands thereby come in contact with the lower portion of this screen, with any part of it, the metal meshing which underlies the entire aisle on which you are currently standing will instantly become electrified. Very strongly electrified, I might add." He peered downward.

"I see that you are not wearing insulated footwear." The nasty grin returned. "You may kill me, but you'll end up just another cinder on the floor, just like the other two your boss sent after me. Only you'll dance longer. So why don't you just leave?"

One hand edged slightly downward toward the activated portion of the display screen.

"Because if I slip, or if I get tired of this little conversation, you won't have the chance to leave."

"What makes you think," asked Loo-Macklin curiously, "that I don't have an explosive or projectile weapon of sufficient power in my pockets?"

"Amateurs," the owner snorted. "That's all I should expect of Lal, I suppose. Amateurs. You poor ghit, even I can see that your hands aren't clenched around anything. Even if one of them was, I don't think the pockets on that cut of trousers are large enough to hold a decent-sized weapon.

"To top it off, you're not directly facing me. You could turn quickly, I'm sure. Physical dexterity is usually present where mental agility is not. But I could fall forward faster. Want to put it to the test?"

"No," said Loo-Macklin with a half smile, "I don't think so. It wouldn't do me any good, because you're quite right. I don't have a projectile weapon in either pocket."

"I thought so," said the owner, exuding self-satisfaction. "More's the pity for you, though, you silly ignorant little ghit." His wrist tendons bulged against the skin as he prepared to slide his hands forward.

There was a small but sharp explosion. Everything happened very quickly.

The owner's hands never moved a centimeter downward. One moment he was standing there, leaning over the invisible proximity field emanating from the display screen and the next he was half imbedded in the fiberstone wall screen behind him, sandwiched in among projections of necklaces and tiaras. Smoke rose from the black cavity that had been his chest, where the twelve-centimeter-long rocket had blown up.

The rocket had come out of the hollow, thick sole of Loo-Macklin's right shoe, which had been pointing at the owner ever since his visitor had entered the shop. It was only natural for a shortish fellow to wear lifters on his footgear.

A very difficult shot, guessing the angle from the floor upward. Loo-Macklin was a very precise person and he practiced hard. He believed one should know the tools of his trade.

He walked around the display screen and examined the body of the jeweler. The man's eyes were wide open. Arms and legs were spread-eagled and the wall cupped the body indenting it like an expensive contour couch would.

Loo-Macklin checked out the hole in the man's chest. He

17

knew there would be a large cavity on the other side, as well as a sizable gap in the wall. The little rocket was *very* powerful.

There was no need to pry the body out of the wall to check the rocket's progress beyond. There was no point in touching the dead man.

The syndicate computer was well-versed in the techniques of protection used by individuals and shop keepers. Loo-Macklin had studied what was known of the store's system for days before deciding on the right weapon to counter it with.

He could have simply walked in and fired, of course, but he felt obligated to make one last try to obtain Lal's money. Lal hadn't insisted on that, wanting to make an example of the arrogant jeweler. "Good advertising," he'd called it. But Loo-Macklin was thorough, and it seemed to him he ought to try to collect just the same.

It hadn't worked. Now there were things to do, procedures to follow. He turned and left the store, careful to close the door behind him. A double glance showed a deserted street. It paid to be cautious. The store owner was right when he'd said that the police in this district were notoriously honest.

The thick walls of the store had muffled the brief explosion the rocket's charge had made. The street stayed empty.

Loo-Macklin strolled casually down the street, found an idling marcar, and eased into the back seat. No one appeared to challenge him as he slipped his credit card into the waiting slot and punched in the address of his apartment. It lay in tube twelve some four kilometers distant, tube twelve of the forty that marched in orderly worm-rows across the smothered terrain of this part of the northern continent of Evenwaith.

As the car sped smoothly along the center street, guided by the sensors in its belly, he reflected on the murder he had committed. It was inevitable in the line of work that society had forced him into that someday he'd be compelled to kill.

He felt no different, nor had he expected to. He'd thoroughly researched the psychological aspects and decided that his own profile fell among those who would not be affected by such an act. He was mildly gratified that his research was now supported by fact.

It had simply been another job, this taking of a life. He had performed it with his customary efficiency. The accomplishment would be entered into and duly noted by the master underworld computer system on Terra and it in turn would probably direct that his status be raised at least ten levels. Perhaps he would even jump into the sixties, status-wise. A successful murder was a considerable achievement.

All he had to do now was get away with it, and that seemed to him no more complicated than calculating the angle at which to fire the foot rocket.

Another car came up alongside his. The single passenger was an Orischian, and the large, ungainly ornithorpe was obviously cramped by the modest dimensions of the marcar. Its cab was not designed to accommodate the alien's two and a half meter height, nor the enormous splayed feet with their gaudy and elaborately tied multicolored ribbons.

A charming folk, the Orischians. They were very gregarious even across racial lines and had mixed easily with mankind since the first mutual encounter several hundred years ago. The one in the cab was male, easily identified by the bright red jowls which ran down the long neck, and by the crest of pomaded feathers running from forehead down its back. Various pouches were slung across the broad back and the long, feather-rimmed fingers were running through the contents of one.

The cab pulled away, accelerated down a main street.

Loo-Macklin leaned back in his seat. He found the Orischians interesting, but then his appetite for knowledge had always been nonspecific. He was interested in everything.

Brrreeeeurrrrrppp . . . the soft, insistent sound came from inside his left coverall pocket, from the device he'd been holding in the jewelry store which the deceased owner had suspected was a weapon. He pulled it out.

The small, flat plate was about two centimeters square. Three LED's pimpled the top: red, yellow, and purple. The purple light was blinking steadily now, in time to the beeping.

Loo-Macklin stared at it, then touched the control on its side. The beeping and flashing ceased. He thought rapidly for several minutes, then punched the STANDBY button on the marcar's computer. It flashed READY at him and he entered a new destination.

He had to detour for one quick stop before returning home. He had an important pick-up to make. Of course, he might be overreacting, he knew. It might be nothing.

Considering the activities of the evening, however, all precautions could be very important. His brows drew together over slightly narrowed eyes. It wasn't that he hadn't been expecting some new threat, only that he'd hoped to hold it off for another year or two. He'd be a little better prepared to deal with it then.

Ah well, if his hand was being forced he would just have to handle it as best he could. Of course, there was always the chance it was a false alarm. If that was the case and his detour proved unnecessary, he could restore the past with little difficulty and only slight chance of being detected.

His apartment was situated on the skin of tube twelve, on the second of five residential levels. It was a cheap district, populated mostly by factory workers and minor status service technicians. The gently curving outside wall gave him a view, however, though there was little more to see at night than during the smog-filled day.

A few stars were dimly visible through the lighter night-time haze, surrounding one of Evenwaith's two moons. A grove of pollutant-resistant trees, a special variety imported from Terra, grew nearby. They gave the otherwise barren landscape an illusion of vitality. At night they gleamed as they exuded water, washing the day's accumulation of pollut-ants from the leaves. Close to Cluria, the only plants that could survive were those that perspired.

He turned his gaze from the window and reached for the illumination control near the door.

"Forget the lights," said a harsh, low voice. "Come inside and put your hands on top of your head."

Loo-Macklin did as he was told and walked into the single room that served as living quarters. Sleeping and hygienic facilities lay in a separate, smaller room off to his left.

The lights came on. Immediately to his right stood a man Loo-Macklin didn't recognize. He was very large and not much older than Loo-Macklin himself. He appeared to be enjoying himself even though nothing had happened yet.

Seated across the carpeted floor on the single decent piece of furniture (the couch was made of real wood and animal skin and had cost Loo-Macklin a great deal) was a swarthy chap he did recognize. Gregor was pointing a very small needler at him. The taller, younger man moved away from the wall and exhibited a similar weapon.

Gregor gestured with the gun. Loo-Macklin obediently moved in the indicated direction until he was standing with his back to the wall.

"I don't understand," he said quietly. "Have I done something wrong?"

"Not my business to say, or to know," replied Gregor.

"I was instructed to kill the jeweler if he refused to pay. He refused to pay."

"Lal knows that," Gregor said.

"Then why are you here?"

"We've been told to get rid of you," said the taller man.

"Shut up, Vascolin."

The younger man looked hurt. "I was only. . . ."

"I said, shut up. He doesn't need to know why."

"I think I do anyway," put in Loo-Macklin. He shifted his stance, careful not to move his hands from his head. "I worry Lal, don't I?" Gregor said nothing. "I've always worried him, since the day he picked me out of the public ward for his apprenticeship program six years ago."

"Like I said, I don't know anything about it," Gregor insisted. "I sure as hell don't know why he'd be afraid of you." There was disdain in his voice, the disdain of the experienced survivor for the neophyte.

"He's afraid of me," replied Loo-Macklin with assurance, "because he doesn't understand me. I don't fit his preconceived mold. He's spent the whole six years trying to get me riled or upset because he feels he can keep control over anybody whose emotions he can juggle. But he's never been able to do that with me.

"So he's decided to use me once for this particular job and then get rid of me. Disposable killer, right? He'll report it to the authorities and gain points with them, so he benefits doubly by the jeweler's death."

Gregor frowned. Loo-Macklin was quite a student of facial expressions. He knew immediately that Gregor, who was after all Lal's number one private assassin, knew that it was true.

But he shook his head and said again, "I told you, I don't know. I just do m'job."

"You're not a bad servant of Shiva, Gregor," Loo-Macklin told him, "but you're a lousy liar. Tell me, do I worry you, too?"

"Nah," said Gregor calmly, "you don't worry me. Nobody worries me, and in a minute you're not going to be able to worry anybody because you're going to be dead."

Loo-Macklin took a cautious step toward the door leading to the sleeping room and bathroom. Gregor's needler rose and he halted.

"Can I at least go to the zeep first? I'd hate to be buried with crap in my pants."

"Tough," said Gregor. "D'you really think I'm going to let you get your hands on anything but dirt?" His fingers squeezed the trigger. His younger companion was a second behind.

Loo-Macklin didn't utter a sound as he pitched forward to the floor and lay there. His hands quivered from the effects of the needler for several seconds and then he was still.

Gregor rose from the couch and walked over to examine the body.

"Well, he wasn't much, was he?" murmured Vascolin, eyeing the corpse.

"No. I expected something more from him. However, he was only a kid. Bright, had a future with the syndicate, but if the boss says. . . ."

Vascolin was frowning. "Ah, Gregor . . . ?"

"What now?" The assassin was holstering his pistol inside his shirt.

"There isn't any blood, sir."

Gregor had just enough time to realize this was so before

his head disappeared. Vascolin whirled and raised his needler, but not fast enough. The gun went off as his hands tightened convulsively on the trigger and punched a tiny, blackened hole in the far wall. Then he crumpled, like a rotten tree, nearly smothering the already decapitated form of Gregor beneath him.

Loo-Macklin came quietly into the room, inspected the two bodies. The silenced projectile weapon he'd used was placed carefully on a small table until he considered how best to proceed.

First he would have to see if the simulacrum was salvageable. The duplicate Loo-Macklin had cost a great deal. The firm which had manufactured it for him was curious as to how he planned to use it. Most of their product was purchased by producers of entertainment shows, since the government still frowned on showing actual murder, dismemberment and other such real violence on the channels.

"I'm going to fool my friends," he'd told them, and they'd nodded knowingly. A simulacrum in bed, for example, was always good for a few laughs.

So he'd stood outside the apartment and manipulated the viewer and controls, seeing the action inside through crystal eyes, speaking through a remote larynx of remarkable precision.

Now there was no question as to who'd sent the assassin, and he'd always had a pretty good idea why Lal might want him killed. He sighed. He'd begun the day with nothing more serious on his history than a few broken faces. Now he'd slain not one man but three.

He still felt no different than he had at breakfast this morning. These last two were more troublesome than the jeweler had been, but only from a technical standpoint. Emotionally, they affected him not at all.

First he would have to dispose of the corpses and clean the

room. Ordinarily, in such situations, you contacted the members of a rival syndicate who specialized in such janitorial specialities, but at the moment he wasn't prepared to trust anyone. The world of illegals was full of gruff competition, but Lal's equals were more allies than enemies. They'd be more inclined to help a powerful syndicate boss like Lal than a mistrusted and unpredictable youth.

It would take quite a while to properly and completely dispose of the bodies, since the apartment's trashall couldn't handle any debris larger than a third of a meter square, but he would have to endure the odious task alone. No, he wouldn't trust any of Lal's counterparts. Loo-Macklin hadn't trusted a human being since he could remember. . . .

II

His mother had been a voluntary whore, which is something quite different from an involuntary one. She enjoyed her work, or perhaps wallowed in it would be a better description. An intelligent woman who could have aspired to something more, she apparently savored the endless and inimitable varieties of degradation her clients subjected her to. It was an obvious case of a profession fully suited to a state of mind.

Loo-Macklin's father remained a permanent enigma, apparently by mutual choice of both parents. He had no brothers or sisters. When his mother had turned him over to the state for raising, at the age of six (just old enough to appreciate what was happening to him), she'd shrugged him off without a parting glance.

He had no idea where she was, if she was dead or alive, and he didn't much care. That day at the ward office was vivid in his memory, if for no other reason than that it was the first and last time he'd ever cried.

He had a very good memory and the conversation was clear in his mind.

"Are you sure, ma'am," the sallow-faced social clerk had asked her, "that you don't want to try and raise the boy yourself? You seem to have the capabilities, both mental and fiscal."

Loo-Macklin had been standing in a corner. That was his punishment for taking an expensive chronometer apart to see how it worked. The fact that he'd put it back together again in perfect working order hadn't mitigated his treatment. He could have turned his head to see his mother and the strange, tired little man talking, but that would result in another beating later on. So he kept his eyes averted and satisfied himself by listening closely, aware that something important relating to him personally was being decided.

"Look, I didn't want the little ghit," his mother was saying. "I don't know for sure why I've put up with him for this long. Anyway, I'm going off on a long trip and the gentleman friend I'm going to be traveling with doesn't want him along. Nor do I."

"But surely, ma'am, when you come back...."

"Yeah, sure, when I come back," she'd said in boredom, "then we'll see."

He remembered the perfume of her dopestick reaching him in his corner, rich and pungent and expensive.

"Besides, maybe somebody else can do something with him. I never was cut out to be no mother. When I found out I was past termination time I thought of suing the damn chemical company."

"If you were so against raising him why wait 'til now to hand him to the ward?"

"I think I was drunk at the time of decision-making," she said with a high laugh that Loo-Macklin could remember quite clearly. It was shrill and flutey, like an electronic tone but with less feeling.

"Doesn't matter anyway. He's here. I know I should've turned him over years ago, but I've been busy. Business, you know. Occupies most of my time. Anyway, I turned around one day and figured out he was always getting underfoot. Besides which I... well, look at him, just look at him. He looks like a little orangutan without the long hair."

The loathing in her voice did not trouble Loo-Macklin as he remembered it. It had been different then, in the office. He'd begun sobbing softly, a peculiar sensation, the warm tears running down his face.

The clerk had cleared his throat. "Naturally, this is your choice as a legal citizen, ma'am."

"Yeah, I know, and it *is* my choice. So let's get the forms together and let me imprint 'em. I've got a shuttle to catch and I'm damned if I'm going to be late."

They'd done so. Then she'd stood, said to the clerk, "He's all yours," and left.

Loo-Macklin blinked and studied the humming trashall. He was almost finished with the last of Gregor's body. Vascolin had gone first. There was only a leg left of the second assassin's body.

He used the tiny arcer, another instrument from his personal arsenal, to slice the leg in half below the knee. He fed the upper half into the efficient unit. There was a soft buzz as the meat was deboned and then the bone itself ground up and shoved into the city sewer system. The last piece followed, the fragments cascading down the ceramic opening in the kitchen chest.

There were dark spots on the counter nearby where Loo-Macklin's fingers had been gripping it. His hands were slightly numb. He forced himself to relax, regulated his breathing. Only rarely did he get so upset.

After concluding the gruesome job he cleaned both rooms and then allowed himself a leisurely hot shower. He put on a plain silver and blue checked jumpsuit with false epaulets and then opened a sealed cabinet by placing the five fingers of his right hand into the appropriate receptacles on it.

There was a *click* and the dual panels slid apart. Inside the cabinet, neatly stored and arranged, were the tools of his current trade. He'd been collecting them for several years now. They shone as brightly as any surgeon's instruments.

Choosing the one he thought most suitable to the task at hand, he closed and locked the cabinet. After spraying both rooms with deodorant he turned off the lights and exited. Loo-Macklin was as neat as he was thorough.

Lal was a small man, but relative physical size is important only to social primitives whose ignorance renders their opinions useless. The guaran lizard of Aelmos is only three inches long, but its bite can kill in two minutes.

The syndicate chief's hair was turning silver. It fit him, gave him a distinguished look, as did the electric velvet suit he wore, its shimmering black field rising a quarter centimeter above the surface of the charged material. The expensive electrostatic clothing bespoke wealth and position.

Lal was a twentieth-class illegal, quite high status for one from a world like Evenwaith. He couldn't expect to break into single number status in Cluria, but he had hopes.

His large private home consisted of many small domes connected to the tubes by security-monitored accessways. Gathered there that night were men and women of all status, from their sixties to their teens, legal and illegal alike.

Unlike some of his underworld colleagues, Lal affected a respectability he could not hope, as an illegal, to actually achieve. But appearances were important to him, and he'd long ago decided that if he couldn't have the real thing, he could at least possess the impression of it. Such grand parties were one way of doing so.

A hand was laid gently on his shoulder and he looked up and around into the face of Jenine, one of his current mistresses. She was a thirty-second-class illegal, a very sharp lady, but one of limited ambition. She was quite pleased with her present role. Her investments in legal corporations were making her wealthy.

In a few years she would probably leave Lal and retire to a life of ease and gentility. That didn't bother him. He understood her desires as clearly as he did his own. There would be other women around. Power and money are ever handsome.

"Something wrong, my dear?"

"No." She leaned over and he felt the warmth of lightly clad breasts against his shoulder, always a delightful sensation. "That elegant young gentleman over there...."

"The one with the mustache?"

"No, the one standing next to him."

"Ah, I believe that's Ao Tilyamet. His father is a twelve and President of the Coamalt Rare Metals Group, Cremgro. They operate out of Bourlt Terminus, down south. Want an introduction?"

A hand ran through his thinning hair. "I never have to tell you anything, do I, darling?"

"No, my dear. Because we understand each other."

"You don't mind, of course?"

"Of course not." He smiled up at her as they started

toward the group of chatting young men. "I would if this
were tomorrow night."

"Tomorrow night is yours, darling, and the night after,
and so forth. But tonight, if you don't mind. . . ."

"Enough said, lady." His voice dropped to a conspiratorial
whisper as they neared the group. "I'll make you out to be
the greatest discovery since the Morilio Screen."

"I am the greatest discovery since the Morilio Screen,
darling," she said confidently.

"When you put your mind to it," he agreed.

"And other things." She smiled.

He performed the introduction and watched admiringly as
she deftly drew the handsome young industrialist away from
several other women. The legals had been fawning over
young Tilyamet all evening, but they were badly outmatched
against Jenine.

Clever girl, he mused. Has to be reminded of her true
station from time to time, taken down a notch, but very good
at what she does. Intelligent, too. He liked that, when he
could relate to it.

As opposed to that insidious young fellow . . . what the
devil was his name? Oh yes, Kees vaan Loo-Mickmin . . . no,
Macklin, that was it. Too bad about him. Showed a lot of
promise. But strange, strange . . . never got excited, never
showed an ounce of emotion, nothing. Dead-panned as the
land outside the tubes.

Couldn't tell for certain where a man's loyalty lay if he
didn't grow a little impassioned once in a while. Whether he
got angry at you or something else was irrelevant. Loo-
Macklin never got angry at nothing, Lal thought. Never
shouted, never got involved.

Robots acted like that, and at least they had the virtue of

predictability. Lal found them more understandable than Loo-Macklin.

He checked his mini-chronometer, an exceedingly finely wrought instrument which he wore on his left pinky finger. It provided not only the time of day and related statistics but also the time on Terra and Restavon. Suitably instructed, it would also offer up computer readouts detailing the various workings of his syndicate.

He left his guests alone for a moment while he used the instrument to see how things were going with the expansion of his drug operations in the southern cities of Trey and Alesvale. Figures blinked at him: production up twenty-four percent, income up 132,000 credits for the first tenth of the year, south quadrant up five percent, north up six, western up sixty-three (have to see who was running western Trey-Alesvale, he thought) and so on, each sector reporting in via the tiny computer link.

Eastern quad up forty-five percent . . . *that was Miles Unmaturpa*, he remembered. *Good man*. Production beginning locally was running a deficit of 42,000 credits for the first half year of operation . . . only normal, start-up was expensive, he knew. Bribes, construction costs running to some 20,000 credits . . . you're going to die, Hyram Lal . . . expansion to southern Alesvale tubes. . . .

He stopped the flow of information, frowning at the tiny screen, and backed the last series of statistics up, then ran them forward again at half speed. The pinkywink was linked directly to the master syndicate computer located in security-sealed A Tube. Either one of his programmers was playing a most humorless joke on the boss (in which case he might find himself suddenly as full of holes as an irradiated programming card) or else. . . .

He gestured across the floor. Two very large gentlemen

who'd been admitting the guests left their positions flanking the single entryway and made their way unobtrusively through the milling crowd of laughing, sophisticated citizens. While he waited for them to arrive, Lal played back the insolent section of material a third time.

... costs running to some 20,000 credits ... you're going to die, Hyram Lal ... expansion to southern....

No, he hadn't imagined it.

"Something wrong, sir?" said the dark man in the brown jumpsuit looming over him.

He held up his finger and showed them the screen, ran through the message for them. "What do you make of this, Tembya?" The two men exchanged a glance, shrugged.

"Beats me, sir. Some foul-up down in programming."

"Maybe something like that. Maybe a sick joke. I don't like sick jokes." He thought a moment, looked sharply at the other giant. "Olin, has Gregor reported back to you, yet?"

"No, sir, not yet." The man checked his own information viewer, which was larger and not nearly as precise as Lal's. It blinked on his wrist.

"No. Nothing from him yet."

"That's your responsibility," said Lal. "Why haven't you notified me before now?"

The man shifted uncomfortably. "I didn't think the delay anything remarkable, sir. Gregor promised to notify me as soon as he'd finished the job."

"You think maybe he hasn't finished yet?"

"Excuse me, sir," said Tembya, "but the delay strikes me as excessive. It's hardly likely that this kid Loo-Macklin, if his habits are as predictable as I've heard, would suddenly up and vanish for a whole day. Still, I suppose it's possible. Especially on the day of his first kill.

"If that's the case then he's probably off somewhere

33

collecting his guts. So maybe Gregor and his bullywot are still squatting there in the guy's apartment waiting for him to show his face. Loo-Macklin may be greenpussed somewhere after sizzling his veins.''

"Not this guy, not this Loo-Macklin," murmured Lal. "He's not the type. Why d'you think I wanted him vaped?''

"I never thought about it," said Tembya dutifully. "That's not my job.''

"I know, I know." Lal waved him off nervously. "I tell you, this kid's weird. Almost like he's not human, 'cept that I know for a fact that he is. I've been watching him for six years. Never saw him get involved in anything except himself. No drugs, no liquor, no stimulants of any kind. Keeps to himself. I think he's been with a woman once or twice. Straight current, no deviations, no aliens, but no involvements of any kind, either.

"He just gives me the shivers. He's too smart for his own good. Tries to hide that, but he can't. Not over six years he can't.''

"If you say so, sir," said Olin quietly.

"Anyway," Lal told him, "you check up on Gregor. Find out where he is now, if he's stuck in the apartment or following this kid around the publicways. I want to know. Tell him no more subtlety. I'll worry about any consequences, witnesses or stuff. But I want it done *now*.''

"Right, sir.''

Lal's attention shifted to the other man. "Tembya, I want you to take a full squad. Get . . . let's see, Mendez, Marlstone, Hing-Mu, Sak and Novronski. Get onto the search programs and find this guy. If Gregor's not finished with him, or tracking him, then something's gone wrong. I've never known Gregor to be this late on a simple vape before.''

"Why don't I just wait until Olin," and the big man looked over at his counterpart, "checks in with Gregor? Like he said, they might just be stuck in this ghit's apartment, waiting for him to come home."

"I don't want to wait," Lal told him firmly, "and I've no intention of leaving the party. I owe it to my guests to stay visible, understand?"

Both men nodded affirmatively. "Yes sir," they said, and turned to leave.

Lal turned away from them, his eyes roving over the crowd. Just a small hitch, he assured himself. Nothing to spoil an evening over. Tembya and Olin would take care of things now. He could relax, enjoy himself.

Ah, there was Orvil Hane Pope . . . "Oppie" to his friends. He was a member of Cluria's Board of Operators, the select group of men and women who ran the master city computer, which in turn followed the programming of Computer Central on Terra. They were the human part of the government.

Oppie was rumored to be absolutely incorruptible. It was said that he attended parties given by noted illegals for the pleasure of seeing what new methods of bribery they would try to invent to seduce him. His weakness and preference for young boys was a very tightly kept secret, an illegal affectation.

Well, Lal would toy with him for a while. No need to rush things. The corruption of Oppie was something he'd had in the works for years.

The presence of the Operator was the principle reason for the party. Oppie's nephew was getting married and Lal had generously offered to throw a pre-ceremonial get-together. You never knew which approach might work best with a legal. Things were so much more straightforward in the underworld. He started toward the Operator.

Alan Dean Foster

The floor jumped up and hit him in the face.

A section of wall ten meters high and as wide caved in behind him. Beyond lay two other rooms and beyond that the polluted night of Evenwaith.

The outside atmosphere immediately came rushing into the open room. Shaken guests, some of them badly injured and bleeding, picked themselves up and began scrambling for masks and shields. Initial cries of fear and pain gave way to gasping and racking coughs as the surge of pollution entered their lungs.

Lal lay pinned beneath a heavy section of steel table. Blood trickled down his forehead and into his eyes. Around him the sounds of wheezing and outrage echoed through the settling dust and smoke. He shouted for Tembya, for Olin, but it came out a croaking gasp.

None of his other people were in sight, not even a waiter. Suddenly a figure loomed shadowy before him, the smoke swirling around its stocky silhouette. It didn't move but stood still staring down at him, as inanimate as a piece of furniture.

Lal's eyes widened and he tried again to scream, but his throat refused to cooperate. The face of the figure was largely obscured by the now dense pollution and the still settling dust, but there was no mistaking that apelike build.

"Stupid, stupid," Lal whispered toward it. "What good will it do you?"

"Quite a lot, I think." The breathing membrane of Loo-Macklin's mask gave his deep voice an unusually hollow tone. "I didn't want to do this. I'd hoped to strike out on my own in a couple of years. You forced me into it."

Lal found he could lift his head slightly. He strained, saw other bodies scattered around the ruined ballroom, looked back toward Loo-Macklin.

36

The Man Who Used The Universe

"For somebody who hadn't killed a soul until yesterday, you're sure as hell making up for lost time, mollywobble."

"I'm not enjoying any of it," came the distant reply. "Just doing what I have to do."

"So I made a mistake. We all make mistakes." Lal tried to raise himself up, to pull free of the table's weight. Something creaked and the pressure on his hip redoubled. He remembered a time when he could lift twice the weight of anyone centimeters taller than him, but that was many years ago. As his physical strength had ebbed, he'd substituted guile, equally effective and far less strenuous. But he wished he had that thirty-year-old body now, for just a few minutes.

He reached up with an open hand.

"You've proved your point. I underestimated you. So did Gregor, or you wouldn't be here now."

Loo-Macklin nodded.

"Well, I confess I didn't think much of you, kid, but I'm going to have to revise my opinion. I'm big enough to admit when I've been wrong. Give me a hand up out of this mess and we'll see about finding you a position more suitable to your abilities. How about Gregor's? You've sure earned it."

"I've earned more than that." Loo-Macklin walked over, reached down and took the proffered right hand. But he didn't move to extricate the syndicate boss from beneath the table.

"That's better," said the hopeful Lal, smiling but only on the outside. *Where the hell were Tembya and Olin?* At the first hint of danger they should have rushed to his side. *Lousy ghits! Well, they'd suffer for it.* Lal had no room in his organization for those who lost either their wits or their guts when the unexpected showed itself.

37

Alan Dean Foster

In the background he could hear the rising whistle of approaching sirens. Rescue teams responding to the scene of the disaster. Good.

"I didn't know you knew a damn thing about explosives," he told Loo-Macklin admiringly.

"I know quite a lot about a number of things you don't know I know about." Loo-Macklin raised the tiny gun in his other hand and touched the muzzle to Lal's forehead.

At that instant the little warning from his pinkywink came back to Lal, together with sudden realization. There was astonishment in his voice.

"You put that death threat in the files. You got into the computer somehow."

Loo-Macklin nodded again.

"But that's impossible!"

"I've been planning that for years, too. I thought access might be helpful, not to mention necessary. I was right. As to your little job offer, sorry. See, I'm promoting myself."

"You can have any position in the syndicate you want." Lal's self-control was beginning to splinter. The plastic muzzle was cold against his forehead. "I'll make you second in line, reporting only to me. You'll be rich and your status will probably double."

Loo-Macklin sighed. "I played fair and honest with you for six years, Lal. I followed every one of your stinking, degrading orders and did everything you told me to, up to and including the murder yesterday. You respond by trying to have me killed. So I'm promoting myself."

"I don't understand." Lal's voice had sunk to a breathy whisper. "None of this was in your profile, none of it. You're not the revenge-oriented type."

"Who said this has anything to do with revenge?"

Lal finally broke. "What then? What the hell are you trying to prove!"

"I am trying to prove something, I suppose," came the thoughtful reply. "Trying to prove something to myself, among the more practical considerations."

"What? What's that?"

"It wouldn't mean anything to you, even if I could explain it clearly. You wouldn't, couldn't understand, any more than a fly can understand why a spider spins its web circular, or spiral, or square, or just haphazardly. It doesn't really make any difference to the fly, of course, but sometimes I wonder if the spider isn't equally curious."

"You're crazy," Lal husked. "I was right about you all along. I should've gotten rid of you years ago, you're completely insane."

"I'm not insane," said Loo-Macklin, "just curious. You're right about one thing, though."

"I . . . anything, anything you want!" Lal was screaming now.

"You should have gotten rid of me."

He pulled the trigger. . . .

The basement of the city was very quiet. Loo-Macklin always relaxed there, away from the swarms of citizens above. His shoulders barely squeezed past the entrance of the narrow ventilation duct. He knew they would because he'd crawled this way many times before.

His backpack scraped against the roof of the crawl tube and he tried to press his belly flatter against the floor. The components and other equipment carefully stowed in the pack were delicate. If they busted against the ceiling his trip would be wasted.

From far ahead came the soft hum of massive machines and the steady whir of powerful fans. The river of cooled air in which he'd been crawling for the past half-hour threatened to chill him.

He turned the temperature control of his sweater up another notch and the thermosensitive threads immediately grew hotter. A light showed ahead, on his right. It took him only a few minutes to undo the seals. Then he was slipping out into the dim light of the basement.

He was careful to reseal the plate behind him. There were guards, but they were stationed at the entrances, outside the doors people normally used. Programmers did not come out of the walls, like mice.

He hefted the backpack higher on his shoulders and started across the polished alumin floor. The room wasn't very big—barely half the size of an average warehouse. It was populated by long, homogenous rows of individual consoles set against information banks that rose from floor to ceiling.

There were usually two seats at each console station, sometimes more, rarely only one. Each station was enclosed in its own transparent plastic dome. The domes would turn away metal-cutting torches, most lasers, and anything else of a portable destructive nature.

A few of the domes were occupied. Their inhabitants were busy and paid no attention to the powerful young man who strode down the aisles. These smaller domes served as communal storage and record-keeping facilities for private citizens. The larger storage facilities, those holding the records of big companies and the government, were located elsewhere.

In addition to the domes owned by communal citizen's groups there were a few owned entirely by single, wealthy citizens. Most served small businesses. Perhaps a dozen or so out of the several hundred were owned by fictitious companies that were fronts for the dozen syndicates which dominated Cluria's underworld. The information they held could be read out from a number of remote stations, such as in-home consoles or marvels of miniaturization like Lal's pinkywink.

But information could only be entered from here, from the basement storage facilities. It made record-keeping safe. You couldn't rob a computer if you couldn't gain access to it.

Loo-Macklin turned down another aisle. No one challenged him. There was only one way into the basement and that was through the multiscreened, security-guarded entrance to the east. If you were in the basement then you had a right to be there, by definition.

He found the cubicle he wanted, number sixty-three, and inserted the code card. He'd spent months working on that card, just in case someday he might have to use it. He waited patiently for the internal sensors to pattern and process the code. Though he exhibited no outward signs of nervousness, inwardly he was worried.

The card would probably fool the identification monitor, but not the far more sophisticated security sensors. What they hopefully would not detect was the unique alarm suppressant instructions built into the code. The machine would read the forgery and sound the alarm, but the security circuitry would feed back according to the card's mobius pattern, cycling over and over on itself. The alarm would go off, all right. It just wouldn't travel any farther than the boundary of the dome.

Only one person would be alerted by the security system to the fact than an intruder was inside: himself.

As he entered, the red warning light on the console came to life. His means of concealing this alert from any wandering guards involved far less than the months he'd spent supervising the design of the mobius circuit for the admittance card. He put a handkerchief over the light.

Then he took the right-hand chair, activated the console, and fiddled with programming for a while in case some hidden monitor he hadn't detected during his earlier excursions chanced to be focused on him. He learned nothing, since he knew none of the proper call-up codes, but to any casual observer he would have appeared appropriate.

It didn't matter that the information that was locked in the computer was sealed away from his gaze. He wasn't interested in stealing information, just as he wasn't interested in stealing the codes. Everyone thought that to gain access to computer storage you had to know the right call-up codes. But you didn't *have* to know the existing codes. They were hard to steal.

When he was certain he wasn't under surveillance he slid the backpack off his shoulders. It yielded tiny cartridges and long, thin cylinders that looked like black pencils. He touched a few contact switches. Tiny doors and panels obediently sprang open above the console.

He studied the exposed circuitry intently, then began removing components and replacing them with selected items from his pack. It took him over an hour, not because he was unsure of location or method but because he wanted to ensure no hidden alarms were built into the fabric of the storage bank itself.

In the event that he missed such an alarm and guards came running down the corridor with guns to see who had illegally entered dome sixty-three, he would use the last device in his pack. It was a small, rectangular blue gadget about the size of a peach pit. Flipped into one of the open panels, it would make an awful mess of the storage bank, not to mention the entire interior of the little dome.

It would also make an awful mess of himself, but that was a necessary risk.

However, no one bothered him, no anxious faces showed themselves at either end of the aisle. Five minutes after the hour he'd entered the dome he gathered up his clutch of substituted components and modules, slipped them into the backpack, and left. Once outside the dome he closed the door and removed the forged admit card. There was no alarm, of course, since the dome was now properly sealed and protected. With the removal of the card and its integrated mobius circuit the alarm system was free to sound once again: only now there was no reason to. No intruder trespassed within range of the alarm.

Loo-Macklin retraced his steps. Two citizens appeared as he was unlatching the cover to the air conditioning duct. They didn't spare him a glance. Why should they? People sometimes attempted to imitate famous people, or guards, or politicians, but no one had any reason to imitate a maintenance worker. There were always maintenance personnel in the basement, keeping it functioning smoothly.

It had been an enlightening if busy night, Loo-Macklin thought. He'd particularly enjoyed the session in the basement. He enjoyed working with computers.

Many a pleasant hour had passed in his apartment while he'd absorbed all the information the city university had to impart concerning his personal computer unit, others both large and small, even up to and including the massive, incredibly complex units which formed the basis of every city and planetary government.

He'd earned more than one masters certificate in both

repair and programming, talents which Lal had not been aware of.

Perhaps someday he might even have the opportunity to make legal use of such abilities. That would be nice. Machines were easy to get along with. They were always reasonable, never subject to human foibles or emotions.

Not that Loo-Macklin wished that he was a machine; robot or computer. He enjoyed being human. It gave you a flexibility no mechanical could ever hope to possess. It was a silly thought, anyway. Might as well be content with the condition you're born into.

But it would have been much easier on Kees vaan Loo-Macklin if he'd been born a machine. . . .

III

They came for him late the next evening. There were twelve of them and they had trouble all fitting in his modest living room. One was sent to hunt him out while the others waited tensely. There were as many different types of weapons in the living room as there were people.

The plethora of devices was unnecessary, since he didn't intend to give them the slightest excuse to shoot him. He knew that wasn't their intent or instructions or they'd all have piled into his bedroom, blazing away. The fact that eleven waited on one was proof they had other ideas.

He relaxed on his bed and changed the channel on the video monitor from the closed-circuit survey of the living room to an entertainment show. The antics of its performers left him puzzled, as usual.

The door whispered and he glanced to his right as the hunter entered. Huntress, he corrected himself. She was very young. He smiled, unconsciously. Typical of the crew in the living room to send the youngest to see how he'd react.

She was attractive, in a hard sort of way, with flat cheeks and her hair done up in a short braid. She carried a spraygun in both hands and was sweating noticeably. A girl, he thought. Not all that much younger than himself, in years. Decades younger in other ways. He kept his attention on her trigger finger and thought how best to relax her. He was more worried about her nerves than abilities.

"I've been expecting you," he told her pleasantly, "though not quite so many."

She stiffened slightly, wondering how he knew that. "Now you just shut up," she said bravely. "You just shut up and come along quietly. There's people wants to talk to you." She gestured with the gun.

Loo-Macklin swung his legs off the bed, continued smiling at her. "I expected that, too. I'm ready. You just take it easy with that vaper because I don't intend to cause you any trouble. I don't like to cause people trouble, especially people as pretty as you."

"That's not the way I hear it."

"Sometimes people cause me trouble, however. I won't try anything. I know why you're in here alone. I don't imagine you volunteered. It's the nature of the kind of organization we work for."

"*I* work for," she corrected him. "From what I'm told, you don't work for it anymore."

"I guess not. Please ease your finger off that trigger. Even if you tried to fire a warning shot with that sprayer, you couldn't aim anywhere in this room without hitting me. A sprayer's not a selective weapon, and it's messy. Your employers would be upset if I happened to get dead before they could talk with me. Besides, why should I try anything? You've got eleven over-armed backups behind you.''

"Am I supposed to be surprised you know that?''

"No.'' He smiled wider. It was a very pleasant smile. He knew it was . . . he'd practiced it often enough in front of the mirror and had critiqued its effectiveness as ruthlessly as he did the technique for quietly breaking a man's neck or programming a recalcitrant computer.

Some of the tension seemed to ebb out of her and her finger did ease off the trigger.

"There now,'' he told her, holding out both hands, "that's much better. Come on, why don't you put a binder on me? It's bound to get you a promotion. Maybe even raise your status a notch.''

She took a step toward him, hesitated. "They told me you weren't to be trusted.''

"That's one thing they've got wrong. I always keep my word. Always. I'm just careful not to give it in situations where I know I won't be able to keep it. It's simpler than lying and makes for fewer complications later on.'' He gestured with his clenched hands at her. "Go on.''

She considered a moment longer, then reached into a pocket while still keeping the muzzle of the sprayer pointed toward him and took out the thin strip of flexible glass. Carefully she wrapped it once around his wrists, pulling the figure-eight tight. Then she flicked the tips off the open ends and touched them together. They fused instantly. A special cutting torch would be required now to free him. No human, not even Loo-Macklin, could break free of that transparent grip.

She stepped back. "There,'' he told her, "now, wasn't that easy?''

"You're awfully calm about this." She was holding the gun loosely, now that he was effectively restrained. "Especially for someone who's probably gonna be dead within the hour."

He shrugged. "Death is nothing but restful sleep. If I'm not going to die then there's no need for me to be worried, and if I am, there's less need to worry."

She shook her head, regarded him pityingly. "They said you was hulled upstairs. I sure wouldn't argue it."

"You may discover reason to change your mind, sweet thing." He stood. "Let's go. Your backups will be getting twitchy."

"You first."

"No problem. But tell your brave colleagues they can put up their guns because I'm restrained. Go on. Enjoy this, for whatever it will mean to you."

She stepped cautiously around him, and for the first time there was honest confusion in her face instead of fear. "Why are you doing this? I've never done nothin' for you. We don't even know each other."

"I'm aware of that," he replied. "But why should I make things difficult for you? It's a hard enough life you've chosen as it is."

"Damn right there." She edged him toward the bedroom door.

They escorted him to the back room of a small dining club on the Upper Fifth Level, the recreation level, of tube E. There were four waiting for him. Two men, two women, all middle-aged.

Loo-Macklin recognized them all, though he'd never met any of them. They studied him openly, affecting an air of non-interest but unable to hid their fascination, the sort of fascination one normally reserved for the snake house at the zoo.

Despite what he'd already done they weren't worried. The glabra restraint was still wrapped tight around his wrists. In addition, half a dozen weapons of varying power but proven accuracy were trained on him from hidden places in the walls. They'd been chosen for silence as well as precision. After all, the club was full of patrons. Music drifted into the room, along with the louder shouts of reveling customers.

He studied them in turn, beamed down at each in turn. "Well, here we are."

When no comment was forthcoming from the four, he added, "Who plans to be boss now that Lal's gone?"

"He badly underestimated you. Happens all the time." The woman who spoke was just a few kilos shy of fat, but was still a handsome individual. Her name was Amoleen and her voice was low, husky. "You got your revenge. That makes it equal." She waved the tip of a dopestick at him. "So you shouldn't mind dying now."

"Why kill me?" he asked her. "My argument was with Lal, not any of you."

"You're dangerous," said a slim younger man from the far side of the oval table they were seated around. "You managed to kill Gregor and Vascolin. You slaughtered at least a dozen other people, including a number of legals who had the misfortune to be attending Lal's soiree.

"In addition, there are at least two dozen others scattered through the city hospitals suffering from severe pollution poisoning." He shook his head. "Reckless, crazy. Why'd you do it? Why couldn't you have stuck just to killing Lal?"

"Couldn't see another clear way to do it," Loo-Macklin explained. Couldn't they see that, he wondered? Probably not. None of them looked especially imaginative. "He covered himself too well when he was alone. He only let his guard down slightly when he was in a crowd, in his own home. Besides, I had time against me. Not much time to plan. I had to move before his people got to me."

The other man nodded. "Revenge isn't a logical emotion."

Loo-Macklin turned blue eyes on the speaker. They were still only half open, giving him that perpetually sleepy look. "Who said anything about emotion?"

His casualness didn't relax any of them. In the past forty-eight hours, the muscular young man standing placidly before them had calmly and deliberately caused the deaths of fourteen citizens to get at the one individual who'd wronged him. They were not about to slumber in his presence.

"He could be useful," said Amoleen. The man next to her shook his head doubtfully.

"Too wild. Too unpredictable."

"On the contrary," Loo-Macklin corrected him, "I'm the most predictable person in this room, if you know me." His gaze passed over them. "Of course, none of you have taken the time to get to know me. Neither did Lal."

"And it looks like we're not going to take the time to get to know you, either," said Amoleen unpleasantly. She grinned at her three associates through bejeweled teeth. "We'll work that out between ourselves, as we'll handle the separation of power. You won't be around to see it.

"You've rid us of Lal, for which we're mildly grateful. He was an average boss, no dumber than most, more generous than some. Knew his business, didn't get greedy like some and try stepping over the proscribed boundaries between the legal and the illegal. Especially the legal. He was a good diplomat, was Hyram. Knew how to deal with the legals."

Music boomed from the direction of the club as Loo-Macklin smiled at her. "Hyram Lal was a pig."

The woman tapped her fingers on the polished simulated wood-grain table. "You're entitled to your opinion. That's about all you're still entitled to. Tell me. If Lal was a pig, and we followed him willingly, what does that make us?"

"Piglets," he told her unhesitatingly.

She nodded as though this comment was no more than what she'd expected from a young fool, turned to regard her colleagues. "I fear Basright is correct."

The older man looked appeased at having his opinion of Loo-Macklin confirmed.

"See, there is no concern for his own safety, no instinct to survive. A person too unstable to protect himself is obviously not stable enough to entrust with anyone else's concerns."

"I'm the stablest person in this room," Loo-Macklin told her. "Also the only truthful one."

"I'm sure," said the slim younger man seated next to the pinched-faced Basright. His name was Nubra and he had an exaggerated opinion of himself. "I appreciate your name-calling. Naturally we have to kill you for reasons other than personal, and now you've given us those as well. Very convenient."

"I'm glad you're pleased," said Loo-Macklin, "but you'll find it anything but convenient for you all if you have me killed."

"And why is that?" asked Nubra.

"Because if you vape me every one of you will be broke within the week."

That pronouncement was just unexpected and absurd enough to make them hesitate.

"What an extraordinary comment to come from a condemned man," observed the fat woman.

"Quiet, Amoleen." This came from the fourth member of the tribunal, who had hardly said a word until now. She sat at the far side of the table and looked like a rumpled housewife. She was clad in clothing as plain as that of the janitorial folk who cleaned the sewers of the tubes. She looked in no way remarkable.

Loo-Macklin knew immediately who was senior here.

Her eyes searched his face, sought hints, clues, leanings. Found nothing. That disturbed her very much. She was very good at reading faces. This strangely confident young man was more than blank. He wore the expression of a vacuum, and yet behind the mask there was a hint of something immensely powerful, a seething, raging emotion held as tightly in check as the fusion reactions which powered interstellar drives.

Draw him out, she thought. This is no time to be hasty, no time to make a dangerous mistake.

"That's a peculiar thing for a condemned man to say, especially one so young. Can you justify it?"

"Oh now, really, Khryswhy," muttered Nubra, "we waste time with this one."

"I want to be sure," she told him firmly, turning back to Loo-Macklin. "Well? We're waiting, and you don't have much time left."

He focused his attention on her, instantly blotting out the presence of the other three. As far as he was concerned, they'd ceased to exist. At last he could deal with someone in a position to make decisions.

"You have at least one monitor recording this meeting?"
She nodded.

"And therefore the usual computer links. Try and call up the figures for, oh, say the number of bribes that are due and payable and to which police officers in the central tubes for the next six months. Also what forms the bribes are to take: jewelry, money, women, men. Where the drops are to be made.

"That's a very small detail but important to the steady functioning of the syndicate. Surely all of you have them memorized and don't even need to use your computer?"

She glanced over at Basright. "Put away that toy pistol you've been holding and ask the question." The older man nodded, rose and walked over to the wall, holstering his syringer as he did so. At the wall he touched a button. A section of imitation wood slid upward, revealing a video monitor and accompanying entryboard.

"Ask again," she told Loo-Macklin, "in case he missed something."

Loo-Macklin obediently repeated the comment.

Basright, who was obviously much more than just an over-age gunman, punched in the complex question. The monitor screen was large enough for everyone to read the information it would display without leaving their seats.

The computer responded promptly to the inquiry.

INFORMATION NO LONGER IN FILES

"Try again," said Khryswhy, while the woman named Amoleen and the suddenly uncertain Nubra began to fidget uneasily.

Basright repeated the query, slowly this time, and again was rewarded with the response:

INFORMATION NO LONGER IN FILES

He looked helplessly toward Khryswhy.
"Pursue it," she said grimly.
He nodded, punched in fresh codes.

WHY REQUESTED INFORMATION NO LONGER IN FILES?
INFORMATION REMOVED 0-4-26: 02:35

Basright licked thin lips, his long fingers working at the entryboard.

INFORMATION REMOVED BY WHOM?

The computer hesitated a second before announcing firmly:

QUALIFIED PERSONNEL
WHAT QUALIFIED PERSONNEL?
INFORMATION NO LONGER IN FILES

Loo-Macklin allowed that to burn on the screen for a minute, then glanced down at the plain, thoughtful Khryswhy. "Want to try something else? How about asking it when and where and in what quantity the next shipment of green screamers are coming into your distribution system? Or for that matter, any other syndicate pharmaceuticals?"

"You lousy, meddling mollywobble!" Nubra started to rise, expressing both confusion and anger.

Khryswhy glanced sharply at him. "Sit down, Nubra, and don't play the idiot." The young man hesitated, slowly resumed his seat and contented himself with glaring at Loo-Macklin.

"How'd you do it?" Khryswhy asked him.

He held up his bound wrists. "I volunteered to permit these. I'd like them removed with equally little hassle."

She nodded, touched a hidden button. The door opened and the girl who'd placed them on his wrists came into the room. She looked at him uncertainly as she used an eyedropper to drip debonder on the binder. The glass dissolved and broke apart.

"Thank you," he told her. She nodded, backed toward the doorway, her eyes never leaving him.

"All the critical information," he told Khryswhy, "and most of what's less critical, has been removed from the ninth syndicate's storage bank."

"Removed to where?" asked Amoleen nervously.

"To a place of safety," he told her. "A place where it will be safe so that I'll be safe."

"What are you going to do with it?" asked Basright curiously. "Turn it over to the government for reward money?"

Loo-Macklin shook his head. "Now wouldn't that be a terrible waste? Lal may have been a pig, but he was a good business pig. I have instant access to all the removed information via my personal coding system. I'm not about to tell you in which private bank the information has been placed, and I assure you you could never find it.

"I know you won't take my word for it." He smiled. "After all, I'm unstable and unpredictable. If you'll permit me?" He approached the console. Basright stepped out of his way.

He looked back at Khryswhy. "Remember the question?"

"Well enough," she told him.

He turned to the board, thought a moment, and then ran his fingers over the keys. They touched lightly on the contacts, delicate as the fluttering of a muscian's hands. Basright and any hidden monitor were shielded from sight of his moving fingers.

Immediately a long series of figures and words, accompanied by matching illustrations, materialized on the screen.

"Very well," said Khryswhy, "so you have access to the information you stole. What if we force you to give us your private retrieval codes?"

55

"You can't do that." Loo-Macklin told her softly.

"Want to bet?" Nubra was starting out of his chair again.

"Idiot," Khryswhy looked bored with him. "I told you to *sit down*."

He hesitated, half pleading with her. "But Khrys, let me have him for half an hour. Give me Mule and Pioptolus. We can make him talk." He looked nastily at the unmoving Loo-Macklin. "He'll tell us everything he knows and wish he had more to tell us when we've started on him."

"Don't you see what we're dealing with here?" she said exasperatedly to the younger man. "Don't you see that he doesn't care? You can't make somebody like that talk. And if you go too far and kill him, which I wouldn't put past you, Nubra, the information will stay hidden permanently. And then where would we all be?"

"Broke," Loo-Macklin told her. "You might even have to go legal, and that would mean starting at the bottom, status one hundred."

She ignored that. "Anyway, he's right about one thing. Business is good. I'd like to keep it that way." She turned to him. "What is it you want, kid?"

"To begin with you can remember never to call me kid again." He strolled over to the table, pulled up a free chair, and sat down facing them, folding his hands on the smooth surface.

"I intend to keep the syndicate running profitably and efficiently. Within a year's time we will see its income tripled."

Amoleen burst out laughing. "Now how do you propose to do that?"

"By having my orders followed explicitly."

"*Your* orders?" Nubra was so furious he was shaking. "If anyone should give orders around here, it might as well be me. I'm a thirty-third-class illegal, I've been in the organized underworld for ten years. I've been. . . ."

"Loud, abusive, and stupid, most of that time," said Loo-Macklin, cutting him off. Nubra ground his teeth and glared at Loo-Macklin, but didn't reply. Not with Khryswhy staring him down.

"If you need proof of that," Loo-Macklin continued pleasantly, "there's the undeniable fact that you've spent the last ten years of your life being ordered about by a pig. Because of my build, I've often been called an ape. I consider that a step up in class. There's no shame in pigs taking orders from an ape."

"You're asking a lot," said Khryswhy. "We're doing quite well right now." She lit a dopestick and he noticed a flicker of real interest in her eyes. "You really think, though, that you can triple the syndicate's income within a year?"

He nodded slowly.

"You know what I think?" she continued, puffing away on the thin red smoke. "I think you're a bold liar and a dangerous maniac"

Here was a woman he could use, Loo-Macklin thought. "Does that really matter to you?"

"Not if you can do what you claim. If you can't, well, we have a year in which to puzzle out a way to learn those new codes. Then we can steal our records back and have you put in your proper element, say, six meters of foundation stone. Time will be working against you, not for you."

"But consider," he said calmly, despite the threat, "what if I succeed?"

"In that case," she told him, "I could give a damn what you've done with the records. You can keep 'em a secret forever if you want, and I'll do everything in my power to assist your efforts."

"Khryswhy!" exclaimed the fat woman, shocked.

"We may as well give him his chance, Amoleen," was the resigned reply. "We have no choice. Be philosophical. Sometimes the insane can accomplish more than the sane. I'd rather be ordered about by an efficient madman than a mediocre sane one."

"But he's dangerous." Amoleen avoided Loo-Macklin's eyes. Such sleepy eyes! Would they never know for certain what was going on behind them?

"To himself, maybe," said Khryswhy, "but I don't think to us. Where would you like to begin . . . boss?" She looked around the table.

"Nubra?" The younger man's anger hadn't subsided, but he nodded reluctant agreement. "Basright?" The older man shrugged, said nothing. "Amoleen?"

"My dear Khrys," the fat woman said, "this all goes against my better judgment. However," she sighed dramatically and glanced at Loo-Macklin, "as you say, whatever our personal opinions, we've not been given much of a choice."

"None whatsoever," said Loo-Macklin firmly.

"Then that's settled." Khryswhy leaned across the table and extended an open hand. Each of her fingernails glowed with a different shade of polish.

"The pig is dead. Long live the ape."

Loo-Macklin noted that she had a very firm handshake. He would watch her carefully. He would watch everything carefully.

IV

The heavily muscled body had not grown any softer. The haircut was still the same. Half-lidded eyes still gave him that perpetually sleepy expression.

But around Loo-Macklin there had been many changes in the five years that had passed.

The conference room was on the uppermost level of G tube, not far from the offices of the city and planetary government; an irony which Loo-Macklin appreciated. The name of the false corporation which fronted for the syndicate appeared in bold iridium letters outside the double doors: Enigman, Ltd. That was as close as he ever came to true humor.

There were no tables in the conference chamber. Loo-Macklin disdained tables. They separated people, put a barrier between personalities and conversation. They also made it difficult to quickly jump anyone pulling a weapon on you.

Instead, there were numerous couches and chairs scattered casually about. They were made of flexglas and a plushdown fungus from one of the Arilian worlds, a non-chlorophyllic growth that was springy and molded itself to every nook and cranny of the body. To sit in such a chair was to experience the sensation of being held in the gloved hand of a giant. The chairs never had to be cleaned, only cropped. They were very expensive.

Loo-Macklin could afford them.

Khryswhy entered. She was eight years older than Loo-Macklin but her figure had remained trim and there were no additional lines in her face. Only in her mind. She pirouetted for him and the new dress danced.

"What do you think, Kees?"

He admired the emerald and yellow creation, a combination of several diaphanous layers of thin material held apart by electrostatically charged layers of air. She seemed enveloped by several ghosts instead of clothing.

"Very aesthetic," he told her.

She stopped twirling and shook a scolding finger at him. The first two years had been awkward, but she'd softened considerably in the last three. She'd warmed to Loo-Macklin and tried to soften him, too.

He was damned if he could understand why. He never encouraged the attentions of such women and for the life of him couldn't understand why so many of them seemed to find him attractive. It was a puzzlement.

Not that he denied normal bodily urges or saw any virtue in celibacy. That was for stoics and Athabascans. It was simply that he had neither the capacity nor desire for emotional entanglement.

He quite enjoyed sex, much as he did good food, entertainment, and especially reading. He also continued his education through privately constructed computer tutorial programming. And the more he learned, the more ignorant he became.

The sign of a truly wise man, which only another wise man could understand.

Coyness was lost on Loo-Macklin. Khryswhy walked over to his chair and stepped behind it, put a hand on his shoulder.

"It took three weeks to make this dress. The electronics for maintaining the layer separation cost five thousand credits by themselves. The least you could do is say that it's pretty, Kees. Aesthetic sounds so damn distant."

He looked back and up with one of his carefully modulated smiles, which no one else seemed to realize was as artificial as the fabric of her caftan. The effect, however, was equally brilliant.

He permitted her the familiarity of using his first name because it allowed her to think she had some kind of personal bind on his thoughts, when in actuality the opposite was true.

Look at her, he thought admiringly as she stepped away from him. *Difficult to believe she is one of the more ruthless illegals on Evenwaith.* Or anywhere, for that matter. She ran all of the Enigman, Ltd.'s illegal prostitution operations and did so with a cool, businesslike hand. She was familiar with every perversion favored by man and woman and knew how best to satisfy them.

If not for her face and figure, he could certainly admire her for her efficiency.

Basright joined them in the conference room. He spared a glance for the revealing dress Khryswhy was displaying, looked away disapprovingly. The older man's tastes ran to the peculiar and difficult, which one in his position could always manage to satisfy. It was a weakness he regretted, but he never let it interfere with business.

Loo-Macklin was aware of it, of course. He admired Basright's control. The man had a center, which few humans did.

"I guess we can get started," he told Basright.

The woman stopped cavorting, hesitated. She looked toward the doorway, then back at Loo-Macklin, and frowned.

"Wait a minute, Kees. Where're Nubra and Amoleen?"

Loo-Macklin swung the small computer monitor up out of the arm of his chair and around in front of him on its flexible arm. He looked sleepily at her.

"Amoleen died yesterday, Nubra just this morning."

Basright took a chair, suddenly nervous. "What happened, Kees?"

Loo-Macklin smiled at him. "I think you know what happened"

The older man's thinness exaggerated his shaking. "No. No, I didn't. . . ."

Loo-Macklin continued smiling at him, his eyes fully open. Basright always had to look away from that opaline stare. It was nothing to be ashamed of. Stronger men and women reacted the same way.

"All right, I admit it. I knew what was going on."

"You didn't tell me about it," said Loo-Macklin, his tone mildly accusing.

The man turned back to him, pleading with his eyes. Off to one side, Khryswhy was dividing her attention between the two men. She looked thoroughly dumbfounded.

"I . . . I didn't know what to do, sir," Basright mumbled. They put me in a very difficult position. They wanted me to go in with them at first. I said no. . . ."

"Go in with them on what?" wondered Khryswhy aloud. "What's going on here, Kees?"

"Be quiet, Khrys. You'll find out."

"Find out, hell! I want to know wh. . . ."

She broke off. Loo-Macklin turned and gave her a particularly sharp look. "Khrys. . . ."

She'd heard that tone before—harsh and devoid of compassion. The pretense of familiarity that had existed between them prior to Basright's entrance vanished. She was now merely another employee, nothing more.

Slowly she took a seat, the folds of her dress collapsing beneath her, while above her body the chiffon-like material continued to drift gently in the air.

Loo-Macklin returned his attention to the now sweating Basright.

"They said they'd kill me," he remonstrated with his boss, "if I didn't go along with them. I didn't know what to do. . . ."

"Why didn't you come to me?"

"They were on me all the time, clockabout, sir. I'm not into violence. I've always been interested in the ledger side of syndicate operations. You know Nubra, what he was like. Always ready for a fight. He never liked me, that wipsipper. He would've killed me right there if Amoleen hadn't intervened. Said they couldn't do anything until after they'd. . . taken care of you.

"So. . . I told them I'd cooperate, but passively. Nubra wanted more than that, damn him, but he wasn't sure what. They hadn't finalized their plans yet. I didn't want to go in with them . . . I didn't want to see you replaced. You've done everything with the syndicate you said you would. You've been fair with me. And I'm neither jealous nor power-hungry, like Nubra and Amoleen are . . . were."

"That's always been one of your greatest qualities, Basright," said Loo-Macklin approvingly. "You're not terribly smart, but you're smart enough to recognize when someone's smarter than yourself. You're a plodder, not an innovator. Talents in themselves.''

The man's shaking stopped. For the first time since the announcement of his colleagues' deaths he started to relax. But only a little. He wasn't sure he was safe yet.

"Well, anyways, sir, that's why you haven't been able to reach me for the past two weeks. I made myself lost. Vanalatan Islands in the southern ocean, actually. I hoped that if I didn't help them *or* hinder them, they'd ignore me until I came back. I could always plead bad nerves. Amoleen would've accepted that, I think. She needed my financial skills to run the syndicate's business end."

"And conversely, if they failed, you could simply have told me you badly needed a vacation. So you covered yourself with both sides, right?"

"It wasn't like that at all, sir!" Basright protested.

Loo-Macklin waved him down. "I'm not mad at you for looking out for yourself, Bas. Survival's nothing to be ashamed of. But lying isn't one of your talents. I think you know that, too."

Basright hesitated, then let out a nervous little half-chuckle. "No, sir. But I did the only thing I could think of. And I sure as hell needed the vacation, though the last couple of days before I came home weren't very relaxing." He managed to meet the younger man's gaze.

"I'm not in your class, Loo-Macklin, and I know it. Nubra and Amoleen couldn't see how well-off they were. They wanted control more than they wanted success."

Loo-Macklin nodded, rose and approached the old programmer. Basright cringed, then relaxed and positively beamed when Loo-Macklin patted him on the shoulder. Save for the fact that his tongue wasn't lolling out, Basright looked for all the world like a gratified dog.

Hard to think that he presided over, among other things, a squad of twelve professional collectors whose methods were less than courteous. Highly efficient, was Basright, but absolutely devoid of imagination. Dutiful and unchanging as the programs he entered into the syndicate's computers. A born administrator.

"That's why you and Khrys are still here," he told the older man, "and the other two are not." His gaze traveled across the room to Khryswhy. "Basright here is smart enough to know how stupid he is, whereas you, Khrys, are smart enough to know how smart I am."

She fiddled with the airborne folds of her dress, uncertain what to say. "You certainly have a low opinion of yourself, Kees vaan Loo-Macklin."

"Have you ever known me to suffer from false modesty?"

"No."

"It's not a question of opinion but of fact. I'm here. Other people who were careless are not."

"I'd be redundant then," she continued, lighting up a blue dopestick of legal manufacture but laced with highly illegal hallucinogens which the Ninth Syndicate imported to Evenwaith, "in saying that Amoleen and Nubra's passing was accidental."

He nodded once.

"How come no one in my section reported any of this to me?" She glanced over at Basright. "What about you?"

He shook his head violently. "None of my people knew about it or had anything to do with it. At least, none that I know of, sir." He frowned at a sudden thought. "They've all been busy with their regular work, and Nubra was responsible for any stronger 'coercive measures' business required. Who did you get to vape him and Amoleen? If something major like that was afoot I should have heard rumors of it, at least."

"Five years," Khryswhy was murmuring. "They worked for you for five years."

"They got tired of me," he said bluntly, folding his hands across his enormous chest. His eyes dropped to study his interlocked fingers.

"I knew they were plotting against me as early as two years back, but they were valuable people. Within their own sections they performed with great efficiency."

"If you knew all this time that they were out to get you," she asked him curiously, "why didn't you ever let them know that you knew? Maybe none of this would have happened."

Loo-Macklin shook his head. "That's not how people's minds work, Khrys. I know a little about human nature. I've been forced to learn. If I'd confronted them with what I'd learned they would have denied everything. Then they would have bided their time and hatched some new plot, which I might have been lax in uncovering.

"Five years ago I told them, as I told you, that within a year I would triple the syndicate's earnings. Well, we're now the largest, most prosperous illegal enterprise on Evenwaith. We've absorbed four of the original twelve syndicates. With some more hard work and perseverance, I think that within another year we will control more than two-thirds of the underworld commerce on this planet. That will put us in a dominant fiscal position vis-à-vis any possible competitors." Basright nodded agreement.

"I've also initiated expansion operations on Helhedrin and Vlox. Quietly, of course, and in such a way that the small local syndicates there are as yet unaware of our intentions."

Khryswhy gaped at him, half-rising from her chair. "But otherworld expansion by syndicates is. . . ."

"Illegal?" He laughed, as he rarely did, a high-pitched sound almost like barking.

"Sometimes I wonder at the way our galactic society is structured, let alone how it manages to muddle along so effectively. Crime syndicates are illegal by definition and are supposed to restrict themselves to a single world. To prevent them from attaining a dangerous amount of power, I presume.

"Meanwhile, legal corporations and syndicates which destroy the surfaces of whole worlds with their operations are permitted to expand wherever they're able. I see little enough difference in our activities." There was unusual passion in his voice and Basright and Khryswhy watched in fascination as he paced the room.

"We will expand. It's vital to our continued security. I see no reason why we can't."

"You'll find out why when word of what you're trying to do reaches the Board of Operators on Terra and Restavon," Khryswhy told him. "But you didn't answer my question, or Basright's." She gestured at the older man, who'd finally regained his composure now that he was reasonably sure Loo-Macklin didn't intend to have him join Amoleen and Nubra. Actually he was quite pleased at the way things had turned out. He couldn't have been comfortable in his dotage with Nubra as syndicate chief.

"What did you do," she asked Loo-Macklin, "borrow killers from another syndicate?"

"No," he told her softly. "That would have been dangerous. Outsiders can be talkative, especially where things of importance and great worth are involved. I prefer keeping such matters as private as possible.

"So I killed Amoleen and Nubra myself. I think that's more honest than hiring someone, don't you? I've never forgotten my early training, nor have five years relaxed my basic instincts."

His associates were speechless. Their reaction was a mystery to him.

"What's the matter with you two?" He made a face. "Have you both forgotten what I was trained to do? I'm quite capable of calling in my own debts."

"But what about your position," Khryswhy pointed out. "If this becomes widely known it will lower your status."

"Ah, status," he murmured. "If I recall last year's determinations I've been accorded twenty-fourth class. Perhaps now I'll fall above thirty. So what? Status means nothing to me."

Khryswhy stared straight at him and said something which made Basright shudder for her.

"You're lying."

Loo-Macklin resumed his seat and, since this was to be a day full of unexpected revelations, it seemed, smiled at her. It was a genuine smile, an expression as rare as the honest laughter they'd heard from him minutes earlier.

"Sometimes you have rare insights, Khryswhy. Occasional real perception. It's one of the reasons I value you and your opinions so highly.

"Yes, perhaps I am lying. Perhaps." He touched a control on the armchair computer console. Matching units came to life on other chairs, though two of them were not occupied.

"Now then, we've a great deal of work to do today." Basright bent gratefully over the glowing screen, Khryswhy more slowly. "There's a new drug being manufactured on Restavon which hasn't been seen here on Evenwaith yet. It's called Endorphin twenty-nine red. I'm told it possesses some interesting side effects and ought to sell fast and at a hell of a profit.

"The Osos and Ti-chin syndicates also know about the stuff and are trying to line up the usual exclusive import rights from the Restavon lab. Whoever gets there first with the best offer stands to make a great deal, not only here but on other worlds as well. You both know the novelty value of a new drug.''

" 'Other worlds,' " murmured Khryswhy. "Like Helhedrin and Vlox?"

"Among others," agreed Loo-Macklin.

Basright scratched behind an ear, grinned at his console. "I wondered what we were funneling all the credit to those two dumps for."

"Those 'dumps' are rapidly growing, well-managed colony worlds," Loo-Macklin informed him. "As to the credit, now you know. You have objections, perhaps?"

That was always a rhetorical question with Loo-Macklin.

"Good. This is how I recommend we proceed. I've had some checking done into the personal background of the chief chemist at the Restavon lab. He's a legal, twenty-fifth status, clean. More important, he has a married daughter who's wed to a twenty-first class Operator who works for the Planetary government. Economics programming, but that's not what matters.

"What matters is that the husband's been involved in some shady dealings on the side. Nothing extreme, but enough to disgrace him if ever revealed. They have two children of their own.

"We can make a straight offer, of course, as Osos and the Ti-chins will, but I'd also like to begin action against the son-in-law. If not him, the father will want to protect his grandchildren from the damage a scandal could cause. Beyond that we also have the possibility of. . . ."

Khryswhy listened to him drone on, one part of her methodically soaking up every pertinent fact while the other tried to fathom the man she worked for.

She was eight centimeters taller than he was but never felt taller in his presence. It was an effect he had on many people. He was relentlessly, eternally demanding, driving himself toward some unknown, unimaginable personal goal.

He drove his employees equally hard, from Basright and herself down to the lowliest courier.

Because of that drive she'd become wealthy and powerful beyond her wildest dreams. True, she was older, but not that much older. And he was not yet thirty. At times she felt protective toward him, at other times openly affectionate. He never reciprocated, was never more than formally cordial toward her.

Sometimes she had the feeling that . . . she forced the thought aside and fought to pay more attention to what he was saying. It would be dangerous to think she had any kind of claim on him, as dangerous as believing she understood what kind of man he was. She didn't. No one did.

The real Kees vaan Loo-Macklin was buried somewhere beneath a hundred carefully constructed layers of deception and camouflage. There were times when she thought she'd caught a glimpse of the real man, only to discover later on that they were false impressions, deliberately manufactured by him. On other occasions she allowed herself to respond to his leads on a personal level, to find out that he was just toying with her.

Back off, she told herself in warning. Do your job and follow orders and stay clear of this creature. Bide your time. Bide it better than poor old Amoleen. She'd known and worked with her for many years. Nubra for nearly as long. All three of them had worked their way up through Lal's organization together.

And now Lal was long gone and this strange, powerful

enigma of a man was in his place. Amoleen and Nubra were gone too, victims of their own greed and impatience. They'd been out-anticipated, out-thought.

She wasn't going to let that happen to her, no, not to her, not to Khryswhy. Loo-Macklin was right when he said that she knew which of them was the smarter. She'd keep that in mind.

For now, at least, she would be content with prosperity and power. . . .

It was a beautiful, functional thing. The spherical extrusion jutted from the flank of the massive space station like a silver flower doomed never to bloom.

The station orbited a particular blue-green world which was instantly recognizable by people who'd spent their entire lives elsewhere. Ships and shuttles hovered about the vast construction like bees around a hive.

Inside the extrusion, which was located above the orbital center of the station, was a sphere of water given shape by gravitational charge. You could jog entirely around the motionless globe of water. Or you could, as several of the naked men and women were doing, jump into it and swim out the other side, landing feet first on the transparent walkways encircling the room.

Most of the men and women were elderly, though not all. Status and power determined admittance to the spherool, not age. There were benches and attendants who offered massage, tranquilization, and a host of other elegant services.

Beyond the curving windows Terra was a verdant background streaked with white, mostly in shadow now.

One of the men swam clear of the spherool, turned, and drifted feet-first to the floor/ceiling/wall. He floated over to an unoccupied lounge and settled into it. The touch of a switch sent a stimulating vibration through his body and he allowed himself to relax.

His manner was gentle and wholly assured. His hair was plentiful and white as an Appaloosa's spots. He was eighty-three years old but his body was as hard and lean as that of any athlete. Great wealth can give health.

Another man emerged from the water on the far side of the chamber and drifted around to greet the first as he toweled himself dry. He was shorter and his hair was only half turned. He was perhaps twenty years younger and not quite so self-assured.

"Hello, Prax." The man on the bench turned to look at his visitor. He adjusted the sun shield covering his eyes, put his hands behind his head.

"Counselor," said the other man deferentially. "I heard you wanted to talk to me."

"Yes, Prax. It concerns some reports I've been getting from Evenwaith about six months running, now. You know of the place?"

"Naturally." The other man began toweling his legs, using a drink dispenser for a footrest. "Second-class industrial world: heavy machinery, machine tools, raw minerals, agricultural production highly on the negative side, a number of productive smaller industries. I could go on.

"Not a nice place to visit, from what I recall. Unrestricted effluency regulations resulting in poisoning of the atmosphere. I wouldn't want to live there, either, but if I was a mid-status worker looking for a place to make some money, it would be one of my first choices as a place to settle."

The older man nodded slightly, turned on his side. "Someone's certainly been making a lot of money there." He paused briefly to smile and wave toward a friend.

The Counselor had many friends. He was a third-class legal, one of the men who actually oversaw the programming of the master computer that ran the planetary government of Terra.

Admittance to the exclusive station health club with its spherool pool and other services was restricted to members holding class ten status and above. To members and their friends. Prax belonged to the latter group.

"Something unusual about that?" he asked the Counselor.

"A fellow, name of Loo-Macklin, has been running one of the syndicate operations there for a number of years now. From the reports I've seen he's an unusual fellow, not your average syndicate boss. In one fashion or another he controls all but one of the four syndicates on the planet."

"Four? I thought there were seven," said the man called Prax. He was a thirty-third status legal and second-status illegal. It was quite possible to hold dual stateship in the society of the United Technic Worlds.

"There used to be," said Counselor Momblent, "just as ten years ago there used to be twelve. I can remember sixteen in existence prior to that. It took forty years for the sixteen to reduce themselves to twelve, but only ten to shrink twelve to four, of which Loo-Macklin controls nearly all. Two of the four aren't even aware that he's infiltrated their organizations so thoroughly with his own people that he knows what they're going to do before their respective bosses do."

Prax finished drying himself. He chose a small chair and slid it under a sun lamp, switched on subtropical. There was a sun shield in the chair's arm and he slipped this over his face. The two men stared at each other from behind dark masks of plastic.

"Are you sure this one person is responsible for all that, Counselor?"

"Quite sure, Prax. You see, we've been keeping an eye on his activities for a couple of years now. Not interfering in any way, of course. Just marking his progress. A very bright fellow, as I said. Exactly how bright we don't know. His background is hazy to the point of being impenetrable. For one thing, he's never taken the standard adolescent intelligence/aptitude tests. No formal schooling other than rented courses and tapes.

"Despite this he's gained control of almost the entire underworld on Evenwaith. That by itself would not be worthy of notice. But he's also gained at least fifty percent of the illegal commerce on Helhedrin, Vlox and Matrix, and has wiggled into small syndicates on at least three other worlds. He's building himself a little underworld empire, Prax."

The other man leaned to his right and dialed a cool drink. The machine set into the wall/floor/ceiling produced it instantly, along with crushed ice. Because of the extra energy requirements, ice was a great luxury on the station. Within the health club, such luxury was accepted as commonplace. Its members did not remark on it. They were used to it.

No one listened to the two men chatting easily in one curve of the spherool. Men and women swam through its diameter or rested beneath warming lamps. In such an atmosphere of relaxation and indifference are great decisions often made.

"Now that is unusual," Prax agreed, sipping at his drink. "But I don't see why it should trouble you, sir"

"Well, it's not that it bothers me per se, Prax. I'm something of an empire builder myself." He smiled slightly. "If someone else, even an illegal with no lineage, wants to expand his activities to half a dozen worlds or more, I can understand that.

"What does bother me," he continued, dropping his voice, "is that some of the projects this fellow has initiated recently border on the legal. Take what's going on at Matrix as an example. He's gaining control of the market in illegal drugs there. No problem. But he's also taking over the section of the public transportation system through which his product moves. He's crossing the line, Prax.''

"Lots of people cross the line," the other man reminded him. "I've had occasion to do so myself any number of times. That's just business."

The Counselor sat up on the sun bench and removed his shield. Prax didn't turn away, as some people did the first time they were confronted with that unexpectedly vitreous gaze. He was not one to be easily upset, as befitted an illegal who'd reached the top of his profession.

So he continued to stare evenly back into eyes made of crystal and circuitry, tiny video cameras which were tied directly into the Counselor's brain via the shortened optic nerve connections. The engineers had been able to give the Counselor back his sight, but had not been able to supply him with pupils.

"I know that it's just business," Momblent replied. "The awkwardness arises from the fact that one of my companies, Intertraks, operates fifty percent of the marcar system on Matrix. This fellow Loo-Macklin now controls a third of what's left and shows interest in grabbing for more.

"As I said, I admire would-be empire builders, but not when their ambitions conflict directly with my own. I think this Loo-Macklin has become very interested in legal business. If that's the case, that's okay, but I think he ought to switch himself over. If he goes legal, I can manage him. His illegal reserves give him too much leverage, too much unmonitorable power to work with."

"Why don't you just get in touch with him," suggested Prax. "Or if you like, I'll take care of it. We'll convince him that it would be healthier to pull out of the transportation business on Matrix."

The older man shook his head. "It's not just his activities on Matrix. He's probing other worlds as well. No conflict there with my interests, but I've heard complaints from friends with similar problems. The man's becoming an irritation. My own objections aren't enough to warrant strong action, but taken in concert with everything else I've been told, the situation changes."

Prax sipped on his drink. "I could have someone pay him a visit," he said thoughtfully, as though they were discussing something no more important than the sports scores. Among men of great power, casual euphemisms for murder are de rigueur.

Again Momblent demurred. "No. The man is well insulated. His personal network is admirable, from the standpoint of a provincial. I don't think he'd frighten easily, and if a direct physical attempt were made on him, things could get nasty. Not that it would trouble me, of course, but there are others whose constitutions are queasier. Understand?"

Prax nodded. "All right. What do you want me to do?"

"The fellow is sharp. Almost as clever as he is ambitious, if I read him right. So we will offer to take over his illegal operations. They are all profitable; I've checked. They should fit neatly into your organization."

"That's very nice of you, Counselor."

Momblent shrugged. "One of these days you'll pay me back for the information. Since I'm entirely legal, I have no interest in such vile commerce myself. However, if you require a loan to cover the amount of purchase...."

Prax smiled easily. "I think I can cover the acquisition, unless you think this Loo-Macklin will be difficult."

"I doubt it. He's a sensible-seeming young fellow."

"What do you estimate his holdings to be worth?"

The Counselor leaned over and sorted through a pile of clothing. He extricated a small cube and punched codes into it. Information appeared instantly on the tiny screen.

"Given his annualized income over the past five years, compared with what is known of his illegal commercial base, I'd say perhaps eight million credits; though if you had to offer as high as ten, it wouldn't be out of line. I would not go higher than that."

Prax nodded, considered a moment, then said, "I can manage that without any trouble. You really think he'll sell out, then?"

"As I said, he strikes me from the reports I've commissioned as a very intelligent young man." Momblent fiddled absently with the cube. "Also, I have considerable confidence in your persuasive capabilities. He could resist, try to hang onto what he's built up for the rest of his life, but any future attempts at interworld expansion would be met with force at every turn. We could shut him down quickly on smaller worlds like Matrix and Vlox, drive him back to his base on Evenwaith. He's relatively impregnable there, but even so we could make things uncomfortable for him.

"No, I think he'll sell out. I don't know what his inner desires are, but I think he'd be happy to turn legal and set out to pasture. For one thing, from the reports I've read, he's spent so much time building up his organization that he's had no time to himself"

"Women?" asked Prax, encompassing much in one word.

"There's a slightly older woman who's around him constantly," replied the Counselor, "but from what I'm told there's nothing between them but business. There have been other liaisons, always brief, never intense."

Prax had no further questions. He rose, drink in hand.

Momblent slid off the bench and they shook hands, each studying the other respectfully, warily: eyes trying to see beyond cameras.

"Thank you for bringing this business opportunity to my notice, Counselor."

"Tut. What are friends for, Prax?"

"Indeed." The illegal stepped back. "You can report to your concerned friends that their interests will not suffer from the attentions of this Loo-Macklin or any of his underlings. His avariciousness will be checked."

"I'm sure it will," said Momblent confidently. "He is a curious personality. I wish I could unearth more of his early background." He shrugged. "No matter. It will be interesting to see what he does with all that money. Quite a sum for a man his age to come into, when combined with his present personal fortune."

"A nice little savings," agreed Prax, to whom eight millions were a matter of everyday exchange. "If I were in his position I'd take it and retire, ease back and enjoy the rest of my life."

"Yes, but of course, you're not him. Your ambitions and your goals rest on a higher plane altogether."

"That's true, Counselor," agreed Prax, smiling broadly. "For example, I'm still not first status. That's important to me, but not to most people. Most people never dream of reaching for the upper rung."

"No, they don't," Momblent agreed.

V

Khryswhy burst into the room. Her hair was in disarray, she was panting hard and the clinging blue nebula she wore pulsed with her breathing.

Loo-Macklin glanced up from the compact work station, his attention shifting from the computer readout he'd been monitoring. "Something wrong, Khryswhy?"

She stalked over to the desk, put both hands on it as she leaned down to glare at him. Her voice was low, intense. "I hear that you've been visited by representatives of the First Syndicate from Restavon."

He nodded slowly, once. "That's right."

"I hear that they're more than a little interested in buying control of our syndicate."

"Also correct," he told her.

"You're not going to sell, are you?"

He looked away from her, back toward the monitor screen.

It was full of crawling figures, little white worms signifying fortunes.

"I've already sold. Completely. Everything. All the assets of the syndicate, not only here but including all holdings on Matrix, Helhedrin, Vlox and everywhere else."

She stood back, stunned, and gaped at him. "But *why?* We were doing so well. We don't need Restavon's interference any more than we do their cash flow."

"Apparently we were doing too well." He looked back up at her. "Interests not only on Restavon but on Terra as well decided we were getting a little too big for our pants."

"And so they frightened you into selling out," she said bitterly, shaking her head in disbelief. "I wouldn't have thought it possible."

"It's not," he told her. "I wasn't frightened into selling. I was persuaded, convinced. These are intelligent, knowledgeable people, these emissaries from Restavon. They made it plain they knew they couldn't scare me. They simply laid out all the fiscal and commercial ramifications. Given the figures, selling was clearly the more sensible course than not selling.

"Besides, their offer was more than adequate. The profit is substantial."

"Profit to you, maybe," she said tartly. "What about me? I'm no more than an employee." When he didn't contradict her, she continued. "What happens to Basright and me and all the others who've followed your orders so carefully?"

"Not always carefully," he corrected her. "You are all welcome to stay in my service. I have established some headway in the legal world."

She let out a derisive laugh. "What headway? That tiny food-service-supply business on Matrix? The environmental design consultancy on Helhedrin? All your legal interests together don't contribute a twentieth of your income."

"I know that, but one must grab a foothold wherever one can. I never had the capital to expand my legal interests properly. I will now." He smiled. "I expect to obtain an additional million very shortly."

"You can never make as much, do as well, in the legal world as you have in the illegal. You ought to know that."

"I disagree with you, Khryswhy. Regardless, there are things just as important as making money."

There was something in his voice, something that momentarily made her forget her anger and frustration to look at him curiously.

"Is there really? What else could you be interested in, Loo-Macklin? Don't try to tell me you're hiding some secret obsession, because an obsession is a weakness and you're never weak."

"That's not necessarily true," he replied, neither confirming nor contradicting her. "An obsession can be a powerful motivating force. Which is not to say that I have one. I wish you would remain with me. Basright has already agreed to do so, by the way."

"That's typical." She gave him a thin smile. "That old relic positively slobbers in your presence. He'd be happy to be your pet, if nothing more."

"He's efficient, very good at what he does. I admire that. No one's forcing you to do anything you don't want to do, Khryswhy. If you choose to remain with the syndicate, you'll find yourself operating under the aegis of some very powerful illegals. That can cut both ways, if you're not careful. I'd rather you stay with me."

"I'll bet you would, but why? Because I'm 'efficient'? I didn't think you thought that highly of me. Deity knows I've tried to interest you these past ten years."

"I'm aware of that. I'm not a complete social idiot, you

know. But I'm afraid it *is* because of your efficiency, because you dedicate yourself totally to whatever project you're responsible for. I'll need people like you, in the world of legal commerce.''

''You'll need more than that. In a year you'll need loans, and in another year you'll be begging. You're not the type, Loo-Macklin, to make it as a legal. Your background is wholly illegal. You're used to having people broken when they get in your way. The legal world's rules are stricter. There's no camaraderie among its leaders, no unwritten codes of conduct and friendship, of mutual respect. It's a rotten, corrupt, evil place. Give me the clean underworld any day.''

''I take it, then, that you will be leaving?''

''You can take it and shove it you know where, Loo-Macklin, because I'm damned if I'm going to airlock out of a two-million-credit-per-year syndicate to go and work in food services or kiddy entertainment or any other pedestrian legal business.'' She turned from him and headed toward the exit.

''I don't give a damn who's buying you out. I know this syndicate's workings inside and out. I think they'll appreciate what I can do. It will be in their interests to.''

''I can't argue that,'' he admitted. ''I still wish you'd cross over with me.''

''Blow it out the orifice of your choice.'' She opened the door, turned to face him. ''I never thought I'd see you frightened, Kees vaan Loo-Macklin, but that's obviously what's happened, no matter how often or strongly you choose to deny it. I'd have thought you'd have fought them.''

''I am making ten million credits,'' he told her calmly.

She spat on the floor. ''Maggot food. You can make that much in less than ten years here, and still be a young man. And that's not assuming any expansion of syndicate business.''

''Expansion can be opposed.''

"So you work with them."

He shook his head. "The people I've had to deal with made it clear they covet the business I've built up here, not my personal services. Not that it would matter. I wouldn't work beneath another syndicate. And there's something else very peculiar about it, but I had the impression they were worried about me."

"That's peculiar, all right," she snorted, "because in selling out you've proved just how stupid you really are. You keep your offer, and your quick profit. I'll take my chances with my new bosses."

"Last chance to reconsider," he said quickly.

"Forget it. Good luck with your fast-food services, Loo-Macklin. It's going to be quite a shock for you, dealing with the legal world for a change. And you won't find a quick route to the top the way you did here."

"You forget that I made my own 'route.' I will do whatever's necessary to get what I want. The legal world is no different from the underworld. Only the conventions differ, and I think I can cope with them. I'm very adaptable."

"Except when force is applied," she said. "Good-bye, Loo-Macklin. You had me fooled for a long time."

The door closed quietly behind her, humming shut on cushioned rails. He paused a moment, still staring after her, before turning back to the patient computer monitor.

A shame to lose Khryswhy, he thought. She'd done such a fine job for him. But he'd given his word to the new buyers that he wouldn't compel a single key person to cross out with him. Those who chose to stay with him, like Basright, were all the more valuable because they did so of their own free will. They would form the nucleus of his new organization.

The first thing that had changed following confirmation of the sale and divestiture of all his illegal assets was his official status. He'd fallen all the way from twentieth illegal to seventy-third legal. That didn't bother him. He expected those ratings to change again, shortly.

He studied the figures displayed on the screen. Ten million credits was a great deal of money. He'd been poised to make the necessary crossover to the legal world for several years now, in case it became necessary, but he'd been reluctant to divert income from the syndicate to finance legal operations.

Well, now he had plenty of income to divert and no syndicate to worry about. His expansion into legal commerce could commence in earnest.

Khryswhy was right about the difficulties inherent in such a switch. Society didn't accept such transitions gracefully. But he thought he'd found a way to manage it. Events were already in motion to smooth his emergence from the underworld into "polite" society. And there would be side benefits.

It was time for the next step. He touched a control on the desk console. The figures were replaced by pleasantly shifting abstract patterns and a fluid voice.

"You desire outcall, sir?"

"Yes. I wish to speak to Welworth al-Razim, Commissioner of Police for the city of Cluria."

"Noted, sir. I will enter your call. I should add that such officials rarely reply to unsolicited personal calls."

"Give my full identity code and name," Loo-Macklin told the machine. "He'll reply. And while you're active, check on the progress of my new business on Restavon and my concurrent application for commercial status there."

"Very well, sir," said the smooth mechanical voice. "Anything else for now?"

Loo-Macklin leaned back in the pneumatic chair and regarded the ceiling. "No. I think we'll be safe for awhile...."

*   *   *

The big, florid-faced man in the shimmering gray jumpsuit burst unhesitatingly into the outer office and confronted the receptionist there. She was human, which was unusual in itself, but then everything about the office was unusual, from the glittering walls dusted with ruby XL to its location on the 230th floor of Manaus' largest office building.

"I'm sorry," she told him, unfazed by his explosive entrance, "the Counselor is not seeing...."

"Oh, he'll want to see me," said the visitor, staring past her toward the distant doorway. "He'd damn well better want to see me."

Prax controlled his temper while the puzzled receptionist buzzed for instructions on how to proceed. There was no point in trying to force his way farther. The door ahead was protected by security devices as lethal as they were complex. He'd come for explanations, not martyrdom.

There were a number of other people and two aliens, a tall birdlike Orischian and a celibate Athabascan, waiting in the lounge. They gaped at the stranger, muttered among themselves. One did not act that way in the outer offices of a Counselor.

I've reason to, he rumbled to himself. He recognized a couple of the supplicants. That one there, she was a famous surgeon. Another represented the Board of Operators who programmed the master government computer that ran Terra itself.

All were here to pay homage to Momblent and to try and get something from him. There wasn't anything lower than a fifth-class legal in the room. Prax was the only illegal, though you couldn't tell by looking at him, despite what some people said.

The receptionist was conversing in low tones with the business end of a communicator. Eventually she put it back in

85

its holder and looked up with a startled expression on her pretty face.

"The Counselor *will* see you, sir." She waved toward the beckoning door. "You can go right in."

"Thanks," he said curtly, striding past her.

The door opened automatically at his approach. He stalked into an office paneled in richly carved wood inlaid with semi-precious stones cut in strips, all brought up from the gem state of Minas Geraes.

To his right, a broad rhomboidal window provided a view of the thick cloud cover currently smothering the Amazon basin. It was the rainy season and the clouds were rejuvenating the vast rain forest preserve that stretched off toward the distant Andes.

Two other office buildings poked tapering spires through the fluffy gray mass, along with the Jorge Amado Memorial. The latter structure, a towering cylinder of native metallic glass, was covered with bas-reliefs of muscular men, voluptuous women, ancient recipes for spicy local dishes, and every word the great native writer ever put to paper. Amado would have approved of the women and the recipes, would have found the scale of the monument and waste of resources that went into its construction appalling. Unfortunately the dead cannot protest their canonization by the future.

Momblent wore a blue and maroon suit, open at the neck, with a ruffled shirt showing beneath. He was standing next to a surprisingly small desk. Both looked lost in the huge, vaulted room.

None of it impressed Prax. His own offices were considerably more elaborate. He supposed a politician needed to affect a little false modesty. Prax had no constituents to worry about.

"Hello, Prax," said the Counselor, extending a hand in

greeting. He was not smiling, but neither did he appear particularly upset. As usual, Prax couldn't figure him. The syndicate ruler hesitated, finally shook the proffered hand.

"Just got the word myself. Haven't had time to finetune the details."

He gestured for Prax to follow as he walked across the room and activated one of several small screens. His fingers worked the simple keyboard with skill. A familiar face appeared on the screen. Prax recognized one of the United Technic Worlds' more popular information dispensers. Privately, Prax thought the man a pompous ghit.

"They've been cycling this broadcast at the standard half-hour intervals," explained Momblent, "interspersed with updated weather. I've run it forward to the section of off-world news we're concerned with."

The article was right at the beginning. It roused no special interest in the announcer, provoked no unusual adjectives. It was simply another piece of provincial news . . . but not to the pair of powerful men watching it in the luxurious office.

". . . Meanwhile, in fourth quad developments, police on the industrial world of Evenwaith have announced the shattering of the dominant criminal organization on their planet. More than two hundred illegals employed by the vicious under-world syndicate known as the Enigman have been tallied and charged.

"Police Commissioner Welworth al-Razim declared that he has evidence of sufficient depth and detail to put every one of the arrested under a truth detector to the point where they'll be forced to pledge themselves to lives of good works.

"The syndicate's operations included the running of illegal pharmaceuticals and other forbidden substances onto Evenwaith, as well as the perpetration of elaborate insurance frauds and the skimming of profits from legalized gambling."

As he spoke, images flashed on a screen behind him. At the moment it showed a rather stolid looking individual shaking hands with a beaming Police Commissioner. The shorter man did not look into the camera.

"All this," the announcer droned on, "was due to the heroic efforts of long-time undercover police operative Kees vaan Loo-Macklin, who has been functioning in close association with Commissioner al-Razim's office for nearly ten years." The journalist cleared his throat.

"Loo-Macklin was finally forced to surface, according to the Commissioner, when powerful off-world interests attempted to force him into selling the vast syndicate he supposedly was directing. In reality, all instructions were emanating from the police board computer, a fact which the underworld never learned.

"In addition to multiple prosecution at the local level, these revelations are expected to lead to indictments of a number of high-level off-world illegals, a blow which is expected to rock the UTW underworld as nothing has since the advent of the truth detector."

"Hyperbole," murmured the Counselor, turning artificial eyes with lenses of glass on his companion. "You're covered, Prax."

"I'm not worried about my mobility," the man snapped. "I'm worried about my money. The money I contributed to buying out that phlembo."

Momblent tried to calm him. "I'm out a considerable sum myself, remember. Don't dwell on it. It's done, and you'll survive the loss without breathing hard."

"It's not the money, it's the principle of the thing," growled the syndicate chief, his hands clenching and unclenching as he stared at the screen.

"Nonsense, Prax. I know you better than that. We both

know that principle has no place in this. It's the money. We have contracted a common cold, not pneumonia. There is no need for surgery of any kind."

"Who knew?" said Prax, whirling and beginning to pace energetically between couch and screen. "Who knew the guy was a police agent? Before I went into this business I had him traced back as far as his personal records ran. He's been functioning in the underworld for fifteen years. Since he was a kid. Nobody can operate as an agent for that long without making a mistake or being traced. Nobody. We would have found out if he'd been recruited. My tracers always find that sort of thing, always!"

"I've been supporting a little research of my own," Momblent informed him. "He's not a police agent."

Rage and fury suddenly forgotten, Prax gaped at the Counselor. "What do you mean, he's not an agent?" He nodded toward the screen. "That Commissioner. . . ."

Momblent smiled. "I know a few people on Evenwaith. Legals, of course. They did some work for me. Favors.

"They tell me that, not only are there no records in the police storage bank referring to this Loo-Macklin as an undercover agent, there are no legal references on him at all. According to my information, he is only what he appeared to be to us from the first, namely, the director of a modest syndicate.

"Furthermore, my sources say that up until a few weeks ago, this Commissioner al-Razim only knew of him as we did."

"But he just said. . . ." The flabbergasted Prax could only gesture toward the screen, where the announcer was continuing to mouth platitudes.

"That performance reflected part of the deal Loo-Macklin made with the Evenwaith Police Computer. Apparently he found a way to converse directly with it, bypassing its board of operators. The computer then contacted al-Razim, who even if he'd been of a different frame of mind, had no choice but to accept a *fait accompli* when it was shoved under his fat ass.

"This ludicrous story of Loo-Macklin being a long-time police agent was fabricated to save al-Razim's skin, not Loo-Macklin's. In return for turning over all his records and computer files on his syndicate's Evenwaith operations, our enterprising young friend has acquired for himself not only immunity but a sizable cash reward.

"The Commissioner will probably get an undeserved promotion out of it, from city to world police council, plus the admiration of his colleagues, who have never believed him capable of such deviousness. Of which he is not, of course.

"All of the indicted people, naturally, were until a few days ago Loo-Macklin's own close associates and employees. Many of them have worked for him for years. They're half convinced he was a police agent, too."

"Casting of the offal," muttered Prax.

"Quite so," agreed the Counselor. "Apparently Loo-Macklin had the entire betrayal set up to go for some time, even before we 'offered' to buy him out. His insurance policy, in case people like ourselves eventually did make trouble for him. All he had to do was key the necessary computer interfaces.

"As to our money, which despite my seeming calm I have been very much concerned about, it has vanished into a thousand different accounts and shielding businesses. He has so thoroughly dispersed it we could attempt recovery and end up stealing from ourselves. The man must have interfaces in his own skull. He is more than merely clever, this Loo-Macklin."

"He won't think he's so clever," said Prax dangerously, "when he can't spend his money. Maybe we can't get that back, but we can sure as hell get satisfaction. I'll send some people after him who'll cut him up so bad there'll be a piece for each of the UTW worlds and enough left over for the Nuel."

"Sure you want to do that?"

Prax frowned. He could tell when the Counselor was toying with him, and he didn't like it. "What do you mean?"

"Look at him. Watch the broadcast for a few minutes." Momblent gestured at the screen, where local Clurian officials were being shown congratulating the prodigal son. All wore expansive smiles, despite the fact that several probably had underworld dealings of their own. Expediency is the hallmark of the political survivor.

"The man's now not only a local but an interstellar hero," Momblent explained. "The Evenwaith government has already voted him all kinds of honors and others are coming in to him from several off-world service organizations, morality syndicates, and so on. You can't just send over a couple of bullywots to vape him. Can you imagine what the repercussions would be? I've already had calls from worried associates more interested in swallowing their losses than heightening their profiles."

"But he's not a hero!" Prax blurted in frustration.

"Indeed. He's a smart young punk who got lucky. He not only sold us out, he sold out his own people. All except a few who've been transferred to legal activities and have applied for status change. Some hero.

"But to the public he's Kees vaan Loo-Macklin, long suffering and ever vigilant police agent, who sacrificed his youth to preserve their interests from the insidious and malignant encroachment of a powerful illegal organization. You can't just vape somebody like that. It's how he's perceived that's critical, not how he is, Prax.

"Wait. Be patient. After a few years the notoriety he's wrapped protectively around him will have faded. Although by that time," and he glanced back at the screen almost admiringly, "he may have himself so firmly entrenched in legal society and commerce it will be impossible to touch him."

"What are you talking about?" Prax's tone turned wary. "Don't you want your revenge?"

"Revenge does not translate well into profit, my friend. I don't like being hurt financially, and I don't like being made a fool of. It happens but rarely. But a good fighter absorbs a blow and waits for clarity. He doesn't walk angrily back into another punch. If he's too badly hurt, he surrenders and recovers to fight again."

"You're the one who told me to buy him out," said Prax accusingly.

The Counselor's lips tightened. "You're a big boy, Prax. You made your own decision. Need I remind you again that I've lost credit in this business, too?"

"Nothing compared to me." Then the syndicate chief seemed to shift mental gears. "I'm damned if I'm going to slink quietly out of sight and let him get away with this. Not only does he sell us out, sell his own people out, but he ends up a public hero because of it."

"Admirable, wouldn't you say?"

Prax looked at the Counselor as though he'd suddenly gone mad. He'd always respected the older man, always relied on him for legalworld advice. Not any longer . . . not after this.

"I'll be damned. You do admire him!"

"He has accomplished a great deal that is to be envied,"

said Momblent quietly. "He's outwitted some very smart people, you and me among them. It may be his pinnacle of achievement. He is now a rich young man with seventy-third legal status. We may hear no more of him. He may be satisfied with the comfortable security he has achieved.

"On the other hand, he may elect to try working his way upward through the legalworld. That will be interesting to watch. He won't find it as easy as he did the underworld. Legal enterprises are differently constructed, much harder to betray, the managerial class far more duplicitous."

"That sounds funny, coming from a Counselor to the Board of Operators to the Central Computer."

Momblent shrugged. "A pity we have not the ethics of our machines."

On the screen a handsome woman in her early forties was being led off under restraint by several Clurian police. She was ranting and screaming obscenities. The announcer offered a disapproving comment.

"If nothing else," Momblent continued, "he has investment capital. Ten million from us, another million in rewards from the government of Evenwaith."

"He'll have to go legal now," said Prax. "Even if he wanted to he'd never be allowed back in the underworld. Never."

"I'm sure he's aware of that," Momblent agreed. He smiled slightly. "We've none to blame for what has happened save ourselves, you know. It was we who forced him to do what he's done. I'm not sure it wasn't worth the price to you. He could have caused you and your colleagues trouble."

"What, that punk?" Prax snorted. "I know he beat us out of some money, but. . . ."

"I've always said it was only money, not principle," Momblent said, interrupting him. "I'm pleased you finally admit to that truth. So you don't send your people after him. You accept your loss gracefully, though I realize it will be difficult for you, as is anything smacking of gracefulness. Be glad you have a potentially dangerous rival out of the way. I suggest we simply leave this peculiar young man alone and let him go about his life as he wishes. We will watch him, and that is sufficient.

"He was an abandoned child. It's quite possible that having come into such a sum of money and having been exposed in his short lifetime to so many pleasures both common and radical that he will elect to erect himself a small palace somewhere and retire quietly to a life of ease."

"Maybe so," admitted Prax grudgingly. "Maybe you're right. You talked about fighting. Your reaction is to dance and wave. Mine's to hit back as hard as I can." He seemed, finally, to accept what had happened. Momblent breathed a silent sigh of relief.

"Can't do much about it now any event, if what you say is right."

"That's correct, we can't," said the Counselor approvingly.

Prax started for the door, thinking hard.

"There is one other thing, though, Counselor. I think this Loo-Macklin's just a punk. Clever, sure, but still just a punk. But if I'm wrong about him and you're right, and I have had a potentially dangerous adversary and competitor eliminated, and if he doesn't choose to retire quietly, well . . . he'll be operating in the world of legals now. In your world, not mine." For the first time since he'd come storming into the office the syndicate chieftan smiled.

"He's gonna be your problem now."

"I'm not terribly concerned," replied Momblent. His artificial gaze turned back to the screen, where the story was playing itself out against a background of distant hosannas. Evenwaith was very far away.

"In fact, I'm rather looking forward to seeing which choice the young man makes."

"He'd better cover himself well," Prax muttered darkly. He was at the doorway now. "Because I still have in mind what you said a few minutes ago about the notoriety surrounding him dying down. When it does, if he gets lazy, I'm gonna see to it that he gets a nice anniversary visit from some of my people."

He departed, the door closing softly behind him. Momblent sighed, relieved the interview was finally over. He despised dealing with things like Prax. Sometimes it was necessary, however. Sometimes it was profitable.

He turned his gaze back to the screen. The names of the arrested on Evenwaith were being paraded across the plastic.

Clever, clever are you, young Loo-Macklin. He studied the names carefully. Might be a familiar one or two on the list of the accused. In that case there'd be quiet work to do, depending on whom he owed favors to and whom he might want favors from.

Yes, it would pay to keep a watch on this strange fellow. From a distance. Nothing heavy. Just a pin-watch. He was mindful of Prax's words, for despite his low opinion of the syndicate chieftan's personality, he respected the man's primitive instincts.

"He's gonna be your problem now," Prax had said.

VI

"Sir, I don't know if I can cope with being legal."

"Oh, come on, Basright," Loo-Macklin chided him.

"Really, sir. Remember that I've been illegal my whole life."

"So have I." Loo-Macklin thoughtfully regarded the ceiling of his office. Images of fish and crustaceans drifted there, three-dimensional imagos born of clever electronics: an upside-down ocean. He'd always had a fondness for the sea, having never seen it.

"It's not all that difficult, Basright. It's not all that different. You just don't shoot people . . . as often. You murder them with lawyers and accountants."

The slim old man leaned back in the chair fronting the wide computer screen, puffed on his dopestick and looked uncertain.

"If you'll excuse my saying so, sir, I'd rather shoot than argue. It's cleaner. I've never had much use for lawyers, nor accountants."

"That's because you've always handled the illegal analogs yourself. I'm not slighting you, Basright. I'm saying you're going to need their help. We have to go legal now. We have to deal with a new set of rules. It'll be hard at first, sure, but not impossible. I have confidence in you. The underworld wouldn't let us back in now even if we wanted in."

"I can't imagine why not, sir," said Basright dryly.

"Besides which it simply wouldn't do for my new public image."

"Hardly, sir. You're quite the hero of the day." He frowned a moment, the wrinkles crinkling in his deceptively kind face. "It's a shame about Khryswhy, though. We go back a long ways."

"Almost as far as I do." Loo-Macklin gave no evidence of sympathy for the indicted lady. "She had her chance to make a choice, just like you and a hundred other key people. She made it."

"I know that, sir, but don't you think she might have chosen differently if you'd explained your plans to her? She was choosing sort of blind."

"No." Loo-Macklin could take that simple, two-letter declaration of negativity and make it sound as final as the Last Judgment. "I couldn't take that risk. Not with her, not with anyone. You know that. She had the same chance everyone else did, yourself included."

"Myself included," murmured Basright.

"I trust no one. That keeps everyone equal in my eyes."

Are we really? thought Basright. *What do you really think of me, of anyone? Will I ever know?*

Not your business, old fool, said a cautionary part of his mind. The part that had kept him healthy during a long life in the underworld.

Loo-Macklin's gaze fell from the ceiling, settled half-lidded on Basright. The younger man was wearing a dark umber suit with a high collar open at the neck. The vee ran down to his belt, exposing a chest of thick, golden curls. The computer screen filled the room with color-coded patterns and soft background music.

"I have made a decision, Basright. Considering the length of our relationship, what we've been through together, you can call me Kees."

Basright's answer did not surprise him. "If you don't mind, sir, I'd rather not."

Loo-Macklin nodded to himself. "Why not?"

"You ask people to call you by your first name in order to establish a false sense of camaraderie with them, sir. It's a psychological lever."

"Not this time," was the reply. "Not in your case."

"If it's all the same to you, sir, I'd rather continue our present relationship unchanged."

"If it's all the same to you, Basright, I'd like to know why"

"Personal reasons, sir." The old man glanced away.

"Look, you're going to be my closest and most trusted business associate, Basright. I operate on a first-name basis with people who've worked for me for far fewer years than you."

"I'm aware of that, sir. It's just that," he kept his eyes averted as he spoke, "I'd rather not be on a first-name basis with you, sir. I prefer keeping our relationship formal, strictly business. I admire you, sir, but. . . ."

"But you don't particularly like me, is that it? You enjoy

working for me, but you've no desire to be a close friend."
He did not sound in the least upset. "Very well. I'm used to that."

"It's not just that, sir. You make it sound too simple. It's . . . well, you frighten me, sir. You've always frightened me, back from the time when Lal was running the Ninth Syndicate and you came to work for him as a runner up, until this very moment. You frighten me now, while we're sitting here talking in this comfortable room."

"Twelve years," Loo-Macklin said somberly. "That's a long time to be afraid of somebody, Basright. If I scare you so much, why do you stick around?"

"Because I've always had a knack for knowing a good thing when I see it, sir."

"And you think I'm a good thing?"

"It's no longer a matter of opinion, sir. Hasn't been for some years. You've proved what you're capable of."

"And you think I can prove the same as a legal that I proved as an illegal?"

"I think, sir," said Basright, openly and unashamedly, "that you can do absolutely anything you want to do."

That put Loo-Macklin slightly off-stride. "Well," he murmured, "that's quite a compliment."

"No compliment, sir. You know me well enough by now to know I don't give compliments. It's not part of my nature. It's just a statement of fact. A fact which I think you're equally aware of, though you may not admit it to yourself."

"Maybe I'm not quite the genius you think I am," Loo-Macklin countered.

"It's not merely a question of intellect, sir, though I know you have more of that than you choose to reveal. Khryswhy was right about that much, at least. You are an obsessed man, sir."

"Really?" Loo-Macklin seemed mildly amused. "And would you be kind enough to tell me exactly what it is I am supposed to be obsessed with?"

"I don't know, sir. I've spent ten years trying to find out, and I'm no closer to knowing than I was when I started. Do you?"

The massive head turned away from the old man. "We've a great deal to do here today, Basright. We've accumulated a lot of credit and we've got to get it locked in place quickly, before our confused friends on Terra find a way to take it away from us, before the authorities think of some new way to tax it."

"Yes sir," agreed Basright obediently. "It's all right if you'd rather not tell me, sir. It's not all that important. I think you really don't know what it is yourself."

Loo-Macklin said nothing. He had moved to the huge screen and was manipulating the complex keyboard beneath it. Hundreds of figures and charts ran rapidly across the plastic wall. Turquoise eyes scanned every one.

"It's only, sir," Basright continued softly, "that I'm curious to see if I'll live long enough to find out."

"Tell me, Basright," said Loo-Macklin briskly as enormous charts flashed across the screen. They showed the economic output and graphic separation of gross planetary production for each of the eighty-three worlds in the UTW. "What is it that people are most interested in, that they desire and need more than anything else?"

"Air," said Basright.

Loo-Macklin laughed, one of those brief, genuine laughs he so rarely experienced. "You were always good at going to the heart of a question, old man. That's one reason why I thought so highly of you when the others thought you were just simple."

"I learned long ago, sir," said Basright, "that appearances are unimportant. Simplicity is the essence of most critical decisions."

"After air," Loo-Macklin prompted him.

"Food, shelter."

"Get beyond the basics, the survival elements. I'm talking about what's important to the mind, not the machine."

Basright considered further. "I should say recreation, sir. Some form of entertainment. Mental sustenance. Relief from the agonies of the everyday."

"Something to make you feel more than just alive, in other words," Loo-Macklin added. "Something to make you feel good. Pleasure."

Basright nodded, bit off the tip of another dopestick and waited for the air to set it alight. "A good general term, sir."

"That's where we're going to begin, Basright." He stared unwinkingly at the burgeoning, helpful screen. "That's where we're going to put our first credits."

"Quite a jump, sir. From killing people who don't do what you want to giving them pleasure they happen to want."

"We've done dealing in the field before, Basright. We have experience there. Drugs, for example."

"I expect there are legal pharmaceuticals we could buy into, sir. On Yermolin, for example. . . ."

Loo-Macklin shook his head, his voice impatient. "Dull companies, cautious R&D. Fiscally sound, I know, but I want something where we can build a solid legal base in a hurry. I've done a lot of research into the entertainment industry. Chances for quick profits there are substantial, if you know how to analyze what people want."

Amazing, thought Basright, how you can analyze what people want so accurately when you want none of it for yourself. Aloud he said, "Entertainment is a high-risk indus-

101

try, sir. You could lose your capital with breathtaking speed."

Loo-Macklin glanced back at him, didn't smile. "Is that what you think I'm going to do?"

"No, sir, I do not. I was merely mentioning the possibilities."

"You're my second opinion, Basright."

"Thank you for the confidence, sir. Where do you propose we begin? Surely you don't intend to put the entire eleven million into pleasure tapes and performance contracts?"

"No. In addition to entertainment, I want to get into transspatial communications. Quietly. We'll make a lot of noise, throw a lot of money around in entertainment. It will divert attention from our more sober interests. I want contacts in communications industries on every one of the eighty-three worlds, from Lubin and its two hundred to Terra and its billions. I want to develop a network of communications contacts from here to the extreme edges of the UTW. They needn't even be related, at first. Just as long as they're communications oriented." His fingers played the keyboard.

"I've already drawn up a list of thirty purchases I'd like you to make under the new company umbrella." Basright noted that Loo-Macklin did not ask for his opinion on those purchases. That was fine with Basright. Giving opinions to Loo-Macklin always made him uneasy. He much preferred taking orders.

"I want all this done quietly," the muscular young man said intently, "so as not to alarm any potential competitors or the heads of the great public service companies. That's one lesson I learned from the underworld. Move surreptitiously and with elaborate indirection. I want companies with false boards of operators buying up other companies with false boards of operators. There should be at least seven separations of ownership between us and the source of revenue."

He touched another key and the figures on the vast screen vanished. They were replaced by a series of interlocking geometric forms. At first glance it appeared to be a modest piece of abstract art. In a way, it was.

"I've already set up a master design for the new parent company." He looked back at Basright, indicated the screen. "What do you think of it?"

Basright rose from his chair, though he could see just as clearly from it, and walked forward until he was standing close to the screen. He started at the top and began working his way down the screen, studying each section slowly and carefully.

"Extremely elaborate, sir. Too much to grasp all at once." He backed up, finally reached the bottom of the screen, rubbed his eyes. "Too much for me, sir. You'd need another computer to figure out the linkages." He glanced over at his master.

"You always did have a way with computers, sir. But it makes it hard for an old man like me to keep up with your intentions."

"Don't give me that 'old man' routine, Basright. I've watched you work that on too many people and then seen you spring your real intentions on them." He nodded toward the screen. "You'll master it, given time. You'll plug away at it until you know it nearly as well as I do. It's too rational for you to ignore it, too much of a challenge.

"You have your own way with computers. We'd be lost without them. Galactic civilization, the eighty-three worlds of the UTW, would be impossible without them. Even the underworld's become so big and cumbersome they need computers to handle their records. They're just not as efficient as the legal Boards of Operators, which is why the legalworld still holds the reins of civilization. The barbarians will always be stuck at the gates if they can't figure out how to open them.

"The elected politicians, the chiefs of the great companies, the syndicate chieftans . . . they aren't the arbiters of civilization. It's the men and women who sit on the boards of operators, who program the computers that program the computers, who run our lives. Fortunately most of them are technicians and engineers, not administrators or would-be generals. That's why our society is protected from any would-be despot. That's why the UTW will never suffer a totalitarian regime. Thanks to the computers there can be no Khans, no Führers, no Caesars in our future."

"Can't there be, sir?"

Loo-Macklin frowned at him. "Of course not." He gestured toward the screen. "I can probably run up the program to prove it. Why do you wonder?"

"Nothing, sir," said Basright quietly. "Just a passing thought. An idleness. I am distracted from business, which is not good." He looked back at the screen and pointed toward a triangle in the lower right hand corner. "What is that for, sir?"

"That," explained Loo-Macklin energetically, turning his attention to the screen, "is the organizational design for administering our titanium, cobalt, and rare metals processing plants on Manlurooroo I and II. I've already opened secret negotiations to buy into them."

"Pardon me, sir, but if we're to make our first thrust into the entertainment industry, why do we need cobalt and titanium ore facilities?"

"To build the shells of our spacecraft with, Basright."

"Spacecraft, sir?"

"Yes. To populate the shipping line I'm going to start. You

remember what I said about communications. We're going to work into that from two different directions.

"To any curious outsiders, legal or illegal, it will seem as though we're concentrating our energy in the entertainment industry. That's natural enough, given our previous involvements with prostitution and drugs. The line there between the legal and the illegal is slim. On some worlds it's merely a matter of convention and abstract moral principles."

"Yes, sir," said Basright, listening and absorbing.

"We're also going to buy into communications industries, quietly and slowly. But then we're going to work our way into those industries which supply the raw materials for communications."

"What does all this lead to, sir?" Basright waved at the screen. "Does this grand design have a point, an end? Or is it an end in itself? What will you do if you fulfill what you have planned? Draw a larger design, a grander schematic?"

Loo-Macklin took his hands from the keyboard, clasped them behind his head. He leaned back, stared up at the screen.

"Basright, I honestly don't know."

"The unknown obsession, sir. I told you."

"Dammit, Basright," said Loo-Macklin tersely, turning to glare at the persistent old man, "I am not obsessed!"

"Call it by another name then, sir," suggested Basright placatingly. "Each of us owns a certain modicum of ambition."

"I will settle for ambition. But let's have an end to all this nonsense of obsession." He thought a moment, asked curiously. "What about you, Basright? In your quiet, plodding way, does some ambition lurk in that outwardly servile brain of yours?"

"Yes, it does, sir. I want to live long enough to find out what your ob . . . ambition is."

"That doesn't sound like much of a life-goal, Basright."

"A modest ambition to fit my personality, is it not, sir?"

Loo-Macklin considered, then shrugged. He turned back to the keyboard, touched controls. A small section of the immensely complicated design was enlarged to fill the entire screen. It was outlined in brilliant fluorescent green.

"Here's where I want you to begin. There are facilities on Restavon that produce a large number of the more mindless and disreputable programs for home viewing. They are as profitable as they are critically declaimed.

"A number of firms have tried to take over the companies in question. I've made them an offer which they will accept." He grinned. "The difference in our offer from those made previously is that the directors of the companies think it would add validity to their product if an interworld hero was sitting on their decision-making board with them. They intend to use me only for public relations value, of course, and to manipulate the capital we will put in as they see fit. I'll change that in due course."

"I dare say you will, sir," said Basright.

"Meanwhile—" He gestured at the screen—"I want you to go to Restavon and buy up the subsidiary suppliers."

All business now, Basright removed a small box from his pocket. He alerted it and began making notes.

"You can begin with those four small firms on Restavon and Tellemark," Loo-Macklin informed him evenly. "Then there are those up-and-coming young performers whose contracts I wish to purchase. On Terra, the singer Careen L'Hi. On Restavon, the comedian Mark Obrenski. On Elde . . .

The production plant on Restavon was quite elaborate. It had to be. No business could survive on that intensely competitive world save the best, and the QED studios had been built utilizing only the finest equipment and most creative individuals.

From the stagesets of QED came forth dozens, hundreds of works of entertainment destined for transmission throughout the eighty-three worlds: dramas and tragedies, classics, adventure tales, science-fiction, mysteries and comedies, in short, every kind of fictional amusement mankind had managed to invent over the ages to distract himself from the vicissitudes of reality.

QED studios were housed in a four-tiered industrial complex located on the outskirts of Nanaires, a large city which bordered the shore of Restavon's Elegaic Sea. It generated profits all out of proportion to the size of its physical plant, for its primary industrial asset lay in the fecund imaginations of its employees.

A creative mind of a different sort was touring the impressive facilities. To Loo-Macklin, QED represented the industry-wide base he'd been trying to acquire for some time. Its purchase had given him a foothold in the private world of excessive finance and would allow borrowing on the scale necessary to gain entry into other areas.

The executive escorting the new owner around the complex was an earnest, perspiring gentleman in his fifties. He owed his present discomfort to a lack of regular exercise and a plaid and white suit cut too slim for his expanding figure. But then, QED was in the business of supplying illusions and comfort was not particularly important.

Loo-Macklin didn't think much of the administrative personnel he'd encountered so far. That didn't trouble him overmuch. As long as his employees did their jobs, turned out their product, he could overlook personal faults. The executive, Cairns, was no different from the rest.

"Over here," the man was saying unctuously, "are our mixing facilities. We can blend backgrounds, special effects, special sounds, music, aroma, tactility, ductility and live or automatonic performers as readily as you'd make a vegetable stew."

Loo-Macklin nodded perfunctorily as he whispered to the tall, older man who followed him as closely as a shadow. Cairns didn't like the old man, whose name was Basright, any more than he did his new boss, but he kept his famous smile frozen on his face. The corporate takeover had come unexpectedly. Now all he wanted to do was satisfy this new owner's curiosity and get him the hell out of Nanaires as fast as possible. He didn't like playing the fawning subordinate, especially in front of his own staff, but the role had fallen to him and he would play it out to its end. Loo-Macklin had insisted on the guided tour.

"Down that corridor," he continued briskly, "are the location sets for our most famous on-going comedies, including Matermon's Family, which has been in production continuously for fifteen years. But I'm sure you're familiar with the show. Everyone is."

Loo-Macklin shook his head. "Sorry. Can't say that I am. I don't watch much screen, and I don't care for comedy."

I can believe that, Cairns thought. The roller that was transporting them took a turn to the left in response to the executive's pressure on the controls.

"Here are the sets for our viewerun series," he said. "They're recording one right now. This is only for Restavonwide exposure, but the size of the planetary market makes it a viable proposition for us. We also produce such series on other worlds where a sufficient number of residences are wired into the studio."

A flicker of interest seemed to waken within the somber-visaged new owner. He stared down through the transparent wall at the pageant being acted out below.

It was a historical tale, involving the wars of settlement which ravaged Ganubria IV some two hundred years ago, before the UTW extended its control over all the human-settled worlds. The participants battled only with old-style projectile weapons.

As they watched, a noisy battle scene, which filled the huge recording room, was taking place. Technicians scurried about out of pickup range, adjusting the lighting and rainclouds. As the weapons discharged, several members of the cast fell bleeding to the ground.

"The wounds look real," Loo-Macklin commented

"Naturally," said Cairns, surprised. "We pride ourselves on the realism of our productions. As to who gets shot, that is determined by the viewers who run the plot from their home stations and who subscribe to this particular service. We never let the carnage get out of hand. Good actors who are willing or desperate enough to participate in viewerun programming are scarce these days."

Something more than casual interest had appeared in Loo-Macklin's face. As he turned to face Cairns, it was clear that the placid, noncommittal expression he'd worn all morning had vanished. In its place was a twisted, almost maniacal stare of glacial fury. Taken aback, the executive stumbled away from him. Even Basright was staring askance at his boss, wondering what on earth had transformed him so.

"Tell them to stop that," Loo-Macklin said tightly. "Right . . . now."

"But . . . I can't do that," muttered the confused Cairns, trying to recover his poise. His eyes traveled from the homicidal expression on the new owner's face to the scenario in progress below. "They're right in the middle of a voted plot twist and I. . . ."

"Right now," Loo-Macklin repeated, somehow colder still. He'd turned back to stare through the viewing glass, his knuckles white where they gripped the guardrail.

Basright stared quietly at his boss. He's so mad he's shaking, the assistant thought in amazement. Not in all the years of their association had he seen Loo-Macklin this angry.

Cairns recovered slightly, found himself mumbling into the nearby intercom. "Hold shooting!" His amplified voice echoed through the smoke-filled set below. "This is president Cairns putting a formal hold on set twelve shooting . . . 'til further notice."

Far below, a woman turned from her position behind a clump of rocks, put her hands on her hips and yelled up toward the glass.

"What the blazes is going on, Cairns? Who gave you the authority to break into sequence? I don't give a damn if you are chief administrator, you don't have the artistic right . . . !"

Loo-Macklin, his voice trembling slightly as he stared down at her, said softly, "Fire that one."

"But that's Weana Piorski," Cairns protested, wondering what had set the new owner off. "She's one of our most talented veteran action directors. If I fire her, Ultimac or Enterprex or one of our other competitors will hire her so fast it will. . . ."

"She's fired," Loo-Macklin snarled, turning a ferocious glare on the executive, "and you'll join her unless you do exactly as I tell you."

"Yes. Yes, *sir*," Cairns said dazedly.

"I've had enough of this," Loo-Macklin mumbled to no one in particular. "Come on, Basright. I want to inspect the duplication facilities I've heard so much about.'' He stalked off down the corridor, disdaining the use of the roller. Basright made placating motions toward the executive, added a look of warning, and hurried off after his boss.

"What's wrong, sir?" he asked Loo-Macklin after they'd turned the far corner. "Surely you don't feel upset by the bloodshed? It's common to such entertainments."

"It's not the killing." Loo-Macklin was starting to calm down, no longer looked ready to demolish whatever might cross his path. His fists had unclenched and the color was beginning to return to his fingers.

"It's just that I will not have that kind of activity taking place under my aegis."

"Your pardon, sir, I don't understand."

"A bunch of smug citizens squat in their hovels and make life-and-death decisions for performers helpless to affect their own destiny. I won't make money off that."

"Sir, those performers are free agents who signed contracts. They understood the dangers inherent in such productions, as well as the considerable rewards. No one forces them to accept assignments to viewerun series."

"I won't have it," Loo-Macklin reiterated firmly. "Let the damn mollymits come down here and make their own choices out on that toy battlefield. Or let the performers and writers decide who gets shot and who doesn't. Not some bored third party. I won't be a party to it." He glanced over at Basright.

"A man's death is his own, even if his life is not." He accelerated, leaving the older Basright straining just to keep him in sight and still wondering just what his boss was talking about. . . .

VII

"Pick it up," the man said.

The stocky, ugly boy hesitated over the bowl and spoon. Other eyes watched him expectantly, eyes of mostly older orphanage mates. The domeister waited and glared down at the twelve-year-old, his helpmate in hand.

"I told you to pick it up." The helpmate crackled dangerously.

The boy named Kees slowly knelt. The older boy who'd tripped him and caused him to spill bowl and spoon sat at his seat and grinned, enjoying himself no end. Loo-Macklin glanced away from his tormentor and down at the spilled stew which made an abstract pattern against the smooth polytier floor. This was not the first time, only the most recent of dozens of similar incidents which had made his life a stinging hell since his natural mother had abandoned him years earlier.

Something inside him burst.

He picked up the bowl as ordered . . . and heaved it straight at the domeister's face. Taken by surprise the man screamed as the remnants of the hot liquid and hard glass bowl caught him across the bridge of his nose. He dropped the dreaded helpmate.

Kees picked it up, jerked the control tab all the way over, past the safety catch. The plastic catch snapped. Then Kees shoved the translucent tube against the domeister's throat.

The man screamed, stumbled backward and tripped over his own feet, crashing to the floor. Behind them, the other boys were screeching delightedly at this unexpected turn of events. They urged Kees on while staying out of the fray, participating only to the extent of emptying their own bowls on the unhappy domeister, on Kees, on each other as well as the walls and floor.

Again the helpmate jabbed, this time catching the domeister in one ear. He howled, clutched at himself. Satisfied, Kees turned and inspected the riot swirling around him.

The older boy who'd tripped him suddenly turned pale. He started to run, got tangled up with a chair, and fell to the stew-sodden floor.

Kees was on him instantly, stabbing with the helpmate at legs, rump, back, groin. The boy screamed as the rest of the mob howled happily. The sounds of running adult feet could be dimly discerned, still far in the distance.

The older boy rolled over and Kees began to swing the stick instead of poke with it. He worked methodically, silently. The older boy's nose shattered, sending blood flying. A cheekbone cracked next, then several teeth. Blood covered his face and he'd stopped screaming.

The amusement was soon gone from the howling and then the shouting itself faded, until the only sound in the room was that of the helpmate stick striking bone and meat. The boy on the ground had stopped moving. Still Kees continued to flail away at him. Aware that something adult and vicious and nasty had entered their midst, the other boys had drawn back from their ugly cluster mate. They were staring at him now with mouths agape in that special childish stare reserved by the young for those who have crossed a bridge in defiance of an unspoken law.

The sound of nearing attendants was loud now. Off to one side the stunned domeister was regaining control of himself. He was a big man and wouldn't be taken by surprise again.

Panting steadily, the muscular boy named Kees studied the bloody mass beneath him with interest. Then he looked back toward the groaning domeister, then at his cluster mates, letting the hate which had been building all his life come pouring out through his eyes.

No one would ever humiliate him again. There would be no more tripping, no more beatings, no more taunts about his face and body. No more. And no more shocks from the ubiquitous helpmates. Never again. Never, never, never.

He ran forward, jumped atop a chair which teetered precariously under his weight. Then he was pulling himself nimbly up into a high window box. Two blows of the helpmate cracked the glass. Two more sent fragments showering into the room. A couple cut his face. He ignored them.

"What . . . hey . . . there he is!" the newly arrived attendants yelled as they arrived in the chaos which had been the eating room. They started for the window.

Kees turned and heaved the helpmate at them, slowing them for the necessary second or two. Then he threw himself out the window, leaving behind the wreckage of the moment as well as that of his early childhood.

It was the only time in his life he'd completely lost his temper. . . .

His hair was graying now but the memory of that burning,

humiliating, stinging helpmate stick was still fresh in his brain. Poor Cairns had never understood the source of Loo-Macklin's violent reaction that day at QED. Neither had Basright.

Loo-Macklin did not yet have interests on every one of the eighty-three worlds of the UTW. Not yet.

The decisions he'd made as head of QED had led to innovations in entertainment which had rocked the industry. The money which they generated had been put to good use, leading to expansion in other areas of commerce. Little of this was evident to observers, so tightly held was the design and detail of his financial empire, so intricately dispersed were his manifold interests.

Only Loo-Macklin himself, Basright, and three top assistants knew how the forty-four companies were actually tied together in mutual support of each other. Even the operators who ran the financial computers which handled the economics of the individual worlds of the UTW had only a suspicion that of the hundred largest companies in the human sphere, the one listed as thirty-third in assets actually ranked number one.

When a company entered the top ten it became a target for intense competition by many smaller companies, who would temporarily combine to try to reduce its power and influence. Many such immense combines came crashing down of their own weight, for it is difficult enough to manage a diversified business on a single world, let alone many.

No one had Loo-Macklin's ability to juggle figures and facts, nor his peculiar genius for organization, nor even less his magic with computers. Information bound his secretive interests together, interests whose common director was able to supply a mental glue no competitor could match.

Alan Dean Foster

Of all the giants of industry and government, there was only one who studied Loo-Macklin's seemingly innocuous operations from afar and suspected. That was Counselor Momblent, now retired Counselor Momblent. He was still Loo-Macklin's superior in experience, but not in much else. Not anymore.

He said nothing of his suspicions to anyone else, held his silence, smiled, and observed. He was on his way to a hundred years of life, still vital and alert, still toying with his private interests more out of paternal concern than real desire.

Counselor (retired) Momblent had seen a great deal in his near century of existence and had grown jaded and indifferent to many things early in life. Little aroused him any more. Of all the new kinds of entertainment which Loo-Macklin's enterprises had developed for the population, none gave Momblent as much delight as Loo-Macklin's own devious machinations.

From solid bases in entertainment and transportation, communications and light manufacturing, Loo-Macklin's concerns reached out acquisitive fingers to buy interests in food processing and shipping, in education and decorative horticulture. His plants built the equipment which supplied the great computer networks. His schools trained the operators and programmers. His utilities ran the fusion plants that lit the cities of two dozen worlds, cities which Loo-Macklin's construction corps had helped to build.

All apart from each other, of course. All independent. As their own employees would have testified under truth machines, because they truly knew no different.

Loo-Macklin was not the only industrialist to practice such deviousness in order to avoid the attentions of rapacious competitors, but he was by far the most skillful and subtle in devising unusual methods of obfuscation. After a while, however, some of his individual holdings became so powerful that they themselves attracted the nervous attention of many people.

Not all of that attention arose from legal sources. In at least one field, that of entertainment, potential profits had caused Loo-Macklin to acquire through his underlings interests in some of the less reputable and most degrading varieties of personal amusement. Loo-Macklin did not hold moral opinions regarding them, of course. Only society at large did that. To him they were simply services he was providing. Supply and demand were his arbiters of conscience.

As far as he was concerned, every thinking individual had the choice to go to hell in his or her own way. He had no intention of standing in the way of anyone who wished to do so. In fact, for a few credits, he didn't mind helping you along your chosen path, be it healthful or destructive. Most citizens had started out in life with far more advantages than he, so who was he to rise up and say what an individual should or should not do? No, no, not Kees vaan Loo-Macklin.

His services were available freely and without prejudgment or for that matter, without caring. He did not create the demand for such services, he merely filled the needs, much as he did the salted fernal nuts requested by the Inner Six Worlds of the Orischians or the giant cargo ships needed by the bulk hauling concerns of the Three-Ring Giants.

All the same to him: product. Whether sex or steel, bread or bitugle building compound. Commodities all, supplied with equanimity to all.

From time to time, individuals within Loo-Macklin's organizations spoke out against his unwillingness to draw a sharp line between the legal and the illegal, the moral and the not. These people soon found themselves quietly demoted, or shunted to minor posts, or otherwise removed from positions where their concerns might be noted. Loo-Macklin had neither the time nor room for such people and he kept watch on his personnel as carefully as he did on his computers.

In truth, he saw no difference between them. All were circuits in the vast machine he was building. If they did not integrate properly, he excised them.

Not every decision he made was right, not every acquisition profitable. There were reversals and set-backs. Sometimes he went against the advice of his employees and they turned out to be right.

In such cases these prescient individuals were always promoted. Loo-Macklin rewarded nothing so lavishly as correctness, punished nothing as severely as failure. He did not like being wrong when someone else was right. Not ever. But he had no ego. Right was right, to be acclaimed no matter who the perpetrator.

He did not live ostentatiously, considering his accomplishments. Nor did he give the appearance or put on the airs of one who has acquired both great wealth and great power.

In fact, he was not nearly as personally wealthy as he could have been. There were many high-level employees who had grown far wealthier from his efforts and would have been startled to learn that their personal incomes were greater than his own.

Wealth had no real attraction for Loo-Macklin. The vast sums he amassed were put back into this or that new enterprise, new business venture. Many of these speculations never paid back what he put into them, but enough did to make even more money for him, which in turn fueled still additional expansion and development.

Only rarely did he take note of anything affecting him personally. His concern was wholly for his businesses, in fulfilling the grand schematic he'd designed so many years ago. Once in a great while something did pique his interest, though.

He didn't see Basright much anymore, both men being too busy for personal contact. They communicated largely by machine, by the intricate electronic communications system Loo-Macklin had designed to facilitate private conversation with his most important personnel.

When Basright arrived he was surprised at how little the office on Evenwaith had changed during the past decade. Once impressive, it now seemed empty and spartan. His own office on Restavon was far larger, the decor far grander. To have seen both, an outsider would have instantly assumed it was Basright who was the master and Loo-Macklin the employee, and not a particularly important employee at that.

"What is it?" Loo-Macklin asked him.

"I had business in Nekrolious, on the south continent . . ." Basright began.

"I know."

". . . and I thought I'd bring this by personally." He set a sheet of printed plastic down in front of Loo-Macklin. "It's the recent printout from the Board of Operators on Terra, Social Census Section, Individual Status." He tapped the sheet. "Check the sixteenth column under the viewer."

Loo-Macklin slipped the sheet into an enlarger. Each dot on the sheet contained thousands of letters, and there were thousands of dots on the sheet.

"Look under the 'L's," Basright urged him.

And there it was, Loo-Macklin's name among the rest of the elevated legals, raised to the rarified domain of eighth class.

"You've broken the tenth level, sir. My congratulations on your accomplishment."

Loo-Macklin removed the sheet and handed it back to Basright. Then he turned his attention back to the computer viewer he'd been studying when the older man had walked in.

"Means nothing to me."

"Nothing, sir? Are you sure?" Basright had been with Loo-Macklin long enough to tease, though he knew it would probably have no effect on his boss. That never prevented him from trying, however.

"I doubt if there is another citizen of the UTW who has risen from illegal status to eighth-class legal in as short a time as yourself. A mere twenty years, sir."

"Twenty years." Loo-Macklin glanced away from the screen. "Has it been that long?"

"It has, sir," said Basright, knowing the question to be rhetorical.

Loo-Macklin turned to stare at him, his eyes wide open. Basright could take that stare now. No one else could.

"We've done quite a lot in twenty years, haven't we, Basright?"

"No, sir, we haven't. You have. Me, I've just been along for the ride."

"I couldn't have done it without you, Basright," Loo-Macklin said appreciatively.

"Yes you could have, sir. Quite easily, I think."

"I don't flatter myself half as much as you do." He gestured at the sheet of microdots. "I don't need that. Status isn't what I'm after, be it eighth class or first."

"I know that, sir, but I still thought you'd be curious to know." He sounded slightly hurt.

"I suppose I was," said Loo-Macklin placatingly. "It might prove useful." He leaned back and thought aloud.

"E.G. Grange, President and principle shareholder in Polpoquel Tool Making. They have seven large plants on Zulong. He refuses to even talk with anyone less than tenth class and he won't talk to representatives at all. Shrewd old bullyprimewot. That's why I've never tried to buy him out before now. Yes, eighth status could prove useful. Thank you for bringing it to my notice, Basright."

"You're welcome, sir." The older man stood waiting a moment longer, then turned and walked out of the room. There was business to attend to in Nekrolious, and then on Restavon and Matrix. There was much traveling, and he was weary of traveling. But it was necessary. There was no one else to handle the sensitive work, and you could only accomplish so much by relay and computer. Sometimes a man's presence was still required.

He glanced back, saw Loo-Macklin once again staring intently into the small viewer, and realized he was no nearer understanding that hard-faced, soft-voiced manipulator of worlds and men than he'd been twenty years ago.

The land had been cleansed and scrubbed. Loo-Macklin enjoyed taking strolls through the parks that had multiplied outside the tubes of Cluria. He derived as much pleasure from the ironic developments which had accompanied the clean-up of the landscape and atmosphere as he did from the solitude and exercise.

Although it had been many years since his companies had initiated the washout of Cluria's pollution, there were citizens of the city who still were not used to the idea of walking around outside the tubes without protection. They still carried breathing masks and safety goggles attached to their belts, just in case.

It was mostly the younger people, the children and adolescents who'd been raised without preconceived fears subsequent to the washout, whom he encountered on his long walks.

They didn't recognize him, of course, though an occasional attentive adult might. That suited him just fine. It offered him the opportunity to study the always interesting antics of the young of the species, whose frivolous activities he found of consuming interest, never having had the chance to partake of them himself. Loo-Macklin had never been young.

Irony, he thought again to himself. Oh, the medals and praise and honors they'd showered on him during and after the washout! Savior of the good life, cleanser of Cluria they called him. The man who benevolently made the valley of the great industrial city safe to walk through once again, to walk through as men were meant to walk, without the appurtenances of plastic and metal which gave them the appearance of insects.

Of course, there had been nothing in the least benevolent about his intentions.

He recalled the growls and angry missives he'd received from his fellow Clurian industrialists, none of whom realized the extent of his off-world interests. Loo-Macklin had caused to have made a number of extensive and expensive studies of worlds such as Terra and Restavon where pollution had been eliminated or at least substantially brought under control. The results were interesting.

In every case, research revealed that the productivity of individual workers was much higher than on such poisoned worlds as Evenwaith and Photoner. Studies revealed a simple equation: clean air and clean water results in greater productivity, hence greater profits.

So the grand, much-acclaimed washout and clean-up of Cluria which he'd instigated had been done not out of any desire to make Cluria a better place to live, not out of any civic pride or philanthropic interest, but simply out of a desire to increase profits through greater productivity. A healthy happy worker is a harder worker, the statistics showed. The increased production would more than offset, in time, the cost of the washout.

That was not what he told the Cluria Society of Journalists when asked to speak to their annual gathering. Nor was it what he said in response to the honors and praise public officials and civic-minded organizations heaped upon him. Combined with his earlier work in the field of crime control, this new accomplishment firmly entrenched him in the public mind as a powerful force for the general good, a perception which by now had spread well beyond the provincial boundaries of Evenwaith.

Those few industrialists who knew better kept tight rein on their cynicism and joined in the praise. They admired Loo-Macklin's duplicity all the more because they understood it better than the public. A few took the lead and commenced their own pollution–clean-up programs on other worlds, and reaped corresponding benefits.

Through it all Loo-Macklin kept as low a profile as possible. He borrowed from his powerful image as freely and astutely as he would from any bank, when he needed a piece of legislation changed in his favor or a concession on mining rights. You couldn't influence the computers, of course, or even the members of the boards of operators. But you could always influence people who could influence the board members who could occasionally influence programming.

It was all a great game to Loo-Macklin.

He turned around a flowering locust tree and started down toward a favorite creek. In addition to giving him the chance to watch children, he enjoyed these walks because they got him out of the city and away from the press of humanity. His wealth and fame had made him a target for those whose business it was to solicit contributions for various organizations and charities.

Not that he didn't give a reasonable amount. He was very generous with truly needy or helpful groups. In addition to the publicity which resulted from the giving of such gifts and which further enhanced his image in the public eye, it put such powerful pressure groups as the Interstellar Family for the Aid to the Poor or The Society for Universal Literacy permanently in his debt. Sometimes when liberal offerings of credit or pressure tactics failed with a certain politician, a word from such highly respected organizations could work wonders.

Getting Things Done, he'd long ago learned, whether through threats of physical violence, bribery, or political pressure, could all be grouped under the heading of Leverage. Leverage ran the universe, and Loo-Macklin was becoming a master of Leverage.

He reached the creek and stood contemplating the frenetic actions of the water beetles who dwelt within. The little iridescent green and black bugs scudded to and fro across the surface in search of small insects to devour. Occasionally a water whit, that peculiar bird which carries an air supply trapped in thick feathers grouped around its nostrils, emerged from its hiding place beneath a rock to snatch this beetle or that from the glassy surface.

A few adults, mostly young couples, strolled along the opposite shore. They ignored him, as did the children.

His close assistants continually remonstrated with him about his solo forays into the parks between the tubes. It was dangerous for a man of his status and importance to take off for long walks into the countryside.

"Really, sir," Basright had scolded him on more than one

occasion, "you could at least have several members of the Bodyguards Guild follow you at a discreet distance. They would remain well out of view and not interfere with your meditations."

"It's good of you to worry about me, old friend," Loo-Macklin had responded, "but out of sight is not the same as out of mind. I'd know they were following me, and it would bother me." He gestured around at the tiny office. It had not expanded much in past years, but the computer network which enveloped virtually the entire building now had grown to such a size that a new and larger building had been erected just outside the tube wall in order to house the special power supply required to run it.

"Sometimes I have to get away from all this. Physically, if not otherwise. I do it by going outside the tube and by shutting off everything that could remind me of it." He smiled at Basright. "That includes bodyguards."

"I am aware of that, sir, but surely you must realize that everything you've accomplished, everything you've built up during the past twenty years, could all be lost in a moment of aberrant fury propounded by a single crazed individual bent on minor robbery."

Loo-Macklin chided him. "You didn't used to speak that way of such activities."

"I didn't used to be legal, either, sir. That's your doing."

"Disappointed? Long for the simpler days of vice and 'minor robbery'?"

"Hardly, sir. I'm more than content. I've risen farther than I ever dreamed of."

"That's the result of hard work on your part, Basright. Nobody's given you a thing."

"Thank you, sir."

"You can thank me more," Loo-Macklin told him, "by

not interfering, however benign your motives, with one of my few personal pleasures. And in case you've forgotten," he flexed massive hands, "I'm still pretty good at taking care of myself."

"I never doubted that, sir. It just strikes me as perverse that you would risk everything merely for the chance to experience personal solitude."

"I don't consider it much of a risk, Basright. There's not much personal crime in the parks. The tubes are safer for the illegals. Trees make poor hiding places. Besides, suppose I were to die? Wouldn't be much of a loss. Few would mourn."

"I would mourn, sir."

"I just think you might, Basright. But it wouldn't bother me." He shrugged. "I've never worried much about death. In the long run, we're all dead. People and stars, even rocks. I was ready for death twenty-five years ago. I'm no less ready today."

"But everything you've built up, sir!" protested Basright. "The vast organization you've worked and pushed yourself to construct, the. . . ."

"Basright, Basright." Loo-Macklin was shaking his head sadly. "You just don't understand, do you? I've just done what was necessary for me to do. I wouldn't miss it . . . and it wouldn't miss me. The company's big enough to run on its own now."

"But what about your *purpose* . . . ?"

"Ah, that old song again." Loo-Macklin's grin widened. "What a memory. You never give up, Basright. You're sure by now that I have a purpose, then?"

They'd had this same conversation in a hundred permutations during the past decades. It was an on-running game with them: Basright suddenly shifting the subject, trying to pry under Loo-Macklin's reticence; Loo-Macklin as easily shunting the question aside.

"Never mind, sir." Basright sighed disappointedly. "Enjoy your walks. I'll speak no more of it. But I do wish you'd reconsider."

"And I do wish you'd stop fretting," Loo-Macklin told him. And that was the last of it, for a time.

There was one incident when it seemed that the old man's worries might be borne out. The two men who'd attacked Loo-Macklin in the south park carried simple stunners. How they knew his path was never learned, because the one who'd confronted him first and pointed the gun at him while saying they were going to take a walk to the nearest credit transfer booth had had his neck broken before Loo-Macklin could ask him any questions. The other one had been thrown through a nearby decorative wall.

Investigation revealed that while both men were illegals of long standing, neither had been operating under direction from above. They were small-time free-lancers who'd tried to step up in status by assaulting Loo-Macklin.

But while they knew of his reputation for wealth and power, they were too young to know of his reputation in the underworld as a cold, efficient bullywot. Now that word was recirculated through the underworld of Cluria and off-world as well. Loo-Macklin considered the effect. Legally or illegally, do not fool with Kees vaan Loo-Macklin. He's older, but not yet old, he'd be willing to tell any assailant.

Wait forty years and maybe he'll be old and feeble. But he's not there yet. Not physically, and not mentally, as so many rival industrialists discovered when the decisions in Arbitration Court invariably went in Loo-Macklin's favor.

So he wasn't especially concerned when the woman strolling nearby shifted her path to bring her on collision course

with him. She was unusually tall. Loo-Macklin, being shorter
than average, was aware of such things.

There was no weapon showing in her hand or elsewhere.
At about the same time he became aware of the men crouched
in the row of decorative and fancifully trimmed bushes off to
his right, and then the others up in the gum trees on his left.
He doubted they were gardeners or citizens out picking
nuts.

He couldn't say exactly how many were hovering about
him, their air of forced casualness now as palpable as the hot
summer sun, but if this was to be a kidnap try someone was
taking no chances.

No illegal had accosted him since he'd personally disposed
of those two unfortunate young ghits several years earlier.
The operation coalescing around him as he walked seemed
directed from a much higher plane, however.

No matter. As he'd told Basright, he was quite prepared for
the next day to be his last. If this was to be it, he was content.
The creek gurgled merrily and unconcerned at his right hand,
and the sun was warm. There was the smell of persiflora in
the air.

Yes, he decided, there were at least a dozen of them
ensconced in the trees and bushes, masquerading as forestry
officials, young lovers, casual strollers. Their actions were
slightly stiff, their eyes always carefully averted from his
own.

The lovers on his right were too interested in his own body
instead of each other's. The tree servicers beyond them held
their vacuum units too tightly. No doubt they were all waiting
to see what the tall woman approaching Loo-Macklin was
going to do, for she seemed the key to their tenseness.

Pity. He was having such a nice walk, too. The moons of
Cluria, rarely seen prior to Loo-Macklin's washout of the

atmosphere, were rising into the evening sky. Clouds were beginning to form, a hint that weather control might have some rain scheduled for tonight.

Probably a competitor wanting a concession on some world, Loo-Macklin thought. All the while he was studying his incipient attackers, the moons, the creek, he had been considering his options.

The nearest tube entrance was a good half kilometer away to his right, where the curving mass of city tube eight gleamed like a silver whale against the sky. Lights flashed within its transparent skin. Somewhere nearby a hovercar skimmed independent of guide rails across a serviceway which ran toward the tubes, its whine receding slowly into the distance as he listened.

He turned his attention back toward the woman now almost upon him. She was black-haired, in her late twenties perhaps and quite stunning. She wore a prosthetic right ear. Not many people would have noticed it. Possibly it had been manufactured by one of Loo-Macklin's own companies. He wondered how she'd lost the original.

The gun which suddenly and efficiently appeared in her right hand was ultra compact: a solid projectile three-shot model. Since it held only three shells, they ought to be especially effective, he thought. Then he recognized the type.

Each shell was about the size of his little finger and contained thousands of fragments of sharp metal. Upon firing, the shell would explode on contact, sending a shower of metal into whomever the muzzle of the gun was pointed at. They would make an awful mess of any individual, or for that matter, any several individuals standing within ten meters. Loo-Macklin and the woman were not that far apart now. Not even a killmaster could dodge the effects of that weapon. Not at this range.

Well, he had to admire the boldness of whoever had ordered this attempt. If it was to be a kidnapping they'd best watch their intended mighty close. His muscles tensed, old reflexes sending ripples through his body. He hadn't used his hands on another human being in quite a while. While he didn't enjoy killing, physical as well as mental efficiency did give him a certain cool satisfaction.

If escape proved unworkable, however, he would simply order their ransom paid. It's all such a game, he thought tiredly, sorry only that his walk was to be so short today.

At that moment he decided to try to break it. Get it over with, he thought tightly. You're tired. Get this part of the game over with, one way or the other.

He studied the position of the tall woman opposite him. If she was the key, was in charge—another set of mock lovers had appeared, rolling and laughing as they materialized from the bushes. They were wrapped in each others' arms but their attention was on Loo-Macklin. Indifference is beginning to break down, he thought. Must be getting close.

Pruners and vacuumers suddenly shifted their hands to disguised instruments which had not been designed to improve the health of trees.

That made at least fourteen individuals in various stages of concealment who encircled him, including the two working behind the tall lady, ready to stop him if he tried to charge past her.

The brief suicidal impulse passed. He didn't think they'd kill him. A kidnap victim isn't much use to anyone if he's dead. And you couldn't use his credcard to draw money if robbery was your motive.

Not all illegals had good self-control, he knew. There was the chance someone might panic, knowing his reputation. But

he'd take that chance. After all, there was work to do
tomorrow and many more days in which to enjoy a walk.

"My name's Selousa," said the woman brightly.

Loo-Macklin stared up at her. "You know who I am. What
do you want and how do you want it done?"

She surprised him with her response. That was unusual.

"We don't want your money and we don't want your
favors. Only your presence at a little private conference.
There's someone who badly wants to talk with you."

He almost laughed. The drama had become a farce. Unless—
he thought of the powerful illegals he'd betrayed many years
ago. Could revenge still be a thought in someone's mind,
after decades?

Aloud, he said, "Whoever it is could have contacted my
offices and made an appointment. I'm difficult to get to see
but not impossible. I make myself accessible if it's important
enough." He looked into the bushes, up into the trees.
"Evidently someone thinks that it is."

The woman shook her head curtly. "There are too many
levels of bureaucracy lying between you and the rest of the
world. Or so I'm told. That's not my department."

She shrugged and looked indifferent, but her eyes were
always on him and so was the muzzle of the little gun.

"In any case, those who've hired me and mine," she
gestured with her free hand toward the trees, "are convinced
you might not consent to meet with them even if they could
reach your private offices."

Now Loo-Macklin's curiosity was beginning to be aroused.
Something here didn't smell right.

"Who is it, then?"

"I am not to tell you."

"I'm not afraid of meeting anyone," he told her. "Is it

Prax of the Terran Syndicate? One of his heirs? Tell me.''

"It is not for me to say," she replied. "I am only following the orders given me." She gestured slightly with the nasty little gun. "I hope you will come with us quietly." She indicated the non-lovers and imitation workers surrounding them. "There are some very fine shots out there. They are under orders to shoot to wound only, not to kill. We're to bring you by force if necessary, but my employer fervently hopes that won't prove necessary."

"You know," he said conversationally, "I'm very quick. I know that fragmentation pistol," and he indicated the weapon she held, "fires what's supposed to be an impenetrable spray. What's supposed to be. Since you know so much about my personal habits, you probably also know about the innersheath armor I'm wearing under this suit."

She tensed slightly, answering his question.

"That would make my face and bare hands the only parts vulnerable to your frags," he continued. "If I were to charge you, turn my back for a second by spinning as you fired, I think I'd have at least a fifty-fifty chance of knocking you down before you could aim a second shot. If I got you down, you wouldn't get up again, no matter how accurate your sharpshooters in the trees are."

She took a less than confident step away from him and glanced anxiously to left and right. He enjoyed her discomfiture. Loo-Macklin could see the gardeners on one side and the lovers on the other tense as their poses cracked and they readied themselves to wield disguised weapons.

"What you do to me is of no consequence. You can't possibly escape," she said slowly. Some of her iron self-assurance was giving way. "My people have orders to shoot through me if necessary to get to you. You'll attend this meeting if you have to be carried there."

"I have no intention of being carried anywhere," he told her. "For one thing, I'm tired. For another, I'd like to meet whoever's gone to all this trouble just to see me. And for the last, you're much too beautiful to be damaged, though I can see that others may have thought otherwise at one time." His gaze rose.

Her free hand went reflexively to the artificial ear and her expression tightened. "That was a couple of years ago. The other woman involved came out rather worse."

"I'll bet," murmured Loo-Macklin. "I'm a rational person. I won't cause you any trouble. Let's go." He started toward the tube entrance.

"Not that way." She stepped around in front of him, gestured. A small free transport appeared. It was individually powered, as was necessary outside the tubes. There were no marcars here in the parks, since there were no magnetic-repulsion-carrying rails.

The production of free transports had only become necessary subsequent to the washout of the atmosphere and the cleaning out of all the pollution, when a number of citizens moved into the newly scrubbed countryside.

The transport rose with the twin moons. The sun had set by now and Loo-Macklin could look down upon the massive, parallel ranks of tubes that formed the metropolis of Cluria. Lights winked on within the multiple metal fingers.

The two moons had shifted across the sky and the clouds were beginning to break up, streaking the land below, farms and newly planted forest alike, with soft silver, by the time the transport reached their destination.

It was a large structure clinging to the landscaped flank of a mountain. A country retreat for some wealthy executive or operator. Such homes were among the newest status symbols of the well-to-do.

It commanded a sweeping view of the Clurian Vale. The twin moons gleamed off the meandering thread of the river Eblen below. Off to the northwest could be seen the hump-backed tubes of Treasury, Cluria's sister city.

The building itself was constructed entirely of white formastone. Rooms and walkways looped themselves around the native rock like frozen sugar syrup.

"Whom do you work for, Selousa?" he asked her again as the transport settled gently to the landing pad.

"You're persistent. I said that I can't give you that information."

"You work for yourself, don't you? These others," and he indicated the men and women who filled the cab of the transport, no longer pretending to be lovers or forestry workers, "all work for you. You're an independent, operating outside the recognized syndicates. That takes guts."

"I'm a twenty-third-class illegal," she told him proudly.

"Impressive." He nodded slowly. "So someone hired you and your party to bring me here, probably going through you because they wanted to retain as much of their anonymity as possible. Or maybe . . . because no one else would try what they wanted? Or maybe because no one else among the formal syndicates would work for them?"

"Maybe," she replied unsmilingly. They were walking through a dimly lit hallway now and she seemed uneasy, glancing toward openings in the walls, toward closed doors, unprofessionally letting her attention wander from her prisoner.

"I'm sure I wasn't the first whixgang leader they contacted."

"Why wouldn't anyone else take on the job?"

"I said that I don't know if that's the reason. Be quiet. We're almost through with this."

"The sooner the better as far as you're concerned, huh?" She didn't reply.

They entered a room. There were several couches, a lounge chair, the ubiquitous computer-video screen and console which glared nakedly into the room. The usual concealing artwork was missing. The lighting was subdued, as it had been in the hallways. It was almost dark. One of Selousa's people coughed and there were several hushed, angry words at the unexpected noise. Somewhere a humidifier hummed strongly. It was tropical in the room, the atmosphere cloying and thick. Selousa shifted about uncomfortably.

"Our host has respiratory problems?" he inquired.

By way of reply she gestured nervously with the gun. He shrugged, stepped farther out into the middle of the room. There were several shelves full of books protected from the dampness by glass. Real books, he noted, made of paper. They looked quite old. Valuable antiques. But then, the location and design of the house hinted at the presence of money. That was merely a fact Loo-Macklin noted and filed for future reference. The trappings of wealth had long since ceased to impress him.

The furniture was protected by transparent, woven plastic. In addition to the couches and lounge chair there were several other pieces of furniture concealed beneath opaque cloth. Their shape was peculiar.

"I just think he likes the climate this way," said Selousa. She was whispering, and he wondered why.

He turned to face her again. Only two of the fourteen who'd guarded him during the flight to this place remained with her in the room. They held their short, stubby rifles tightly and their attention was no longer on him. Everyone was frightened of something, and he didn't think it was him. Not now.

He commented on the disappearance of the rest of his escort.

"They're outside now," she told him, gesturing with her head. "There's only the one entrance to this room, so there's no way you could break past them even if you could get past Dom, Tarquez, and myself."

"Suppose I don't try to break past you," he said, testing her. "Suppose I managed to incapacitate you three." He used the word delicately. "Suppose I just locked the four of us in here." He gestured toward the blank computer screen. "If that goes outside, and I'd think it would, I would have my own people here inside an hour."

"I wish you would not do that," said a new voice. It sounded as though it was rising from the bottom of an old stone well, intensely vibrant, guttural, echoing.

Loo-Macklin turned to his left, noticing as he did so that Dom, one of Selousa's backups, was edging toward the doorway. He was a big man, young and competent. Now he was sweating profusely, and he wore an expression of extreme unease and disgust.

One of the darkly draped pieces of furniture lifted the material from itself and tossed it to the floor.

VIII

Kees vaan Loo-Macklin was rarely taken by surprise. This time he was.

"I was hoping that," the gurgling voice continued, "we might have a conversation." A tentacle, gray and damp with mucous, gestured toward the nervous figure of Selousa. "Hence the need to bring you here quickly and in ignorance, lest you refuse the invitation or insist on having others accompany you."

"This wasn't necessary, but I understand the reasons for your actions. Not many people would agree willingly to such a meeting."

"But you it troubles not?" the voice asked.

"No," Loo-Macklin replied softly, "not in the least."

A rich burbling sound that might have been a sigh came from the speaker. Enormous, bulging eyes flicked in opposite directions, gold flecks sparkling around slitted pupils.

Alan Dean Foster

"Parum met mel noma," the alien rumbled. "I had hoped this might prove so. Thus far it appears."

The representative of that exceptionally ugly race known as the Nuel turned on thick cilia and used a tentacle to pull another protective covering from a strange, horseshoe-shaped piece of furniture. It settled its gross body into the wedge thus proffered.

The Nuel ruled an unknown number of worlds farther out on the galactic disk than the eighty-three human worlds of the UTW. They had been pressing against the UTW's borders for several hundred years, probing and testing, seeking weak points and withdrawing when none were found, instigating incidents and in general attempting to gain influence over the UTW's citizens in any and all ways possible. They were aggressive yet cautious, paranoid yet willing to take chances.

Much of their drive derived from their shape, which was no less than repulsive to every other civilized race. The Nuel had therefore resolved, back when they first began to explore the stars around them, that they could insure their own safety only by taking control of everyone else. This end they had been pursuing for some time now with considerable success ... until they came up against the powerful federation of peoples that formed the UTW. Their advance slowed and their paranoia increased proportionately.

They had reached the point where they were willing to try anything to gain a tentaclehold within UTW commercial or government circles. As they became desperate they grew more inventive.

Where confrontation had failed, perhaps a meeting might succeed.

The Nuel shifted in its peculiar chair. Slime dripped from the edges of the cup-seat. One of Selousa's assistants made a

138

strangled sound, choking back the gorge rising in his throat.

The Nuel extended two of its four tentacles.

"A custom you have of shaking hands. Would you make the supreme sacrifice for a human and touch flesh with mine?"

Loo-Macklin strode over to the cupouch, studying the alien with intense interest, and unhesitatingly extended a hand. As his fingers were wrapped in a pair of slimy tentacle tips the bullywot named Tarquez put his hand to his mouth and burst out the only door. Dom watched him retreat, then glanced anxiously at his boss.

Even the tall, self-assured Selousa appeared ready to break as the tentacles slipped away from Loo-Macklin's fingers. Delicately, he wiped the residual ooze clean on one leg of his coveralls.

The two oversized eyes moved in that lumpy, silver-gray head. The supporting cilia were wrapped around the central pole that rose from the center of the cupouch seat and the tentacles spraddled loosely around the body. There were no visible ears or nostrils, only the serrated beak protruding from between the great, curving eyes.

"You may depart, Selousa-female," the Nuel told her. She hesitated, glancing empathetically at her former captive. Loo-Macklin ignored her stare, fascinated by the sight of the Nuel. He could feel her relief, however, as she and her remaining assistant fled the room.

Turning, he searched until he settled on a chair fashioned of spiderweb steel, pulled it over and sat down deliberately close to the alien. The Nuel regarded his action approvingly.

"Thus far comes the night, bringing with it everything we had hoped you might prove to be, Kee-yes vain Lewmaklin," said the alien in that reverberating voice.

"How can you know this?" He shifted in the comfortable seat. "I haven't done anything yet."

"You touched flesh with me," said the Nuel. "Few, oh few humans can do that. Fewer still without forming on their faces expressions of extreme displeasure, to mention not the reactions that overcome their physical functions. As did happen with that one male," and a tentacle pointed toward the door.

"I don't consider that I've reacted in any way remarkable," Loo-Macklin told him honestly.

"All the more remarkable for that," the alien replied. "You sit across from me, almost close enough for touch, and exhibit no evidence of distress. Can it be that unlike the majority of your kind you do not find the Nuel repulsive to look upon beyond imagining?"

"Now that's an interesting thought," Loo-Macklin informed him, for a him he thought it was. "You see, most human beings," and he ran a hand down his Neanderthaloid body, "find me unpleasant to look upon."

"Had not thought, had not hoped," murmured the Nuel, "to find a physiological as well as psychological analog for facilitating communication between the two of us. You surpass my wildest expectation, Kee-yes vain Lewmaklin."

"And I'm curious to know what those expectations are," he told the alien. "Obviously you have high ones or you wouldn't have gone to all this difficulty and expense. Not only that required to bring me here, but that required to slip yourself surreptitiously onto an intolerant human world like Evenwaith."

The Nuel made a gesture with its tentacles which Loo-Macklin hopefully read as a sign of agreement.

"We are not at war, human and Nuel. Not today, anyway. Tomorrow, perhaps." It was watching Loo-Macklin closely for any hint of reaction to this pronouncement. When none was forthcoming, it continued.

"It is difficult but not impossible to arrange such things. Even a single world is a vast place. This one is a planet of large cities and many open spaces, easier to penetrate than most. By the way, I am called Naras Sharaf. Your calling I know already."

"What is it you want of me, Naras Sharaf?" asked Loo-Macklin. "More than a casual early morning's conversation and polite discussion of our mutual ugliness, I'm sure."

The squat gray body shifted slightly, cilia rippling on seat and center pole. As it moved, the weak illumination drew forth an isolated flash of purple or maroon iridescence from the otherwise dull epidermis, a momentary redeeming spark of beauty too infrequent and isolated to much mitigate the extreme repulsiveness of the Nuel's form.

"Indeed more than casual conversation, Kee-yes vain Lewmaklin. We have done much expensive and thorough research into your personal history and career."

"There's nothing in it that I'm ashamed of or would want to hide," Loo-Macklin told him.

"Nevertheless, it was required. It is hard for us sometimes to obtain such information, although we have learned during our years of contact with your kind that with sufficient monies we can purchase a great many things supposedly not for sale."

"Better to bribe than kill," Loo-Macklin replied. "I've done both when necessary."

"As have I," the Nuel told him unthreateningly. "I too prefer to purchase rather than take through violent action. Though there are among my kind many who feel otherwise.

"However, I have been able to persuade sufficient of the Heads of the Families (from his studies, Loo-Macklin knew that in Nuel society, a "Family" might consist of several hundred thousand individuals, a Great Family of millions) to allow me to make this contact with you. We occasionally find the rare human with whom we can work."

"Work how?" Loo-Macklin leaned forward, interested.

"I have what amounts to a business proposition for you, Kee-yes vain Lewmaklin. Would such coming from me interest you?"

"I am always interested in good business," was the calm reply.

"Even if it entails dealing with filthy, slimy Nuels?"

"Filth and slime are often personal, not physical characteristics," said the industrialist. "I know many humans who could be so described. Go ahead, make your proposition. My acceptance or rejection will be based solely on its merits, not on its source."

"Equitable is this creature," growled Naras Sharaf.

"Always equitable where business is involved."

"Even with a Nuel."

"Your credit line intrigues me, not your shape, Naras Sharaf. I do business with Orischians, Athabascans, half a dozen other non-human sentient races. Why not the Nuel?"

Naras Sharaf blinked, quite a production considering the size of his eyes. Loo-Macklin had no idea what the gesture signified; if it was full of meaning or merely a reflex. The Nuel did not blink often, so he suspected the former. Double lids closed like doors over those vast orbs, slid slowly open again.

"And not the Orischians, the Athabascans, or any of your other half dozen will have anything to do with us," commented Naras Sharaf, "as they find our shape and appearance as abhorrent as do your own kind."

"Such prejudices are common misfortunes. I fear intelligence and common sense are not the same thing," replied Loo-Macklin. "I've told you that I'm not subject to such primitive emotions."

"Told I was you were a most extraordinary human. The reports did not lie."

"I'm not extraordinary at all." Loo-Macklin shifted in his chair. "I'm just a good businessman, always on the alert for a way to enlarge my holdings."

"Would access to a virtually unlimited supply of iridium enhance your holdings?" asked Naras Sharaf.

Loo-Macklin offered no outward show of emotion. Inside, he was churning. A rare and expensive member of the platinum family of metals, iridium was an important component in the compact, efficient fuel cells which ran half the independent motors in the UTW, everything from household appliances to free transports like the one which had brought him here.

Access to a substantial quantity of iridium would give him control of a vital industry which he'd heretofore been able to penetrate only weakly. It would also give him an inside line on every company that manufactured products requiring the metal . . . though he wondered how exaggerated was Naras Sharaf's claim to have access to a virtually unlimited supply.

"I can see that it would," said the alien, without waiting for a verbal response. The Nuel possessed an impressive panoply of expressions, so it came as no surprise to Loo-Macklin that they might have studied those used by other races.

"We can promise you that, at a price absurdly low by UTW standards, and more. Much more."

Loo-Macklin's attention was distracted by the three caterpillar-like creatures crawling across the bulging front of the alien's body. Each was extruding a continuous silken thread. One was crimson, another yellow, and the third a bright orange.

As they moved in tandem across the lumpish form they wove the Nuel a new gown, simultaneously devouring the old material that lay in their paths. The effect was like those perpetually changing advertising signs which dominated commercial streets inside the tubes.

He'd heard about such well-trained creatures. They could weave four or five new sets of clothing a day, converting old material into new silk. Wardrobe was a matter of training.

No human could have tolerated the constant crawling sensation, but it was typical of the Nuel to work in such fashion. They were arguably the finest bioengineers in this part of the galaxy, preferring to alter or create new organisms to provide services for them rather than develop the extensive physical technology mastered by humankind and most of the other sentients.

When the periodic, almost ritualized little wars broke out between the two groups, men dealt death with energy rays and high explosives while the Nuel utilized poison projectiles and selective diseases. As man tried to deal with the latter, which he found unnatural and insidious, the Nuel struggled to cope with the former, which to them outraged nature and was unnecessarily destructive. Meanwhile the dead of both sides watched and laughed. The morality of the methodologies of murder is of little concern to the victims.

Neither side succeeded in gaining an advantage over the other. Mankind fought with new biology, the Nuel wrestled with complex physics, and each side shouted a lot.

Loo-Macklin had also noticed the organic recorder in the back of the room. A small, flattened creature about half the size of his head, it rested in a transparent acrylic container open at the top. Tiny cilia flowed underneath it. It was photosynthetic, bright green, operated almost wholly on sunlight and water. It was an auditory sponge, soaking up conversation, music, and any other sound within its range and storing them in its copious memory.

When stimulated it could reproduce from its formalized memory anything heard earlier. It was independently operated with fuel-cell storage, wore out only when it died, and functioned on sunlight and water. Another example of Nuel bioengineering substituting for the more familiar tools of human civilization. As to which method was the more efficient, Loo-Macklin could not say.

It was yet another thing that made the Nuel so alien to mankind where the tall Orischians, for example, seemed like feathery, attenuated cousins. It didn't trouble Loo-Macklin anymore than did Naras Sharaf's appearance. He found both fascinating.

It would have been impolitic to enter into a long discussion with the Nuel on such peripheral matters. Despite his seeming calm, the alien was on a hostile world and risking considerable personal danger. Such risk had been taken on behalf of Loo-Macklin. He wasn't flattered by this knowledge. Flattery was something he did not respond to. He merely found it interesting.

"Naturally I'm intrigued by your offer," he said politely. "What in return would you require from me? I know that the Nuel are deficient in certain areas of hard physics. I have access to a great many plants and facilities dealing with the products of such knowledge. We can trade finished goods for raw material, goods for goods, or. . . ."

"Something of a rather different nature is what interests us," said Naras Sharaf. He leaned over and touched a fuzzy object which might have been a tail or a bristly switch: Loo-Macklin wasn't sure which. You couldn't tell with the Nuel. Touch a button and it might leap up on tiny feet and scuttle over to settle down on some other unsuspecting instrument. Some Nuel devices were chemically coded for secrecy. If the main control didn't recognize you, it might bite you. No wonder so many humans found Nuel technology disconcerting.

"Secrecy circuit," said Naras Sharaf, confirming Loo-Macklin's suppositions. "This room has been carefully shielded, but I still check circuits frequently." The vast, slitted eyes gleamed glassily in the dim light. The suns of the Nuel worlds were dimmer than those of Sol.

"You are of course aware of the disagreements between our races that have pockmarked our mutual past."

"Hard not to be," replied Loo-Macklin.

"An impartial observer might almost say we are in a constant state of argument, rather than war. We fight each other as often as we pause to catch our collective breath. Words I will not mince with you, Kee-yes vain Lewmaklin."

"That usually makes them unpalatable," he responded.

The Nuel hesitated. His upper folds of flesh and barnacle-like structures seemed to quiver beneath the steadily changing gown. He emitted a peculiar grunting sound that was probably laughter.

"I see, yes, a humor. Unpalatable. So we will be worbish with one another."

And it was Loo-Macklin's turn to ask for an explanation.

"There are ways to conduct wars without inflicting pestilence or bombs on each other. Ways that preserve life instead of canceling it. After all, war is simply a method by which opposing governments seek to gain control of each other.

"Some peoples have no interest in such expansion and control. The Athabascans, as you know, are quite content to remain within the sphere formed by their ten highly advanced worlds." Naras Sharaf's body shifted, the cilia gleaming with lubricating slime.

"At times I would prefer the Great Families to feel the same way, and humankind likewise. It would benefit both races enormously if the Board of Operators responsible for the destiny of the UTW would simply realize that their future lies with the benign and fraternal administrative talents the Nuel can provide, rather than their own fractious and highly erratic selves."

"Doubtless they feel the Nuel would benefit by the guidelines their computers can provide, judgments rendered by impartial machines with only the general welfare at stake."

"The machines impartial may be, but the wishes of their programmers are in question." The alien waved several tentacles. "However I did not come here to discuss philosophy but commerce. We agree that our governments disagree. The result is this constant fighting which only widens the gap between our peoples. Wasteful of lives and material on both sides.

"My aim is to reduce that waste and bring us closer together."

"Still sounds like philosophy to me, not commerce."

"A tool, a tool," said Naras Sharaf impatiently.

"Sometimes war can be a useful tool."

"Death is never useful," said the Nuel. "Life is ever-giving."

"I disagree with your statement on death."

The alien digested this. "You are strange as well as extraordinary. Some time I would enjoy debating the Pentacle with you. Let us to business now, however.

"What we want to acquire from you, Kee-yes vain Lewmaklin, is not produce but information. Certain details involving the programming of your computers, for example. The commercial networks which tie together and dominate various worlds and clusters of worlds. Information regarding the likes and dislikes of the inhabitants, for no two worlds are the same. Information on the individual boards of operators, the movements of ships and goods through UTW space, the attitudes of races like the Elmonites with special regard to how they might react to the Nuel way of government as opposed to that propagated by the UTW.

"This would not be a first for us. We have a number of 'employees,' human included, working for us in the UTW. This even though your formalized underworld refuses to deal with us."

"Like the young lady." Loo-Macklin turned in his chair and gestured toward the doorway.

"Yes, like the young female. A few strong-willed individuals who have managed to overcome their personal feelings in return for good pay. They are all of little importance, however. Minor functionaries at best." The Nuel leaned forward, tentacles curling wetly around the supportive bend of the horseshoe. Loo-Macklin had no way of knowing if the gesture signified anything other than a change of position for comfort.

"You, Kee-yes vain Lewmaklin, are something different. You could provide us with a great deal of the information we wish to have, for you have that which is most important to any seeker-after-knowledge. You have Access."

"Why should I help you prepare for a major war against my own kind?"

"No war, not war at all." Naras Sharaf slumped back into the cupouch. "You misread my intentions completely. I am disappointed."

"Sorry."

"A nothing, no matter. We Nuel dislike armed combat. We much prefer to reach our desired goals through peaceful methodology whenever possible, and will go to great lengths to avoid physical combat."

"Such methodology to include subversion, propaganda, and the like?" asked Loo-Macklin.

"Efficient words." Naras Sharaf did not sound embarrassed by the confession. "You now grasp the situation. At this time you may, if you so feel inclined, launch into an angry diatribe against me and take your leave by stalking from this chamber. I will be not surprised."

Loo-Macklin steepled his fingers, stared across them at the alien. "I have no intention of doing anything of the sort." He waited quietly.

Tentacles fluttered and he interpreted the gesture as one expressing surprise, though it could as easily have been satisfaction, or something unknowable.

"You will give our offer serious consideration?"

"As long as there is to be no war and I can satisfy myself that is the truth, yes. War is bad for business. Propaganda, whether for a people or a frozen food, is another matter entirely. The important thing is for the flow of commerce to remain inviolate."

"So it shall, so it shall," said Naras Sharaf, now clearly excited. "Our business interests also are strong."

"In fact," Loo-Macklin went on, "I find your offer, providing we can come to precise terms as to surreptitious methods of exchanging goods and services, quite beguiling."

"Really, I did not expect . . ." began Sharaf.

"Such a reaction is unbecoming in a hard bargainer, Naras Sharaf." Loo-Macklin was feeling good enough to tease the alien slightly. "Though I don't doubt it is a shock to you to discover I am the individual you hoped to find. Should our situations be reversed I'm sure I would react in the same manner." Loo-Macklin had always been the smoothest of liars.

"True, oh true. You will truly then take credit for information, material for money, technology for knowledge?"

"I don't have access to everything," Loo-Macklin warned him. "I know some people in the government. I have holds on certain of them that vary from weak to strong, legal to illegal. I have to be very careful when working such sources of information. I'll need to concoct reasons for using them which won't arouse suspicion in those whose business it is to monitor such sources. But I will do my best for you. I pride myself on being a good supplier as well as a good consumer."

The Nuel made a gesture of agreement, thought a moment, then inquired hesitantly, "It does not then trouble you to become a traitor?" Naras Sharaf could still not believe his good fortune.

"I owe allegiance to nothing and no one," Loo-Macklin told him softly. Soft and cold, so cold that even the alien who was not terribly well versed in human voice tones was conscious of it. "I owe responsibility only to myself. I have no more, no less fondness for the Great Families of the Nuel than I do for the Board of Operators, the Orischians, or anyone else."

The Nuel asked a highly (to it) personal question: "Are you then . . . familyless?"

Loo-Macklin nodded. "In both the Nuel and human sense of the term."

"Well, it needn't concern us. We have our own prejudices, you see, but as an alien they needn't apply to you."

"I don't care if it does or not. I'm used to it."

A tentacle toyed with an arm of the horseshoe-shaped chair. "You are fully aware, I am sure, of what the reaction would be among your own kind if your work for us were ever to be discovered."

"That's my problem and worry, not yours."

"Quite truly." The lids half-closed over those vitreous orbs, sliding in from the sides until only the long pupil showed between them.

"You are also aware that we will check back on all information you supply to us. We will check as thoroughly and in as much detail as possible. We have enough sources within the UTW to do that much, at least. Your veracity will be ever on trial.

"Should we discover that you have agreed to work for us only to go in turn to the human government and function as a double agent for them, well, we have numerous ways of dealing with such duplicity, with those who would break a contract made with a family. As bioengineers I can tell you our methods are unpleasant in ways humanity has not imagined."

"I never break my contracts, Naras Sharaf, no matter who they're forged with. Feel free to do all the checking on me you wish. I won't disappoint you. And all knowledge of our business will remain hidden from my own people, let alone the government."

"Why should I believe you, Kee-yes vain Lewmaklin?" asked the alien, heedless of courtesy. "If you will betray your own kind, why should you not also betray those who are alien to you?"

"Because it is to my advantage not to betray you, Naras Sharaf. If you should somehow succeed during my lifetime in taking control of the UTW, which I have no doubt is your eventual aim, or of the Orischians, or any of the eighty-three worlds, I know that there are not enough experienced Nuel in all the worlds of the Families to direct the human government efficiently. You'll still need human operators and bureaucrats."

"Light enters through the window and opacity is vanished!" exclaimed the alien. "You would be a Family Head, then? Pardon . . . a chief of the Board of Operators."

"No, I would not," was the unexpected reply. "I don't like the kind of attention and publicity that attends such positions. I prefer to operate from the background, quietly. I would like very much to maintain the fiction that a Board of Master Operators still consults on the majority of planning decisions which program the life of the United Technologic Worlds."

"While you," said Naras Sharaf approvingly, " 'quietly' program the Board."

"Without their knowledge if possible; with it if not," admitted Loo-Macklin.

"You are quite right in your assumption that the fulfillment of the grand design of the Great Families requires the cooperation of human operatives." Naras Sharaf was enjoying himself. It was a delight to dispense a favor that might not be called in.

"Ambition is a powerful instrument. Yes, I believe you will hold to your contracts."

"My word on it." Loo-Macklin stood and approached the Nuel. Heedless of the slime oozing from the alien's tentacles (which after all was nothing more than a hygenic cleansing gel which helped to protect its sensitive skin from bacterial infection while also aiding in locomotion) he extended a hand.

Naras Sharaf hesitated. "I would take the word you offer along with your family's, but you have no family."

"You have it by me as an individual, that I will do whatever I'm able, provided the Nuel keep their end of the bargain, to see to it that some day the members of the

Families can travel without fear and with impunity throughout the eighty-three worlds of the UTW.''

The Nuel extended its pair of right-side tentacles and wrapped the flexible tips wetly around Loo-Macklin's hand, the rubbery tips entwining with his fingers.

''That will suffice for me, Kee-yes vain Lewmaklin. You shall regret not the decision you have made.''

''I know that,'' said the man matter-of-factly, ''or I wouldn't have made it.''

He withdrew his hand and, again, inconspicuously wiped it dry on the back of a pants leg.

''Now as to the details.'' Naras Sharaf shifted the transparent plastic cube containing the organic recorder so it rested on the little table between them. ''There are fees to be set for specific items, arrangements to be made for private communications, members of my own Family to contact. This is a great day for me.''

Turning, he activated a screen of a thinness Loo-Macklin had never seen before. As he would learn, it was composed of electrostatically charged chemophotic microbes, each one lightening or darkening and changing color on command to form a beautifully clear image.

The communications tightbeam Naras Sharaf employed was transmitted to a tiny, shielded satellite orbiting Evenwaith. From there it was relayed to a shielded vessel standing in far orbit and thence via concealed booster stations scattered carefully among the eighty-three worlds into a vast section of space that held the swirling of stars ruled by the Eight Great Families of the Nuel. The message was scrambled and extensive, but what Naras Sharaf in essence was saying to his brethren was this:

''The man has been bought.''

153

Alan Dean Foster

*   *   *

After Loo-Macklin had departed, sent on his way back to Cluria, Naras Sharaf allowed himself the pleasure of leisurely elaboration. Verily a great day for him as well as for the hopes of the Families.

The Nuel at the other end of the Long Talking had eyes flecked with azure instead of Naras Sharaf's gold. His voice was weak with distance and crinkly with age. But his several whistles of astonishment reached through the speaker clearly enough.

"Truly," it said.

"Truly, Fourth Father," replied Naras Sharaf to the high-ranking Nuel, "has the man been purchased to us." This Fourth Father was a member of both Sharaf's personal family, which contained a modest 243,000 individuals, as well as the Fourth of the Great Families.

There was a pause at the other end. Then, "Why do you think he has done this thing? Tell me not it was only for the money, for by all reportings he has no need of it."

"It is difficult to say," replied Naras Sharaf thoughtfully. "For power, I think, but I am still not certain. I was never certain with him at any time during the interview. He is quite complex. For a mere human. I should say, without intending blasphemy, that in certain ways he is more Nuel than human."

"That much alone is obvious," agreed the voice at the other end of the stars, "or he would not have done this. Beware, beware, Naras Sharaf, that 'mere human' or not, this one does not deceive you."

"I will become the name Caution," Naras Sharaf assured him. "And the human has been warned of the consequences of betrayal. Naturally though, we will depend not on his word alone. We have sufficient operatives to keep watch on him.

154

Pessimissm becomes you not, Fourth Father," he added with respect. "Better to be hopeful in this matter than not."

"Concurrence," admitted the elderly Nuel, "but the humans have attempted this business of double agents before."

"And failed every time."

"Yes, but this one seems so promising, both from the reports and from what you tell me yourself." The eyes moved, oceans of blue, examining something out of range of the distant pickup.

"Great, great would the triumph be if this human were to deliver what he promises, if he truly has not the treasonfear which is so prevalent among his kind."

"From the little I have learned in my studies of human verbal inflection and face-body gestures," Naras Sharaf said, "I have the impression that he was quite sincere in his wish to work with us."

"I would still like a stronger rationale," the elder persisted. "Generalizations make me nervous, especially in a matter as important as this."

"Too early to say." Naras Sharaf refused to be drawn into commitment or opinion. "I hold still to the power theory. Many humans live by it, though they admit it not even to themselves. Most of the bipeds would be more than sated with the power this man has already gained. Apparently he is not. Power is the most addictive of narcotics, Fourth Father."

"Nothing is said I would argue with." He seemed to relax slightly, his skin flow increasing. The gel was opaque with age. "I worry overmuch when I should be overmuch joyed."

"We will watch him constantly," Naras Sharaf said placatingly, wishing for his Fourth Father to pleasure in this moment with equal fervor. "The man will be monitored. The information he supplies to us will from the beginning be most carefully checked to make certain that he feeds us no falsehoods.''

"Did you even mention the possibility of an implant?" inquired the elder. "That would finalize my happiness, for then I would worry no more."

"I thought it premature, Fourth Father," Naras Sharaf told him honestly. "I was wary unto stiffening that I might not secure his cooperation, and thought it best to do that alone this first meeting. You must know that humans have a particular horror of other creatures, however tiny, living within their own bodies."

"And yet their own systems," murmured the elder, "are alive with endemic parasites and all manner of independently functioning organisms."

"That is so." Naras Sharaf leaned back in his cupouch and idly cleaned one eye with a tentacle. The other remained focused on the screen. A Nuel could look in two directions simultaneously, like a chameleon—another trait which did not endear them to races like mankind saddled with more conventional and restrictive vision.

"There seems to be a critical size. That which is invisible to sight is not offensive, nor is anything as large as a small *nming*. But if it is small enough to live within the body cavity, yet larger than microscopic, it is something to be abhorred."

"How strange," the elder muttered. "I would not know what to do without my plaaciate."

"Nor would I." Naras Sharaf patted his lower abdominal bulge where the tiny inch-long creature made a home, living off residual food consumed by the Nuel while filtering out dangerous poisons and rendering them harmless before they could damage its host's body.

"You would think that something comparable engineered

for the human system, which has no counterpart to the plaaciatoma, would be welcomed by them with great delight. Yet they are not only not interested in but are made ill by the thought of such products."

"This man may be different, Fourth Father, but even he may need time to adjust to the idea."

"It is very strange," the elder mused. "We must change all that in the future."

"Verily we must," agreed Naras Sharaf. "Farewell, Fourth Father. Carry tidings of our great achievement to the Family Councils."

"That I will do with the greatest of delightment," said the elder.

"With the greatest of delightment, Fourth Father," echoed Naras Sharaf as he ended the clandestine transmission. He touched a control, and the creatures who formed the broadcast screen gratefully went to sleep.

IX

As the months traveled down to the vanishing point of time neither Naras Sharaf nor his Fourth Father nor any of the members of the Family Si which was in charge of covert activities among non-Family worlds had any reason to regret the time and effort they had put into recruiting the human Kee-yes vain Lewmaklin.

The information that came from him in a steady stream was every bit as valuable as anyone could wish. Furthermore, he refused their offer to transmit the information through an intermediary because, as he said, of the danger of detection.

Thanks almost entirely to Loo-Macklin's information the Nuel were able to defeat UTW forces in three out of four small battles in free space, and to accomplish this with surprisingly light casualties.

These unusual successes, for usually the results were reversed, emboldened the more militant among the Families to call for the all-out war they had put off in favor of numerous small-scale skirmishes. They were voted down unanimously in the private chambers of the Council of Eight.

It was pointed out to the hotheads that the recent modest successes their forces had secured had been made possible in large part because of information obtained from a highly secret source. Expanded conflict would make the always nervous humans extra wary, would jeopardize their source, and would make it unlikely he could supply enough information to assure the success of such a risky and dangerous enterprise.

Besides, there was no need to take such a chance. Patience was a strong Nuel virtue. An occasional defeat in combat might have a deleterious effect on human morale, but it would be slight at best. Most citizens of the huge UTW paid little or no attention to such news bulletins, repetition having long since inured them to the effects.

More important by far was the information their special source provided the Council about psychological motivation, the fragility of computer programming on some of the less affluent worlds, and related matters.

For example, there were the worlds of Mio and Giyo, where Nuel-manipulated businesses were able to gain control of local commerce. Again, thanks to information supplied by the mysterious source. It was the first time commercial penetration had achieved such a result.

Using such methods, some among the Nuel predicted that within the next fifty birthing cycles the Families might gain enough influence within the eighty-three worlds to affect decisions not only among planetary boards of operators, but also on an interworld level.

Alan Dean Foster

Within a hundred and fifty cycles it was not inconceivable that complete control could be gained of the UTW. This with little loss of life, commerce, or material.

The predictions were not idle, not dreams, for the source of critical information necessary to grease the path to quiet conquest was likewise still comparatively young. Nuel physiological engineering could extend his life an extra fifty or sixty years, and thus his usefulness.

There was no reason to fear for the plan. The Great Families were hard pressed to constrain their delight. Many looked forward to the day, though they personally might not live to see it, when a new era of Nuel expansion would reach out to encompass a hundredth of the known galaxy.

Skepticism was greatest among the Si Family, which was responsible for interspecies intelligence work. Years of frustration in dealing with humans had made them irritable and inclined to criticize as a matter of course. Gradually, however, their famed surliness gave way to an unbridled enthusiasm greater than that of those Family members who'd voted to support the enterprise, as Loo-Macklin's information continued to flow freely and prove in every instance to be accurate as well as valuable.

For his part, Loo-Macklin's interests prospered mightily. His employees could only shake their heads in wonder at their boss' incredible ability to continually locate new sources of rare metals and earths, or to provide the groundwork for the development of new techniques in gene and bioengineering which confounded the experts employed by his own companies. Particularly when one was aware of Loo-Macklin's non-existent background in such fields.

Those who had watched him over the years, however, were surprised by nothing Loo-Macklin did. Basright, for example, accepted such miracles without comment. They were simply

160

a part of the endless river of surprises that flowed from the remarkable individual he worked for.

Basright suspected that Loo-Macklin had put together a private, sequestered research team of top specialists in many fields and that they labored out of sight (and out of any competitor's bribery range) to produce one explosive discovery after another. It was the sort of thing Loo-Macklin would do, in order to enjoy his competitor's confusion and frustration as much as the fruits of his think tank's labors.

In fact, Basright was not far wrong. He erred only in not suspecting the inhumanity of those unseen researchers.

Naras Sharaf continued to function as intermediary between Loo-Macklin and the worlds of the families. Oftentimes Loo-Macklin preferred to deliver really important information in person, so a private resort station had been set in orbit around Evenwaith.

Whenever man and Nuel were to meet, the station's guests were given good-byes and its personnel sent on vacation. The freefall display chambers were shut down, the rooms for logi exercise turned off.

Naras Sharaf always arrived in a shuttle vehicle of human design and manufacture, adapted for Nuel use. It was impossible to shield so small a vehicle from detecting equipment. Therefore the captain of the starship which delivered Sharaf to such meetings nervously kept his own much larger craft many planetary diameters out from the surface.

None of the station's employees ever became suspicious of the periodic shutdowns. They were glad of the frequent, if sporadic, vacations which came their way and accepted them with good grace. It was hardly their business, was it, if the station management chose to turn the entire facility over to some rich executive or operator for a private party?

Even the shuttle crew which carried Loo-Macklin up to the

station remained innocent of the real purpose of their boss' journey. They did their job quietly, efficiently, without questions. They made too much money for too little work to trouble themselves with questions.

They didn't worry about their boss flitting about an empty space station. His reclusiveness was famous, and such stations were largely automatic, computer maintained and run. And in truth Loo-Macklin often went up early so he could roam the empty, silent corridors in peace prior to the arrival of Naras Sharaf.

It was he who'd insisted on the meetings to hand over especially important or sensitive information. Though he and Sharaf employed the most modern of tightbeams for their communications and encoded them with sufficient complexity to baffle even those who performed the encoding, he still worried about a message being accidentally intercepted by some idle, unsuspecting communications prober far out in interworld space. Personal contact was expensive, time-consuming, and dangerous. The Nuel agreed at once, however. The cost was nothing, the time well-spent, the danger an inconvenience compared to what was gained. The important thing was that secrecy was assured, and Loo-Macklin's status rose in the eyes of the Si because it was the human who had proposed it.

"Greetings, my friend." Naras Sharaf stepped out of the large airlock into the station, his cilia moving damply across the velcronite floor. The Nuel were slow and not particularly agile. What they lacked in athletic ability they more than made up for with exceptional digital dexterity. A Nuel tentacle was capable of feats of manipulation no human hand could hope to equal.

Loo-Macklin extended a hand and Naras Sharaf enveloped it in a tentacle. When they separated, the man spat in the

palm of his left hand and touched it to the edge of another
tentacle, the mingling of bodily fluids being the equivalent
among them of a friendly greeting.

He walked patiently alongside the bulky alien as they
strolled toward a large chamber which no station guest had
ever entered. It had been adapted to serve Nuel as well as
human comforts.

Behind the two, several other Nuel clad in freshly spun
uniforms were unloading tightly packed precision instruments
designed to aid in the manipulation of cellular material,
Loo-Macklin's reimbursement for today's package of information. The equipment had been built with Loo-Macklin's
specifications in mind. The Nuel engineers had become
experts during the past few years in supplying him with
requested instrumentation. They looked on it as a challenge,
for not only were they constructing much new machinery but
every piece had to look on close inspection as though it had
been built by human hands.

Naras Sharaf settled into the powder blue cupouch and
leaned his gross, warty form back against the inner curve of
the horseshoe brace. He touched a control on the nearby
dispenser. It served up a triangular drinking vessel filled with
a liquid any human would have found unpalatable, if not downright corrosive.

"Well, my friend," he finally said after sucking the
triangle dry and ordering up a refill, "I hear from sources that
our long association is leaving you more prosperous than
ever."

"I've been raised to status Second Class. It is supposed to
be quite an honor, though I find such affectations distracting
as well as meaningless. Odd how people will take the measure of a man by what words tell about him, without ever
meeting the person in question themselves. I'm sure there are

hundreds of people who have fully formed opinions about me, whom I will never actually meet. But this must be meaningless to you as well.''

''Not so, not at all at all,'' replied Naras Sharaf. ''You forget what a student of human culture I be. There is much that I find confusing, admittance be made.''

''No more confusing than most humans find your society,'' said Loo-Macklin. ''They wonder at sixty inhabited planets ruled not only without the direction and wisdom of advanced computers, but by a family system they consider archaic.''

''It has served the Nuel for thousands of years.'' Naras Sharaf's voice assumed an unaccustomed solemnity. ''It serves us still.''

''And very well, too,'' Loo-Macklin agreed. ''You're looking well.'' His gaze dropped and he said politely, ''I see that you've added an inch to your skirt.''

The Nuel shifted in the cupouch. The several flaps of gray flesh which hung from his lower abdomen to overhang the upper cilia moved from side to side like the wings of a manta under water.

''Not unfortunate have I been. Why deny that our association has brought glory to me as well as benefits to you? I gain praise from it. Now then,'' he said eagerly, ''what new delights do you have for me?''

''Always in a hurry, Naras Sharaf.'' Loo-Macklin smiled thinly. ''Later. First I have a request.''

''Ah. Something in addition to the agreed-upon shipment.'' The alien seemed uncertain. ''Well, ask. I suppose the Families would grant you a bonus now and again. They owe you much.''

''It's nothing involving Family expenditure; no credit or instrumentation or pharmaceuticals. Nothing like that, at least not directly." He leaned back in his chair and regarded the ceiling, his voice assuming a falsely wistful tone.

"You see, I've made it possible these past years for the Nuel to participate extensively in the commerce of the eighty-three worlds of the UTW. What I want, Naras Sharaf, is the right to do the same on the worlds of the Families. There are already a few human firms who've managed to gain access to your markets."

"Little things," said Naras Sharaf nervously. "Minor trading at specified and restricted interworld ports. They run no products directly to Family worlds."

"Well, I want to." Loo-Macklin looked hard at the alien. "You say what a student of human culture you are. I've not been idle these past years. I've studied you, Naras, and everything I could obtain about the Nuel." He made a gargling sound.

Naras Sharf twitched and his eyes performed acrobatics. "I did not know you could do that, Lewmaklin!"

"A difficult language," Loo-Macklin confessed, "but not an impossible one to learn, if one persists. It would be easier with water in my lungs, but I can't drown and speak at the same time the way you can."

"But that was the calling for converse," muttered the astonished Naras Sharaf. "I understood you clearly."

"There's a way of compensating that my own linguists have been working on for some time," Loo-Macklin told him. "It wasn't as difficult to accomplish as some would think. The main block was the fact that electronic translators do a perfectly adequate job of translating human and Nuel words. Also there's not much call to master a language when there's little opportunity to use it. Contact between our peoples remains minimal."

He leaned over, sipped at a drink and added some new words. "It's an intimate way of speaking and it takes care and practice," he told Naras Sharaf. "But if I concentrate, keep a glass of water or some other liquid close at hand, and learn how to form the tones properly, I can reproduce almost any sound in the language of the Families."

"A remarkable accomplishment, Kee-yes vain Lewmaklin," said Naras Sharaf honestly. "Such efforts convince me you truly wish to do commerce directly with the Family worlds."

"Truly," gargled Loo-Macklin, adding in terranglo, "I think it's only fair. I've made it possible for the Nuel to do it on numerous human worlds. I ask only the same privilege. It's not as though you'd be opening the Family worlds to general commerce. Only my people would have the right, a right you know I won't abuse because our interests are the same. I'll screen everyone chosen, from the ship pilots down to the factors."

"A powerful request," Naras mumbled. "Naturally, I have not the authority to grant it."

"But you'll put it to the Council of Eight on my behalf?"

"Well, to the Si and Orlymas, at least. Those are the families that regulate commerce."

"Tell them it's not something only I would benefit from," Loo-Macklin urged him. "Any trading families involved will likewise benefit. I'd think they'd jump at the chance to trade directly for UTW products on their home ground. It would mean my people would be absorbing some of the transportation expense and troubles."

"I know, I know. There have been many who secretly if not openly have wished for such a thing. But continuing hostilities between our peoples. . . ."

"That won't be a problem because you'll be dealing

166

strictly with my companies," Loo-Macklin reminded him impatiently. "The Families already know me, know what I've done for them and will continue to do. It's only that I don't see any reason why all concerned can't increase their profits while the Nuel increase their penetration of the UTW."

"So simple you make it sound; simple and inevitable." Naras seemed to be gaining confidence in the idea. "Yes, possible this may be. Truly will I communicate your request to the Orlymas, though the Si must clear it first. I think it may take a full vote of the Eight to make it happen, however." He paused, then asked curiously, "Tell me, my friend, why have you waited this long to make this request? I suspect it is not a new thought with you."

"I can't hide anything from you, can I, Naras Sharaf? No, it's not a new thought. I had it in the back of my mind on the day we first met outside Cluria."

"Then this is the end you have been working toward all along." Loo-Macklin nodded. "It makes great sense. An interesting place to visit must be the back of your mind, Kee-yes vain Lewmaklin."

Loo-Macklin shrugged. "Not really. Crowded, certainly. But not especially interesting. My desires are quite basic, really. Uncomplicated."

Naras Sharaf made a sound the man could not interpret. Then, "I admire your patience. You have so firmly insinuated yourself into the intelligence network of the Si Family that I suspect they could not do without you. I think the Eight will grant your request. Once you begin, there are many small trading families who will swarm to do business with you."

"Think of the propaganda benefits to be gained by the Families, too," Loo-Macklin hastened to point out. "You'll be able to make a grand pronouncement over UTW channels that after many years the Nuel, as a gesture of friendship between our peoples, are opening up their internal trade to human entrepreneurs."

"Of course, that means only those companies owned or controlled by you," said Naras.

"Of course. But it will look excellent in the human journalistic channels. The Families will gain in ways other than commercially by granting my favor."

"Of myself, would I grant it this moment," said Naras Sharaf, now positively enthusiastic about the idea, "but as mentioned, I have not the authority."

"That's all right." Loo-Macklin dialed himself a non-alcohol drink from his own dispenser. "I've waited years for this. I can always wait a little while longer. . . ."

There was much debate among the Eight Great Families over Loo-Macklin's extraordinary request. The more insular among the Nuel were opposed. But Loo-Macklin, via Naras Sharaf, assured the heads of the Families that there would be no flood of humans, of potential intelligence agents, traveling among the sixty worlds of the Nuel. There would be only Loo-Macklin's chosen representatives, chosen ones on whom he would keep a close personal watch to make certain no UTW government agents infiltrated their number.

When they asked for reassurances he informed them that several agents for the Board of Operators covert activities bureau had already approached him for permission to work with his trading factors on the Nuel worlds. Instead of turning down the request, he'd agreed.

Now he supplied their names and likenesses to representatives of the Si, so that a close watch could be kept upon them. The Si were delighted, pronouncing Lewmaklin almost as devious as themselves, and almost voting to make him an honorary member of the family.

That would have been too much, however. After all, a *human*.

Loo-Macklin was not troubled by the slight. Honorary family status meant no more to him than the Second Class status he'd achieved among his own kind.

At any rate, the Council of Eight was convinced, and Loo-Macklin was granted his trading privileges.

Within three years he had thirty different trading establishments on twenty of the major Nuel worlds. As he had predicted, the propaganda victory for the Families was considerable, and they were able to insinuate themselves ever more deeply into human affairs. Profits exceeded the expectations of Loo-Macklin and Nuel trading families alike.

It was when he was making a personal inspection trip to Molraz, one of the largest Nuel worlds, that his guide, Naras Sharaf, drew him away from a just concluded business meeting and conducted him to a place of privacy.

When he was certain they were alone the alien turned both vast eyes on the man. "If you are still so inclined, Kee-yes vain Lewmaklin, I have a special treat for you."

"Still inclined? What are you talking about, Naras?"

"Something you mentioned to me a number of years ago. Something which I naturally ignored at the time and never remarked upon again, but which I did not forget. My mental file is almost as large as the one I employ for food." He caressed his protruding abdomen. His skirt almost hid his cilia now, dragging on the floor. A handsome specimen of mature Nuel maleness.

"I wonder if your interest remains." He glanced around the circular room once more. "There are those who would think it heresy and have my skirt for it, but I feel that as friend as well as associate, I owe you this chance."

169

Loo-Macklin wondered what the alien was being so secretive about. As he watched, the two *el* spinning their way across Naras Sharaf's upper body switched to silver and gold as they consumed his old attire of black and white polka dots. Naras automatically lifted his left upper tentacle to allow them access to his flank and back.

The el were one bioproduct humanity did not take to. The idea of inch long bugs constantly crawling over one's flesh was not appealing to the majority of mankind, not even to the more fashion-conscious among them. Besides, the *el* tickled the more sensitive human skin.

Loo-Macklin found them unirritating and had bought several dozen of the industrious little creatures early on in his trading relationship with the Nuel. The sight of his clothing changing constantly during the day was as fascinating as the material, a fine silk, was comfortable. The special *el* he wore had been trained and bred by Nuel designers to clothe the human body.

"Enough toying about, Naras Sharaf," he said, more curious than impatient. "What desire have I forgotten that you have not?"

"Your wish to observe a Birthing," Naras Sharaf told him in a low voice.

Loo-Macklin felt a rising surge of excitement, rare these days. Any hint of something new and special was an event.

"Very much would I like this. Are you truly serious?"

"Truly much so," said the alien. "But there are complications."

"I am not surprised. What kind of complications?"

"To the best of my knowledge," said Naras, hesitating to answer, "no alien, human or otherwise, has ever witnessed a Birthing in person."

Loo-Macklin saw no reason to argue with that. A Birthing was an event of importance and privacy.

"But you," Naras continued, "have become such a vital part of our efforts to infiltrate and control the UTW, and have proven your loyalty on so many occasions these past years, that you have made many friends among the families. So I have been able to secure permission from one such for you to observe one of their Birthings." He hesitated.

"But there is a condition. A strong condition."

"Name it."

"Restrain your compliance 'til you have heard." Loo-Macklin hadn't seen Naras Sharaf this serious in some time. He listened carefully.

"The observer psychologist in charge, with whom I had contact, was most reluctant, but he agreed to pass favorably on the request if you would accede to one condition. His superiors agreed and think it a valuable idea even if no Birthing view was involved.

"Recall you that a number of years ago I mentioned to you the possibility of your taking on an implant?"

Loo-Macklin's memory sought. "Vaguely, yes. You never told me what kind of implant."

"It was first proposed by the Si. You are a remarkable human, Kee-yes vain Lewmaklin, but I do not know if you are remarkable enough to agree to this.

"There is a very small, empathetically sensitive creature we have bred. A symbiotic non-motile insect about the size of the claw in your smallest digit."

Loo-Macklin looked thoughtfully at the nail adorning his little finger.

"Somewhat smaller than that, actually," said the uncomfortable Naras. "There is a technique by which it can be sensitized to a particular thought. It is then implanted behind the cerebral cortex of any oxygen breather. An Orischian, for example, or myself, or a. . . ."

"Or a human," Loo-Macklin finished for him. "Myself, for example."

"Truly, for example," Naras admitted, watching him carefully for reaction. As usual, there was nothing. Naras had grown adept at recognizing the meaning of human gestures and expressions. Loo-Macklin was neutral as ever.

"You would be asked to think a certain thought at the moment of sensitization. There are ways of checking on such things. We have equivalents of your truth machines. The sensitization process, by the way, is a chemical one and utterly painless."

"What kind of thought?"

"That you would agree never to do anything that would be contrary to the best interests of the Nuel. The actual insertion is performed under local anesthetic. You would never feel or be aware of the presence of the *lehl* in your skull."

Loo-Macklin reached back and rubbed his neck. "How long does this little visitor stay with you?"

"For the life of the implantee or until it is removed by Nuel surgeons. I assure you that only my own people are capable of making such an implant work. If anyone else, human doctors for example, were to attempt to remove the *lehl* the process would affect the creature's emotional stability and it would react by defending itself."

"And how would it do that?"

"By hiding in the only place it knows. By leaving its assigned position and burrowing as deeply as necessary into its host's brain."

"Then I'll make sure I don't sign up for any surprise operations." Loo-Macklin smiled slightly.

"Then you consent?" Naras Sharaf was startled in spite of himself.

"Why not?"

Naras performed several elaborate gestures and eye movements indicative of astonishment mixed with delight.

"That is wonderful to hear and a great relief to me personally. I can tell you now that for over a year there has been much talk of testing your loyalty by asking you to undergo such an implanting. The Si were against it, not wanting to risk losing your aid should you decline. They will be most pleased and your decision will strengthen their position within the Eight.

"The problem arose because whether you realize it or not, Kee-yes vain Lewmaklin, you have become so deeply entrenched in not only our intelligence service but also general commerce that your humanness itself became enough to condemn you in certain circles. Many grow nervous to see a human wield such influence. Now that you have agreed to accept an implant, even those voices raised most vitriolic against you must cease their complaining. Your ability to work freely among the families will not be questioned again."

"What happens if someone goes back on their sensitized thought but doesn't try to have the *lehl* removed?" Loo-Macklin asked curiously.

"The disturbance will register with the creature. The chemosensitive receptors within its body will become irritated and the body will release a nerve poison. The action is instinctive and reflexive. The creature has no more control over it than you do. The host dies quickly. There is no effective antidote. The mind dies first."

"Unpleasant. Yet you regard the *lehl* as a beneficial creature."

"All creatures, no matter how seemingly insignificant or

unimportant, have their uses. That is a lesson your kind has yet to learn.

"As long as you do not try to have it removed and do not retract the sensitized thought, you will not even notice its presence, save for one small side effect."

"Which is what?" Loo-Macklin asked.

"The *lehl* prefers calm surroundings, as does any sensible creature. It secretes other chemicals to make its 'home' a comfortable place. While it remains with you, you cannot suffer cerebral hemorrhaging. If you receive damage to the skull, the *lehl* will assist your natural bodily mechanisms in healing any wounds.

"And another headache you will not have for the duration of your life." Naras Sharaf sounded pleased at being able to cite a beneficial effect or two for the implant.

The former sounded good to Loo-Macklin. He did not tell Naras Sharaf that in his long and complex life he had never experienced a headache. . . .

X

Sharaf was right. The operation was painless. Loo-Macklin was even able to watch, disdaining general anesthetic, as the incredibly deft Nuel surgeons opened the back of his head and inserted the tiny, dark blue creature. It did not move about, resembling a scrap of blue sponge more than a living animal.

Then they sealed the opening so smoothly that within a couple of hours it was impossible to tell where the initial incisions had been made. A brief session under the programming machinery, during which he dutifully complied with all instructions necessary to sensitize the *lehl* to the indicated thought, and then he was up and walking about.

He put his hand to the back of his head. Only by pressing very hard was there even the slightest hint that something other than flesh and bone lay beneath the skin. He hadn't even lost any hair.

For a few days he scratched at the spot, but the itch he rubbed was psychological only. In a week he'd forgotten about it.

Then came the day when Naras spirited him out of the central city in a Nuel ground car. Loo-Macklin had to scrunch down low to avoid bumping the curved, claustrophobically low ceiling.

Compressed air powered the car through a plastic tube, sent it speeding out into the countryside toward a distant range of spectacularly rugged mountains. It was raining outside the tube, most Nuel worlds being subject to periodic deluges. These the Nuel manufactured themselves when they did not occur naturally with sufficient frequency. The Nuel were evolved amphibians. They couldn't breathe water any longer, but they still liked to be wet.

"Where are we going?" the cramped human asked his guide.

"There are certain traditional places," Naras Sharaf explained. "New worlds give rise to new traditions. We go to one such place.

"A pregnant female has her choice of where to give birth. On the original eight worlds of our forefathers there are ancient sites which have been used for this purpose for thousands of years. Birthing at such places is rumored to endow offspring with such virtues as good luck, fine appearance, thick cilia, sexual potency and other desirables. Nonsense, of course, but entrenched superstitions die hard."

"We have plenty of our own," Loo-Macklin assured him.

"I am aware of that." He turned great eyes on the tube ahead. "In witnessing of a Birthing you will learn one of the great secrets of the Nuel, learn why such events are so closely guarded from the sight of aliens. You are to be the first, Kee-yes vain Lewmaklin. A great privilege. No one is worried about this. Not now, not since the implanting." One eye continued to study the route before them while the other swiveled independently to stare at Loo-Macklin.

"The implant gives you no trouble?"

"None whatsoever. In fact, I think you must have understated the beneficial side effects the *lehl* induces. Since the implanting I feel better than I have in years."

"No human has partnered a *lehl* before, so though the probable results were carefully schematized before the operation, they remained only theoretical."

"In fact, I feel positively buoyant."

The tube rose into the mountains, carrying the car with it through passes and around sheer cliffs no road could have traversed. At night the single large moon shone on coniferous trees whose branches curved upward, giving the forest they were traveling through the appearance of an army of emerald candelabra. Loo-Macklin slept soundly on the pallet that had been arranged for him near the back of the thin, long car. The creature inside his head which could kill him instantly saw to it that he always had a good night's sleep.

Two days later they'd left any semblance of flat ground far behind. Occasional Nuel communities were visible, built in scattered mountain valleys or on the less precipitous flanks of snow-capped crags.

The car slowed automatically and was shunted into a smaller tube. They sped on alone, no other car visible ahead or behind them at the usual preset interval.

Eventually they slowed. The car slid out of the tube into a docking area inside a building decorated with baroque carvings and mosaics. Arches were everywhere, employed more for their aesthetic than architectural use.

A pair of subtly armed Nuel approached the car. They wore

two *el* apiece, the busy spinners constantly changing the shape of the stars that dominated the alien's blue and brown uniforms. They looked askance at Loo-Macklin as he wrinkled his way out of the confining vehicle and drew their stubby projectile weapons.

One recognized Sharaf. "Truly this is some kind of bad humor, brother."

"Truly there is no humor to it," Sharaf replied.

"But surely you cannot mean to. . . ."

"It is all right, brothers," Sharaf assured them. "He has been spoken for."

"Hello," said a new voice. The Nuel who joined them now was younger than even the two guards, considerably younger than Naras Sharaf. He was barely beginning to gain control over the viscosity of his excreted slime and other bodily fluids and his interlocking eyelids occasionally stuck together longer than was completely polite. In addition to the iridescent purple which occasionally flashed from the skin of a Nuel, a bright yellow sparkle also appeared on his body from time to time, a particularly attractive surface coloration.

"Greetings, Naras," he murmured. Then both eyes examined the foreigner. "So you are Kee-yes vain Lewmaklin."

The stocky human extended a hand palm downward, fingers tightly pressed together, as he'd discovered was the preferable approach among the Nuel. The newcomer hesitated, then extended two tentacles and crudely managed the shaking motion. Loo-Macklin spat into his other hand and offered fluid, studying the other in turn.

"From what I have been told," the newcomer said, "it is difficult to believe that you are not a Nuel biologically re-engineered by our scientists to resemble a human."

"I'm quite human," Loo-Macklin assured him. "As human as you are Family."

"I am Chaheel Riens. Nuel psychologist and student of alien thoughts and actions."

"So truly are you then here to observe me as much as anything else."

"Truly," admitted Chaheel, showing no surprise at Loo-Macklin's mastery of the guttural Nuel tongue. That much he expected, having studied it in the records pertaining to this remarkable creature.

"I am to understand that you have submitted to a *lehl* implant?"

Loo-Macklin said nothing.

"Well then, I suppose you are as assured of as any biped could be. Come along, and please lower your voices to a respectful level."

Naras and Loo-Macklin trailed behind the psychologist as he exited the car dock and entered the main structure. The human's presence attracted many stares and set others to talking. He smiled inwardly at some of the comments which were whispered openly in the belief that he could not understand them.

The Nuel were quite conscious of the fact that all other civilized races regarded them as exceptionally ugly. For their part, the Nuel had never thought of themselves as very attractive, either. The attitudes of other peoples coupled with the Nuel's own insecurity combined to produce a racial inferiority complex unmatched among any other intelligent race. It also served to bind the Nuel tightly together.

Three other sentient species had been taken over by the expanding Nuel society. These three now kept their true opinions of the Nuel appearance well hidden. It is not healthy to make disparaging remarks about one's conqueror.

The Nuel could do nothing to make themselves attractive. Very well then; they would settle instead for power. One day mankind, too, would be forced to hide its contempt for the Nuel. One day the bipeds of the eighty-three worlds of the UTW would kiss the ground a Nuel slid upon, if so ordered.

Until then the Nuel would bide their time, endure the continuing flow of insults inspired by their appearance, and keep silent.

Soon the visitors had left behind the smoothly crafted rooms and corridors and had entered a dimly lit passage hewn out of the solid mountain. They continued down the long tunnel. Loo-Macklin could see ancient signs and paintings covering the walls, some carefully protected by a transparent shield to prevent accidental damage.

"This is a very old place," Naras Sharaf told him reverently. "The Nuel have held Birthings here for several hundred years."

"Surely those patterns are older than that?" Loo-Macklin indicated the tunnel decorations.

"No. They are old enough, but are only duplicates of those appearing on similar tunnel walls on the Motherworld, on ancient Woluswollam. These were painted here by the first settlers of this world. So they are old but not truly ancient. Old enough, though, to be worth preserving. The inhabitants of this world take pride in their origins."

"Lucky them," said Loo-Macklin, but Sharaf's curious look did not make him elaborate further.

The passageway wound deeper into the mountain before opening into a large natural cavern. Stalactites and stalagmites grew in profusion, and there was even some butterfly calcite hanging from a nearby flowstone curtain. Geology's the same everywhere, he thought. There was running water somewhere ahead, and close by.

They were met by a Nuel clad in a peculiar conical cap and an unmoving, prewoven garment, one of the few Loo-Macklin had seen on a Nuel. It was deep brown shot through with black metal thread. Their host had been told of their coming, since he glanced only briefly at Loo-Macklin before addressing himself softly to Naras Sharaf.

"It is almost time. Truly should we hurry." He added almost imperceptibly, with a half-glance at Loo-Macklin, "I like this not."

Then they were jogging down the path leading deeper into the main cavern. Surprisingly, it began to grow lighter even though the artificial lights faded to insignificance. The cavern narrowed, then opened into a still larger chamber. Filtered sunlight entered from the far side through a translucent green glass window of impressive proportions and multi-sided shape.

They had gone completely through this part of the mountain. Here an underground stream rambled through a section of cavern exquisitely decorated with long limestone straws and thick masses of twisting helectites.

It was not the colorful formations which drew Loo-Macklin's attention, however, but the deep, still pool formed by a gaur dam on the far side of the running stream. It was the first time he'd ever seen a pregnant Nuel.

Her lower abdomen was swollen three times normal size. The loose folds of skin which formed the cilia-shielding skirt, of which Naras Sharaf was so proud, had expanded to encompass the increased volume of flesh.

The Nuel in the hat escorted them to a molded formation which hid several observation cupouches and instructed them to keep out of sight. Particularly Loo-Macklin, whose presence could be disturbing to she-who-was-about-to-give-birth.

Loo-Macklin studied the chamber relentlessly. Despite every attempt to make the setup look as natural and unaffected as it had been for Birthing Nuel females thousands of years ago, he quickly noted a number of alterations not made to the cavern by nature.

There were slick areas set in both the ceiling and side walls, one-way glass behind which monitors and machinery were likely concealed. Cave formations concealed transmission lines and conduits for substances other than electricity. There was nothing primitive about this Birthing site, despite its appearance. Vast obstetrical technology was hidden everywhere, ready to watch, monitor and assist if necessary. It seemed like a lot of equipment to aid one birth. The reason for it would become clear soon enough.

He asked Naras Sharaf about it.

"You are correct in assuming that the appearance of the place is more designed than real. The mental health of the mother is every bit as cared for as the physical.

"That pool, for example," he gestured over the barrier, "appears to be a backwater of this underground stream. In fact, the pool water is heated some thirty embits warmer than the stream flow. Warm water in a sheltered place was the preferred spot for giving birth among our primitive ancestors. There are no warm springs on this world, however. So we help nature along a little.

"Everything you see before you, even to the shape and appearance of the midwives clustered around the mother, has been designed to provide her with the maximum comforting, psychologically as well as physiologically. Notice the color of the formations, the shape? They are not natural either." That surprised Loo-Macklin. He couldn't tell them from the real cave formations.

"Chosen by the mother, for her family will pamper her all she wishes. A Birthing is a great event in any family."

Loo-Macklin strained to obtain a better view while at the same time making certain he kept well out of sight. He was also aware that the psychologist Chaheel was devoting considerably more attention to Loo-Macklin than to the Birthing in progress across the stream.

He'd been the subject of studious attention on numerous other occasions. The fact that the eyes now concentrating on him were not human didn't trouble him in the least.

The lighting in the cavern was even dimmer than the usual faint haze the Nuel preferred and he had to work to see anything at all.

There was a quickening of activity among the many attendants surrounding the site. Tentacles moved efficiently; to prepare, to help, to do whatever was necessary to ensure that things ran smoothly.

A great shudder passed through the object of all this attention. There was no warning, no series of intensifying contractions as there would have been in a human female in the same situation. A vast, gurgling sigh issued from the swollen bulk and then the enormous body heaved several times, like a huge bellows.

Suddenly there was a flurry of activity in the water of the pool and a corresponding rush by the Nuel attendants. Loo-Macklin could see dozens of small shapes thrashing on the surface, churning the once placid pool to foam. The attendants needed every one of their tentacles to aid the young to the surface so they could breathe.

An oceanic origin of quite recent development had been postulated for the Nuel by human xenobiologists, but until now there had been no proof for it. Cephalopodian shape and exterior construction was not proof enough.

Loo-Macklin noticed that the cilia of the young Nuel grew as much from the sides of the body as from underneath. As the young matured the cilia would shift until they gave support to the form, acting as legs instead of oars.

And still they tore at the water even as dozens were carefully, lovingly moved to shallow bassinets of warm water. As their heads were lifted into the air they emitted a sharp whistling. It filled the cavern with a snapping sound as if a million castenets formed a background to the whistling: the sound of dozens of tiny beaks biting at the air.

"This is our secret." Chaheel Riens spoke softly. "Not all females can give birth. This selective sterility is an evolutionary development designed to hold down the population. We have tried to adjust it to suit our wishes but cannot." Coming from the finest bioengineers alive, Loo-Macklin thought, that was a sobering assessment.

"Furthermore," the psychologist continued, "those who are capable of delivering young can do so only once in a lifetime. But a single female can give birth to as many as fifty healthy Nueleens."

It explained so much about the Nuel, Loo-Macklin thought as he watched the newborns being moved out of the cavern toward hidden incubation areas. The stability of their population, the extended families which formed the basis of the more complex and, to humankind, absurd form of interworld government, and the exaggerated courtesy the rare Nuel trader showed to a pregnant female of any species.

"No wonder birth is spoken of with such veneration among the Families," he said to Chaheel Riens.

"You understand then why the process is treated as such an event, far more so than among your own kind," the psychologist replied. "Truly, a miscarriage, as I believe it is called among humans, is cause among us not only for unhappiness and mourning but for great despair. The female in question is finished forever as a mother, again unlike most of your kind.

"A miscarriage among us is the tragedy of whole families with relatives lost. Indeed, a whole family is never born. A series of miscarriages threatens the stability of a community's population and in primitive times, its very survival. As soon as pregnancy is confirmed, it is treated with the utmost attention.

"We find your obstetrical procedures careless and indifferent," he added, "though you no doubt consider them as modern as your computers. We could save eighty percent of those humanettes, those infants who still perish in childbirth.

"Of course," he added, bitterly sarcastic, "no human female would allow a Nuel attendant near her body, much less her sensitive regions, no matter how experienced the attendant or benign its intentions."

Loo-Macklin noted that each newborn was carefully cleaned with a variety of substances before being placed in its individual bassinet. The young seemed vigorous and active, much more so than human newborn at the same stage of development. That was only natural, given the comparative infrequency of Nuel birth. He'd been counting steadily while listening to Chaheel Riens. There were thirty-eight young so far, all seemingly quite healthy.

He remarked on it to Naras Sharaf.

"Yes. Once the young are free of the mother's body, the survival rate is excellent. In primitive times it was much less so, of course. Now few perish in the pools or from post-natal disease."

There seemed to be a hundred attendants swarming around the pool now, caring for both the newborn and the exhausted mother; cleaning, taking temperatures, preparing bassinets, reciting litanies . . . a host of tasks. In addition, one was aware of all the activity taking place out of sight behind walls and one-way panels: the flurry of physicians attending to each newborn, the recorders monitoring health, the special equipment controlling with precision temperature, light, the circu-

185

lation of water. There was even a special group preparing names for each of the thirty-eight children.

The support facilities for this single birth put those of the most modern human hospital to shame. The efficiency and scope of the operation fascinated Loo-Macklin, though not quite for the reasons Naras Sharaf suspected.

"Everything is so thorough," he murmured. "There seems little room for mistake. It's like a starship, full of backup systems for its backup systems."

"Which is why nearly every newborn survives," said Naras Sharaf proudly. "Thousands of years of necessity have taught us how to optimize everything for a successful birth. The process is expensive, traditional, and very effective."

"Quite a production," Loo-Macklin admitted. He glanced at Naras. "Tell me: is the process controlled from start to finish by certain families, the way a branch of the Si is responsible for Intelligence? Or is it divided among all the families according to those who do the best job of it? I'm not talking about the rituals but the products involved; the monitoring equipment, the cleansing liquids, the schools that train the attendants, that sort of thing."

"Efficiency is a matter of competition, though there are some old, venerable favorites for certain items, such as the water salts mined on Veraz. You should be familiar enough with our commerce by now to know this, Kee-yes."

"I always want to make sure."

Naras Sharaf seemed slightly disappointed by the man's questions. "As always, you see in the highest glories of nature only a new path to potential profit."

"That's never troubled you before."

"Indeed and truly not," confessed Naras. "I've profited much by my association with you, far more than I should have without it. Yet still after all these years I. . . ."

Loo-Macklin rose slightly. "Is it safe to leave now?"

Naras Sharaf took a last look at the pool. The mother had been removed to a place of resting, where she could recover and contemplate her thirty-eight offspring in peace. Only a few attendants remained, bustling around the pool and tidying up.

"Yes, it is."

The supervisor, the Nuel with the inflexible attire and pointed cap, came to see them off. They thanked her profusely and Loo-Macklin exchanged substance with both her and the young psychologist Chaheel Riens. Then he and Naras Sharaf retraced their route up the painted tunnel.

Behind them, the supervisor chatted idly with Chaheel Riens. "What did you think of this? It truly troubles me still to permit a human so intimate a knowledge."

"The Council of Eight itself passed on the decision to allow the human attendance," the psychologist replied. "He is bound to us tightly, I was told."

"Truly, I suppose I worry overmuch. It is a characteristic of my work." Her expression lightened somewhat. "I am sure there is naught to be concerned about. I have heard he carries a *lehl* implant sensitized to prevent his doing anything contrary to Nuel interests. No surer bind could be placed on his actions."

"All truth, all truth." Chaheel Riens paused, then said conversationally, "You know I have made some small study of this race called mankind, both on my own out of personal interest and also on commission for the war department. I have never before encountered a specimen quite like this Kee-yes vain Lewmaklin, either physically or mentally. His physiognomy compares with that of far more primitive

187

human types, but his mind is clearly highly developed. The first does not trouble me, but the actions of the latter give me cause for concern."

The supervisor turned one eye up the tunnel which had swallowed the human and his guide while the other remained attentive on the psychologist.

"I must truly confess I see no real reason for worry. Why should we trouble our sleepings on his account when he has been passed by our own Intelligence service?"

"His interest in the commerical aspects of Birthing worries me."

"He is apparently a creature of commerce," remarked the supervisor, "a type not unknown among our own kind. I would say he has more in common with Naras Sharaf than many of his own people. It is only natural that he would be interested in such aspects of Birthing, or of anything else."

"But why Birthing?"

"Perhaps because it was unknown to him. He strikes me as an intensely curious individual, though quiet in manner and speech."

"Too quiet, perhaps truly," muttered Chaheel Riens. "Why Birthing I ask still?"

"As Naras Sharaf observed, the human sees profit in everything. Of such dedication are great fortunes raised. Besides, everything he does which involves family commerce binds him to us from a business standpoint much as the *lehl* does from a physical. So long as he aids us against his own kind, what matters how much money he amasses? Surely his interest, therefore, is all to our benefit."

"Surely," mumbled Chaheel Riens.

The supervisor seemed satisfied that she had soothed the thoughts of her young visitor and scuttled away to assist in the naming of the new offspring, always a pleasant task.

Chaheel Riens stood by the entrance to the pool cavern, thinking. After awhile he removed the tiny unit, part organic, part solid-state, he carried concealed in a fold of his clothing and murmured into it.

Family work had provided him with enough money to have some spare time. He had been planning to devote it to a study of the minterfin war rituals of the ancient Uel family on Nasprinkin. His professors looked forward to the resultant report, for Chaheel Riens was a brilliant student.

Now a new project had come to mind. He had studied humanity in general and, occasionally, free or captured individuals. Something about this Kee-yes vain Lewmaklin intrigued him in a way none of the other alien bipeds had.

Wasting your time, he argued with himself. Better to devote it to the Uel study, as the fatherminds suggest. Si intelligence has checked this one out for years, almost more years than you have been alive. Who are you to second-guess them?

And he carries a *lehl* implant. Not even all Nuel would voluntarily submit to that. Yet this member of an antagonistic race has done so of free will, truly truly.

If nothing else, our knowledge of his traitorous acts has tied him to the Nuel as securely as any *lehl* could do. Should he betray us, his own people would dismember him. Mankind is a vengeful race.

What so troubled Chaheel Riens and what apparently had escaped the good people of the Si in their eagerness to recruit so valuable a human agent was not the fact that Kee-yes vain Lewmaklin was overly interested in the Nuel, but that the man gave the impression of not being interested in anything. An ideal state of mind for a traitor, perhaps, but troubling to Chaheel.

Lewmaklin was interested only in himself. Again, a good

sign in a traitor. Such individuals are more easily bought, truly.

I worry too much, truly, the psychologist thought. That's why my matings seem dull and why intellectual exercise is the only thing that gives me pleasuring. Do I therefore identify with this joyless human? Is that why I am so interested in him?

Regardless, it had to prove more interesting than the somewhat dry study of the Uel rituals. If not, well, he could always drop it.

But Chaheel Riens did not drop his new interest, because the more he learned about Kee-yes vain Lewmaklin, about the incredibly intricate web of commercial and political ties the human had spun among both the eighty-three worlds of the UTW and the worlds of the Families, the more the psychologist resolved to press on. And the more he pressed on, the more frightened he became.

Yes, frightened, though there seemed no overt reason for such an extreme reaction. True to his word, the human seemed to have done nothing contrary to the best interests of the Nuel. Many members of the Great Families had become wealthy beyond imagining thanks to Lewmaklin's assistance. Nuel beliefs and attitudes had worked themselves ever deeper into human society, laying the groundwork for the day when the Nuel would seek to gain control of the UTW government.

Naturally, Lewmaklin also benefited by such activities. He'd made huge investments in many family businesses, most notably in those concerned with supplying the vast range of products utilized during Birthing. A good profit he truly turned, but his interest in the process of Birthing still worried Chaheel Riens. No one else he consulted with seemed concerned, however. Birthing was merely one business in which the human was involved.

But such interest . . . or so it seemed to Chaheel. There were other family businesses where his investment could have brought him a greater return. Why then did he not enter into them?

"Who can fathom the human mind? He must have his reasons. His successes speak for themselves." The replies to his worried questions ran along those lines. "And besides," they would inevitably say, "he has the implant, and it is checked on periodically. The man cannot do harm to us."

"Is a *lehl* so final, then?" he would ask. "Do we know that much about human biology? True, it was tested on human prisoners. True, it cannot be removed or affected by external factors such as irradiation or sound. But what about slow poisoning, carried out under the supervision of human doctors? Couldn't that kill the *lehl* or render it insensitive?"

And he was told, "The *lehl* is too sensitive for that. Any hostile activity, however gradual or subtle, would be detected immediately. There is no chance for the human to experiment, either, for a false move would result in his death. Even a slow poisoning attempt would be detected by our sensors during the man's regular checks. The *lehl* is always healthy, shows no signs of tampering."

"For an individual supposedly dedicated only to profits," Chaheel had argued, "to forego other investment opportunities to concentrate on a lesser industry like Birthing does not make sense in light of what I have built up of his psychological profile."

"Obviously the human sees commerce differently than you," they had chided him. "He clearly senses a chance for greater profit still. There is nothing evil in his obtaining control of any family business, so long as he is carefully monitored. He could not do anything malign even if he so wished, because all the employees close to actual Birthing or

191

production of related material are Nuel. They owe their allegiance to family and their own race, not to their employer. Truly—especially as he is a human.''

Chaheel's arguments availed him nothing. His persistent pessimism made him unwelcome at many government offices. Even his professors turned from him. He grew morose and lost eye color.

He had to confess there was no factual basis for his suspicions of the human Kee-yes vain Lewmaklin. If such evidence did exist to support any such suspicions it was clear that the human had concealed it too well for it to be discovered on the worlds of the Families. Therefore, Chaheel Riens decided, he would have to conclude that he was wasting his time or he would have to seek out such evidence elsewhere.

He would have to travel to the eighty-three worlds of the UTW.

As a psychologist he was more aware than most of the loathing humankind had for the Nuel. The mere sight of one still caused many to turn away in revulsion and horror, and there could be uglier reactions. It was not as dangerous to travel the UTW as it had been years ago, however. Ironically, it was Lewmaklin's efforts on behalf of the Nuel which had made such travel safer.

His knowledge of human psychology should help him, however. He would know better than most of his kind when to approach and when to retreat, how to defuse a potentially dangerous situation. Perhaps he even knew enough to get some answers.

His professors were shocked when he applied for the grant to study human society from within instead of from a distance. They remonstrated with him, not wishing to lose a valuable pupil and brilliant mind to the mob violence which oftentime plagued human cities. But he persisted and, reluctantly, was given the grant. His record of achievement made it possible.

He booked passage on a ship to Restavon. It was one of the two capital human worlds. He would begin there and make his way, as inconspicuously as possible, to Lewmaklin's headquarters world of Evenwaith, which under his direction had become such an industrial goliath that it now ranked third in production and importance only to Restavon and Terra themselves.

He would take his time. Persistence and not genius is often the hallmark of the successful scientist. . . .

XI

It was fortunate that Chaheel possessed scientific detachment as well as expertise. Sometimes that was the only thing that allowed him to cope with the many blunt refusals and outright racial insults his attempted inquiries met with. Fortunately, the profit motive (i.e., greed) was common to both races, so with persistence he was able to find individuals whose love of money enabled them to overcome any personal loathing they might have felt toward the nagging Nuel.

The Orischians were too old an ally of humanity to be of much help, but among the less rigid Athabascans and others he found programmers filled with discontent, real or imagined, who were able to gather information for him from supposedly inviolate computer sources. This gave him levers with which to pry further at his human contacts.

Slowly, inevitably, his work led him to Evenwaith. By now the human scientific community, at least, had come to accept his presence. He was a student of culture and psychology. They did not resent his presence. There were even a few who sympathized with his work and assisted him, without ever becoming aware of his real purpose.

He never saw Kee-yes vain Lewmaklin. Most of the time the great man was not on Evenwaith but was off inspecting his innumerable interests on other worlds or attempting to close some major new contract or merger.

All the while, Chaheel kept tabs on the activities of Loo-Macklin's concerns within the worlds of the Families and in particular those businesses related in some way to the Birthing industry. He discovered that by dint of surreptitious purchasing, outright merger and careful acquisition Loo-Macklin had gained control of some forty percent of all Birthing related commerce.

Not enough to constitute a monopoly: not quite, but large enough to influence methods of buying and selling, and certainly enough to influence the products of smaller subcontractors and suppliers.

Among his Nuel employees he found the same kind of dedication Loo-Macklin inspired in his own kind. And why not? Most of them were unaware their efforts enriched, at the top of the scale, a human. Their loyalty was to their company and to their immediate superiors, all of whom were Nuel. Few had any direct contact with humans, none at all with Loo-Macklin himself.

Those family agents assigned to keep watch on him showed no alarm. Family economists actually welcomed the fresh infusion of outside credit while the Si approved of this new evidence of the man's interest in his allies. Truly was Loo-Macklin's destiny interlocked with the continued well-being of the Nuel!

So large had the human's investments among the families

grown that the potential threat of confiscation of those holdings had become at least as powerful a weapon for controlling him as the implanted *lehl*.

Yet still was Chaheel troubled, for Loo-Macklin continued to pour money into Birthing-related businesses when he stood to enjoy larger profits elsewhere.

Then occurred an event which shocked Basright and those nearest Loo-Macklin as much as it pleased the Nuel. Kees vaan Loo-Macklin announced his intention to marry. To the Nuel, the prospect of a Birthing to their vital ally was greeted with much rejoicing, for no sentient being responsible for young of its own was likely to risk its life on wild adventures or dangerous betrayals.

Her name was Tambu Tabuhan. Loo-Macklin encountered her on Terra. His car was passing through a plant which manufactured computer components when he stumbled on the altercation. That there was a single woman involved, and a slip of one at that, battling three men was enough to make him step in and put a stop to the fight. That she had been holding her own at the time was enough to lift her out of the seething mass of humanity high enough for him to take notice.

Her hair was jet black and straight, her eyes reflective of her Oriental heritage.

"Who asked you to interfere?" she snapped at him, breathing hard and holding the top of her factory jersey together. Behind Loo-Macklin the plant manager nearly fainted as he frantically tried to indicate by signs and grimaces how important the man she was berating was. He failed. Her attention was solely on Loo-Macklin.

"No one," he admitted.

"Then why did you?"

"I don't like unfair fights, even if they're not my own."

"This one's finished." She turned to go.

He put out a hand to stop her. She tried to shake him off, discovered she could not. That in itself was unusual.

"My name is Kees vaan Loo-Macklin."

"So what?"

"I own this plant." That softened her pose, but not her tone.

"That doesn't give you the right to paw me, any more than rescuing me from the likes of those three wimbs does. '

"What would give me the right to paw you?"

"Not a damn thing. I don't care if you own the whole planet."

"What if I told you that I did, more or less?"

"I'd say you were a liar as well as crude."

"I won't dispute the crudeness, but I'm not lying." Then he added the phrase which caused the onlooking Basright's heart to miss a beat.

"I'm alone. I've always been alone. I'd like to try not being alone. How would you like to be my wife?"

She cocked her head to one side, studying him. "You're serious, aren't you?"

"I'm always serious."

"You own this plant?" She gestured, taking in the extensive production facilities stretching off into the distance.

He nodded. The numbed manager confirmed it.

"Other plants as well?"

"I am not poor," he told her.

"Well I am, and it stinks. There's neither grace nor nobility to it, as some fatuous fools sometimes say."

"I couldn't agree more, having once occupied such status myself."

Alan Dean Foster

"So." She considered a moment longer, then shrugged. "Yes, I'll marry you, Kees vaan Loo-Macklin. You're tired of being alone, fine. I'm tired of being poor."

So the bargain was struck. Basright pondered over it for many days thereafter. There had to be a reason besides loneliness, he knew. Loo-Macklin might be experimenting with life, as he so often did, or he might be trying to placate the Nuel, who were ever suspicious of unmated friends. But there had to be a reason. Depend on Loo-Macklin to think it through carefully and do the right thing at the proper psychological moment.

He was only partly correct.

After four years of work among the eighty-three worlds of the UTW, four years of enduring insult and imprecation, four years of unnatural working conditions, Chaheel Riens was ready to return home.

For nearly a year now he'd been forced to consider the embarrassing possibility that he'd been wrong about Kees vaan Loo-Macklin. He wasn't positive he was wrong, might never be, but he was becoming certain he'd never be able to prove anything. Loo-Macklin's taking of a mate had removed the last vestiges of concern among his family superiors. The human was clearly bent on founding a family of his own, on producing offspring who would inherit the great position that would accrue to the family of Loo-Macklin once the Nuel assumed dominance over the affairs of men.

Chaheel Riens was sick of worrying about it, as he was sick of the UTW, of alien food and culture, of the sight of creatures striding about on only two spindly solid legs instead of properly flexible cilia.

Chaheel Riens, xenopsychologist extraordinary, was intelligent enough to recognize the symptoms. He was homesick.

The four years had been anything but a failure, however. No representative of the Nuel scientific community had spent anywhere near that length of time among the humans. The papers Chaheel could now dictate at his leisure from his copious notes would fill several whole information chips. Acclaim and reward would greet his monumental work, the first extensive research ever done on human culture and psychology from the inside.

Still Chaheel felt the pain of failure. It was not humanity he'd come to analyze. It was one human.

So intent was he on returning home that he'd nearly forgotten the modest network of contacts he'd so laboriously woven during his first three years in the UTW. When it came, the breakthrough was presented to him not by an Athabascan or Eurtite, as he'd felt it might, but from another human being.

He was in his quarters, the walls and cabinets now stripped bare, his possessions packed and ready for outship, when he got the message. The contents were as startling as the source.

He was perusing his personal messages with boredom. They flashed across the monitor screen set in one wall of his chambers. They were in terranglo, a simple language Chaheel had mastered during the past four years. He had no need of the built-in translator unit. Once, he'd felt pride in the accomplishment. Not any longer. There had been no accomplishments in some time and he was not the kind to linger over old ones. It was only work now.

The special message was tucked inconspicuously among his other calls. Most of them were from home; requests for information on this or that aspect of human society. Chaheel had become quite a source for the curious stay-at-homes. A few came from human scientists. Exchanges of knowledge

Alan Dean Foster

had followed the trail blazed by exchanges of goods. Knowledge often followed greed, instead of the other way 'round.

What the peculiar message said was simply, "Recall your initial interests in certain humans commercial activities. Would request personal audience to discuss ramifications presented by same. Most truly. Thomas Lindsay." Beneath was a call number. An Evenwaith number.

The seemingly ordinary communication was full of too many buzz words for Chaheel to let it slide by. It had been a while since he'd thought seriously about his original purpose in traveling to the UTW. Now this terse, somehow anxious message renewed it.

Ramifications . . . commercial activities . . . things that had first piqued his own fears and interest were thrown back at him by an unknown human to haunt him all over again. The key was the apparent misspelling of the word "human" as the plural "humans." If one added proper punctuation it became "human's." Possessive. Someone's activities in particular then.

Chaheel debated with himself. He was packed and ready to leave this miserable place, ready to return home to acclaim and praise. Possibly the message was placed by an unstable mind. A crank call, as humans termed it. Chaheel had received plenty of those in his four years within the UTW. Such psychological aberrants were common among mankind, he knew. Why waste his time with one?

And yet . . . this "Thomas Lindsay," which might or might not be the caller's real name, had taken the trouble to search Chaheel out. It was the preciseness of the message's language, carefully calculated to attract the attention of no one *but* Chaheel, that finally persuaded him to put off his departure for at least another day.

On contact the human refused to show his face, likewise refused to meet Chaheel in his quarters. Security reasons. Chaheel concurred, suggested a small eating establishment where he was not unknown and where his alien presence would attract little comment. The human agreed, broke off the transmission abruptly.

He, for it was male, was not a particularly impressive representative of his species. He was very short and thin to the point of emaciation. Though not particularly old he was losing his head fur.

There were many other things which would have been missed entirely by an ordinary Nuel but not by the human-wise Chaheel. Things which told him this human was irritable, nervous, worried, and generally unpleasant to be around. And the man had said nothing as yet. Really, the inferencing Chaheel performed was impressive.

The noise from the electronic music generator permeated the oval entertainment and eating chamber. It was quite deafening. Chaheel hated the music but enjoyed the noise because it kept him from hearing the comments other patrons often made about him. A human performed ritual gyrations on a stage which further attracted the attention of most of the humans in the establishment.

The emaciated one did something with a small electronic device, passing it through the air, over the table, beneath it. Satisfied, he slipped it into a pocket. They sat in a corner booth, human-designed chairs being quite impossible for Chaheel, but large booths providing acceptable if stiff-backed support.

The human pushed aside the drink he'd ordered and leaned close toward Chaheel. This was a human gesture signifying trust and confidence. The psychologist knew this because there was nothing wrong with his hearing or with the human's voice.

The man wore a dark indigo set of coveralls with a dull green shirt beneath the suspenders. Chaheel was clad in a single-piece black-and-yellow striped non-renewing suit. *El* were difficult to keep alive past a certain time and there was nowhere on the eighty-three worlds to purchase new ones.

"You're very interested in Kees vaan Loo-Macklin, aren't you, alien?"

"You know that I am. That's why you have contacted me. You have information for me?"

The man glanced nervously at a nearby table, quickly back down at his own. "Maybe."

"Why do this?"

The man looked up, his eyes hard. " 'Cause I hate the ghit's guts."

"A great many humans do, I am told. Why should you be able to do more for me than anyone else?"

The man smiled slyly, an expression Chaheel had not encountered often. "Because I know a lot of things that most of the people who hate him don't. Things which the Nuel ought to be interested in."

Chaheel, who had come to the meeting convinced he was wasting his time, felt himself stirring inside. "Large words, truly. What things?"

"Not so fast, slimeskin. You'll believe me better if you understand why I hate Loo-Macklin and how I come to know what I do. See, I worked for Tommotty for five years. It's a services outfit, mostly storage and information processing."

"One of Loo-Macklin's companies, ' Chaheel said, drawing on his store of information about the human they were discussing.

"Yeah. Not the biggest, but high-profit. Lot of money in

information processing. Investment's in personnel more than material.

"Anyway, I worked there five years."

"You said that already."

"Shut up and listen, will you!" The man shot another nervous glance at the patrons nearest them. No one *seemed* to be looking his way.

"Never had any trouble with my work, never had any complaints. I worked *hard* for that outfit. You had to, to stay in. Well, I was using some of the spare capacity on the side. Everyone does it. You run a few programs for friends, maybe make a little credit above your salary. Nothing but electricity to the company.

"I was doing it one day and stumbled into a code. Happens sometimes when you're hunting for a place to hide your clien . . . your friend's information. Normally you just ignore it and dig up another place, but I punched into this thing and I mean, the information came flooding across that damn screen! Just flooding. You wouldn't think so much would be stored under such an innocuous code."

"Making something obvious but difficult is a good way to discourage inquiries about it," pointed out Chaheel.

"Yeah, well, I wondered about it. It was a slow day and just for the hell of it I slowed the stuff down and looked at it. Thought I'd skim it quick. You never know." He smiled in a comradely way. "Sometimes you might stumble across something that could tip you to an impending merger or other big deal. Something you can make a little credit on. Just for yourself, of course. I wouldn't have considered selling it to a competing company."

"Of course not," said Chaheel politely.

"Well, some of the names in the thing—" the man lowered his voice still further—"I recognized 'em. I mean, who wouldn't. Important people, really important. In the government, on *the* Board of Operators. Not just business stuff. It all pertained to you people, to the Nuel.''

Chaheel tried not to tense. His tentacles tried to retract up against his body.

''Naturally I am interested in anything that pertains to my people, especially if as you say Kee-yes vain Lewmaklin is involved as well.''

''I'm getting to that,'' muttered Thomas Lindsay with maddening deliberation. ''What I saw shocked me. Truly. I suppose it shouldn't have, but it did. I didn't know what to do about it. I mean, some of those names. . . . So I just packed it in, you know, kept it to myself, and went on about my business. One time I tried retrieving the code again. I couldn't. Probably it was changed daily.

''Couple months after that I got fired.''

''Fired?'' Chaheel had an image of the man going up in flames.

''Discharged. They threw me out. No job.''

''Oh.'' Chaheel's knowledge of human idioms was still imperfect. There were so many different ways of saying the same thing.

''Yeah. Five years of sweat and hard work. The thing that gets me is that it had nothing to do with the code I'd stumbled across. Far as I know nobody knows that I saw any of that stuff. Far as I know.

''No, it was because of my using excess capacity to make a little play money. Like I told you, everybody does it. They just don't talk about it. Not only did they fire me,'' he said angrily, ''but they noted it in my resume file. I haven't been able to get another job since. Nobody'll touch me, even though most of 'em look the other way when the people they've got working for 'em now do the same damn thing.''

"Truly it sounds as though you have been unfairly singled out, Thomas Lindsay." Privately Chaheel knew he would never have recommended hiring this thief either.

"Truly, yeah. Well, since nobody wants to buy my abilities—and I'm good at what I do—I thought I'd sell a little knowledge. I heard stories about you being interested in this Loo-Macklin . . . I'll bet he approved firing me personally. I know what I know is valuable to the Nuel. Valuable, hell." He took a long swallow of the liquid he'd ordered, then suddenly turned reticent.

"You can pay, of course?"

"If I think your information is worth knowing." Chaheel went to great pains to affect a casual air. "I have a line of credit with various government and educational agencies."

"Okay." The man put his glass down. "I want a million UTW credits."

Chaheel was glad the human was not well versed in Nuel expressions. "That . . . is a great sum of money. '

"How much is the survival of your race worth to you?"

The psychologist was beginning to think the human he was dealing with was loaded with intoxicants as well as delusions of persecution. He was wrong.

The human took his silence for indifference and hastened to follow up.

"Tell you what I'll do. This information's no good to anyone else. I hear the Nuel, even though they are the ugliest things in the universe, are honest business folk."

"As honest as any human," said Chaheel.

"Yeah, well, of course that ain't good enough." The man let out a nervous little chuckle. He knew enough about Nuel society to have Chaheel swear on his family line all the way back to his first father. "If you think the information is worth it, you pay me."

"You have a great deal of confidence in what you learned by accident," observed the psychologist.

"I ought to. You know, Loo-Macklin's done a lot of business with you Nuel. Stuff about it on the newscasts all the time."

"That is so." He repeated the official line. "It binds him closely to us."

"Particularly a lot of business with those outfits that deal in Birthing ceremonies."

Chaheel wondered how the man had learned that, but kept silent. Talk, human. Let it spill out of you.

"What would you say," whispered Thomas Lindsay the human, "if I told you that Loo-Macklin had been doing all that, insinuating himself into your commerce all these years, with the intention of betraying the entire race of the Nuel to the UTW government?"

"We are naturally concerned with protecting ourselves," said Chaheel calmly. "Precautions truly have been taken with regard to Loo-Macklin especial."

Would this unimpressive specimen understand the function of a *lehl* implant? Probably not, the psychologist decided. He contented himself with a simpler explanation.

"If Lewmacklin does anything contrary to the best interests of the Nuel he will die instantly. There is no way he can prevent it."

"I've heard the stories about the thing you guys put in his brain. But suppose he doesn't give a damn about dying?"

"Every sentient is interested in self-preservation."

"I understand that you actually met the guy."

"A long time ago, though I have followed his activities with interest these past years."

"Then you know he ain't your average human being. He ain't your average anything."

"So I've been led to believe," admitted Chaheel, trying to prod the man.

"Everybody knows his story. How he rose out of the underworld in Cluria, made himself legal, all that garbage. Privately I think it's all mystmit put out by his PR people. But he's got about everything a guy could want out of life. Suppose he wants more? Suppose he'd like to go out one of the greatest heroes in human history? A martyr to mankind's expansion in the galaxy? D'you think he'd sacrifice his life for that?"

Chaheel considered thoughtfully. "I don't know, but it's an interesting idea. We the Nuel consider life sacrosanct. An individual's life belongs not only to him but to his family. Survival is important to others besides oneself."

"Yeah, well we the Humans think different. Some of us do, anyway. Some of us are downright eager to give away our lives for something we believe in."

"It does not matter." He tried to explain to the man. "Lewmacklin would perish as soon as he *thought* any inimical thoughts toward the Nuel. He would not have time to actually do anything."

"Yeah, you think not? Well tell me what you think of this.

"Among other things Loo-Macklin has control of the firms that supply the special food your newborn—Nueleens, I think you call 'em—is fed in the nurseries." He grinned nastily. "See, I did my homework pretty good."

Chaheel could not keep his tentacles from retracting this time. They curled up flat, tight against his gross body. "I know now all you say is truth, Thomas Lindsay. Or you would be dead by now."

"Yeah, I know." The cause of the human's nervousness was now explained, the psychologist thought.

"This information could be false, designed to be discovered

207

so that leaks in human security might be detected, contacts between Nuel and human friends discovered."

The man shook his head violently. "I did my checking. This is for real, slimeskin. I saw the people's names. It's all been done real careful, real clever.

"They've developed a chemical that's going to be inserted into the Nueleen food. It's slow acting, no side effects. Every young Nuel will get some while it's maturing. It'll make them . . . mentally pliable, I guess is the best way to describe it. It won't have any results until the individual matures. By then," he shrugged, "the Nuel will do whatever mankind asks them to do. Racially, the Nuel will lose their competitive edge. All of you will be, well, anesthetized. Only you won't be aware of it happening to you because your young will grow up acting that way. You'll all become very content, very happy, and easily handled, which is what the UTW government wants."

"Monstrous," said Chaheel Riens huskily. "Why are you telling me this? Apart from your dislike of Lewmaklin, are you not betraying your own people in return for money?"

"Hell, no. I'm not going to cause anyone to be hurt. At worst, I'm just helping to maintain the status quo. I don't give a damn about you slimeskins," he added frankly, "and I'd never betray my own race. I'm not giving you information that's going to help you overthrow mankind. I'm just keeping a bunch of alien brats from growing up lobotomized.

"You'll want more proof." He reached into a pocket and handed the Nuel a small plastic box.

Chaheel extended a shaky tentacle for it. "That's full of chips, information storage chips," the man told him. "I did some copying that day. You have access to human data processing machinery?"

The psychologist performed a gesture of assent that the human could recognize.

"Okay then. Run 'em yourself. Have your own experts check 'em out. They're not fakes."

"I will do so," said Chaheel, "and if they are not, I shall arrange for the transfer of funds requested."

"Here." The man slipped him a code plate. "That's my account. My special new one. It's on Restavon, not Evenwaith, and don't transfer everything at once. Do it a hundred thousand a year."

"You trust me to do this?"

The man rose from the table. "You've sworn to me on the line of your first father. That's good enough."

"Lost I am," whispered the stunned Chaheel. "Lost and disbelieving. If Lewmaklin has done truly what you claim, has participated in this monstrous evil aimed at the innocent unborn, then he should have perished long ago. Yet he lives."

"Don't take it so hard," Lindsay advised him. "Look, I'm a programmer and researcher. I probably wouldn't understand how or what you guys stuck in his brain even if you explained it to me slowly. But even you Nuel can't make new laws of biology. All you can do is use the existing ones.

"You know what I know: that Loo-Macklin, the sorry ghit, ain't dead. Maybe he found some way to circumvent or short-circuit whatever kind of check you put inside his head. I wish I was wrong. Wish he was dead. You guys better check up on whatever it was you did to him, 'cause it sure as hell ain't working."

Those were the last words the psychologist heard from Thomas Lindsay. The man vanished into the crowd, leaving a stunned Chaheel slumped alone in the booth. Hastily he concealed the packet of information chips. Then his great eyes scanned the room.

If Lindsay was wrong, if he hadn't covered his actions with sufficient thoroughness, then there would be work here for assassins soon enough. Chaheel doubted they would hesitate to kill an alien visitor. Not one carrying the information just passed to him. He vacated the table and the establishment as fast as his cilia could carry him.

The information chips were transported to a Nuel vessel, run through human-designed computers, then reprocessed and scanned by Nuel instrumentation. Chaheel carried them aboard himself, not trusting them to anyone else to deliver safely and certainly not to ground-based transmission. There was too much at stake.

It was all there, everything Lindsay had claimed and more. Loo-Macklin himself making arrangements with high government officials, records of dates and delivery schemes, the design for the distribution of the soporific chemical to Nueleen food suppliers and when it was to commence: all in stomach-turning detail.

It was estimated it would take thirty years for the drug to reduce the maturing Nuel to a state of racial complacency through manipulation of the hormone balance in their brains. A plan as perfect as it was insidious, for while it was being carried out the otherwise normal young adults would never suspect a thing.

When the last information chip came to an end, several of the ship's prime officers turned in shock to Chaheel Riens. The psychologist was only slightly less stunned by the scope and sheer malignancy of the plan.

"It is clear," one of the junior officers finally said into the devastated silence, "that the *lehl* has failed. The humans have either found a way of extracting it without harming the host or neutralizing its reactions."

"Impossible, impossible truly," countered another. "They have not the medical skills necessary."

"A renegade Nuel physician could do the operation," suggested a third.

"That does not explain how our periodic checks on this creature continue to show positive," Chaheel pointed out, trying to restrain the rising air of panic in the meeting chamber.

"In any case there is one advantage we retain." The officers listened closely. "This creature Lewmaklin may by now know of this Lindsay individual's actions, but he cannot be certain that said information was conveyed to me. He should still think that he holds our trust, that his position is unchanged. We still have time to destroy this intended assault upon the minds of our young." A few outraged murmurs rose from the assembled ship's officers.

"We will alert all the food distribution firms as well as those companies who produce the food. In addition, there are Nuel who monitor incoming shipments from the UTW. They can be on the watch for this additive and stop it before it reaches any family world. Surely this creature has no Nuel in his pay. I am certain those who work for him are unaware of this plan.

"And lastly, there is a simpler way to prevent this and any future such troubles." When no one said anything, he explained further.

"Once long ago I actually met this Lewmaklin thing. He was friendly enough but his attitudes troubled me even then. Still he makes his residence on the world below us." He indicated the slowly rotating globe of Evenwaith, a mass of white clouds and sapphire seas filling the sweeping port off to his right.

211

"Likely he is traveling now. He travels much, to attend to his vast interests. We will wait for him to return."

"And when he returns?" prompted one of the officers.

"When he returns I will see if I can call upon that long-ago meeting to secure an appointment with him," said Chaheel quietly. "I am sure he will suspect nothing. I will kill him. No physician, be he human or renegade Nuel, can prevent me from accomplishing that intention. The *lehl* has failed. I assure you that I shall not. . . ."

XII

He had no trouble gaining the appointment. Loo-Macklin, the secretary in charge assured the psychologist, would be pleased to greet an old acquaintance. Further proof, to Chaheel's mind, that the human knew nothing of the meeting with Thomas Lindsay.

He traveled by marcar from Cluria. Soon the car slipped free of its tube and raced across a field of ripe, waving grain. The wheat concealed the magnetic repulsion rail which kept the car aloft and moving forward.

Chaheel studied the well-cultivated fields with interest. He knew that many years ago this world of Evenwaith was a cesspool of pollution which was forced to import such products as grain because they couldn't grow in the poisoned atmosphere. He knew also that Loo-Macklin was the one principally responsible for cleaning the planet's surface. Looking at the endless fields of golden wheat, the clear blue skies, it was difficult to imagine what this land must once have been like, choking under a permanent pall of dioxides and particulates.

It was no wonder Loo-Macklin was idealized by many humans and had been raised high within their society. His greatest accomplishment, of course, lay ahead: the silent subjugation of the Nuel.

His status and intent would have given him access to secret government files and records, all of which he no doubt employed to enhance his business dealings. The government would find it repayment enough, and his competitors could only wonder at his seeming prescience. All little things, insignificant things, beside the vast evil the human intended.

A spur off the main marcar rail dead-ended atop a rocky bluff overlooking Evenwaith's South Sea. Automatic switching devices made insect-noises beneath the tall cliff grass as Chaheel's car was shifted to a private rail. Then he made a breathtaking descent down the cliff face, leveled off, and found himself skimming over the waves booming on shore.

Glancing out the side of the car he could just make out the rail running beneath the surface. Ahead lay a large, igneous plug whose vertical gray sides rose sharply from the sea.

The core of the long-extinct volcano which comprised the island was wholly owned by Loo-Macklin. From twisted lava rose his private estate, a forest of thin, gleaming towers coated with precious reflective metal enamels. Sunlight turned the island into a forest of wild mirrors.

As he neared the fortress home Chaheel decided the towers were more than merely decorative. No doubt many contained components of an elaborate defense system. That was only to be expected. It was hardly likely the most powerful human in the eighty-three worlds of the UTW would chose to live in a defenseless fairyland.

That did not trouble Chaheel Riens. He never expected to get off the island alive.

He was compelled to endure several checks of his person. Not all the polite guards who scanned him for weapons and made certain of his identity were human. There were two of the tall Orischians and one Orophite. No Nuel, however, much to Chaheel's relief.

They found no weapons on the psychologist because he was carrying none. From the beginning he'd assumed anyone as important as Loo-Macklin would maintain an elaborate system of personal protection and had given up the idea at once of trying to smuggle anything lethal, even a sophisticated biological agent, into the great man's sanctuary.

His plan called for something as simple as it was primitive. Though no athlete and half a foot shorter than the human, he was a good hundred pounds heavier. He would wait for the right instant, work his way as close as possible to the creature, and before any automatic device or living guard could react, he would throw himself on Kee-yes vain Lewmaklin and break the man's neck.

What happened subsequent to that did not concern Chaheel Riens.

The room they ushered him into as he flexed his powerful tentacles a last time was obscenely large. The soaring, vaulted ceiling was several stories high, forming a peak of transparent gemstone which permitted the entrance of an altered sun. It curved down in a fine sweep to meet a broad, transparent wall supported by glass buttresses. It was far too large to be called a window.

Beyond lay a panoramic view of setting sun, endless ocean and the curving point of headland known as the Mare's Eyes. Evening approached and the lights of expensive bluffside

homes began to wink on, sprinkling illumination on the edge
of the continent.

He flowed on relaxed cilia across a floor of richly polished
wood composed of millions of hardwood chips gleaned from
all of the eighty-three worlds. Probably some from the worlds
of the families as well, he thought bitterly.

At the far end of this cathedral-like office a man sat on
either a very small couch or very large cushion. He sat
motionless until the psychologist had drawn quite near. Then
he rose, smiled, and extended a hand.

Patience, patience, the psychologist warned himself. *It's
too early, too soon. Now is when his protective devices will
be most alert. Relax this monster, relax his shields, relax the
conversation. Then slay him.*

"Chaheel Riens, it's been many years." The monster's
hand touched a tentacle and exchanged liquid with the psychologist. Chaheel felt unclean but forced himself to handle
the exchange calmly.

Then he took a moment to study Loo-Macklin. The body
appeared unchanged, unusual for a human of his age. It
looked very much as he'd seen it years ago in the Birthing
cavern. Some skull fur was missing, however, mostly in front
of the head. It had not been artificially replaced, a crude
bio-engineering technique the humans clumsily practiced.
The most noticeable change was in fur color, which had faded
from gold to white.

There were a few additional wrinkle lines in the face,
comparable to the changes that took place in a Nuel's skirt as
it aged. And that was all. He measured himself carefully
against the human. It would have to be quick. He doubted
Loo-Macklin's security personnel would permit two attacks.
The human was very strong for his kind, but Chaheel had

weight and two extra limbs on his side. There should be no difficulty.

"Good to see you again," Loo-Macklin was saying cheerily. He turned his back on the Nuel and waved toward the sky. A large cylindrical metal cylinder rose from the floor. It was brightly lit in changing patterns. Tiny spigots encircled its upper section. "Can I offer you some liquid or near-liquid refreshment?"

"No thank you," Chaheel said. "I will take up but little of your time."

Loo-Macklin shrugged and waved emptiness again. The floor obediently swallowed the cylinder.

"I was told you wanted to question me for some report you're preparing. Something on the psychological effects of human/Nuel commercial interaction, I believe. I've always been interested in stuff like that. Be glad to answer any questions I can."

Truly you will, thought Chaheel. He was examining the room for the location of the expected surveillance machinery. It was well-hidden and he couldn't locate so much as a spyeye.

Well, no matter. It would only take a second to slip all four tentacles around that fragile human neck. Then it wouldn't matter how many cameras or weapons were trained on him. Only an instant. A little pressure and he and Loo-Macklin would experience the last moment of life together.

All my work, he brooded. All the research, all the old desire to found a family of teachers, lost in the need to slay a single alien biped. How ironic are the workings of the universe.

If Loo-Macklin suspected Chaheel's intent he'd given no indication of it.

"Now, what is it you wish to know?" He turned from the ocean wall. "How may I help you?"

You can come just a little closer, Chaheel thought. What he said was, "There are certain aspects of trade in luxury goods which I find especially interesting. It's a question of perception on the part of both races. Neither seems certain what the other regards as luxury versus necessity."

"Which do you think my imagined plan to poison the food of your now-unborn falls under?" asked Loo-Macklin casually, hands folded behind his back.

Chaheel nearly jumped for him at that moment, except that the Nuel are not constructed for jumping. They move slowly and tirelessly on their hundreds of thick cilia, but always they move close to the ground. The Nuel record for the high jump was somewhere under ten inches.

"You know. A thousand curses on your family line, monster, if you know."

"Just found out recently," Loo-Macklin informed him. "Good thing, too. The man could have ruined everything. Fortunately he drinks a lot. Alcoholic stimulants make humans voluble. But I'm sure you, as a student of our culture, are aware of that.

"Anyway, I found out about your little meeting. I don't expect you came here to chat about commercial interactions or psychology, did you?"

"No." Chaheel saw no reason to prolong a failed deception. "What I do not understand is how you managed to neutralize the *lehl*," he said, sorry only that he'd failed and certain now he didn't stand a chance of getting within grasping distance of the man before some hidden weapon cut him down.

Loo-Macklin grinned narrowly. An honest and rare grin.

"Who said it had been neutralized?" He rubbed the back of his skull.

"It has to have been," muttered the psychologist, "or it would have killed you long before now, because you have contradicted the thought it was sensitized to."

"Who says I'm contradicting it?"

Chaheel's well-ordered mind was coming apart. He wanted to scream. This human's dealings were more complex than the maze of coming-of-age tunnels on Merenwha.

When he could not find a response, Loo-Macklin gently tried to help him form one.

"You met with this Lindsay, the programmer. He told you certain things, supplied you with certain stolen information."

"A great deal of information," Chaheel finally said. "I had it all checked prior to processing. Everything he gave me is truth." A glimmer of confused hope began to rise within him. "Can you deny that?"

"No. Not the meetings, the discussions. Those all took place. The only thing that's missing is the fact that I'm not going to do anything contrary to the best interests of the Nuel." He tapped his head again. "Wouldn't want to upset my little passenger."

"You say that poisoning the minds of our children is not contrary to our best interests?" the psychologist replied sarcastically.

"I have no intention of poisoning anyone. But my government thinks otherwise. I will supply you with some of the 'additive.' It does indeed seem to produce the gradual softening of competitiveness the stolen information talks about. But what the government scientists I've been working with do not know, because they have no access to Nuel patients, is that upon introduction into the Nuel system the chemical bonds

219

holding the additive together are broken down in about ten months time by your body's enzymes. The resulting three components are harmless. They remain in the Nuel bloodstream for several years, but affect nothing. Certainly not the minds and motivations of your children.''

Chaheel felt dizzy. A Nuel could faint, but it could not fall over. Nevertheless, he wished for some support.

"I . . . I understand this not, Kee-yes vain Lewmaklin. Why would you go to such elaborate lengths to prepare a false attack that can avail you nothing?"

"Who says it avails me nothing? Truly are you full of misconceptions, Chaheel Riens.'' He seemed to be enjoying his visitor's confusion.

"Here I am,'' he gestured widely with massive arms on which the hair had also turned white, "a single human being, working closely with mankind's most dangerous enemies. I visit the Nuel worlds, ostensibly on missions devoted only to commerce. I talk with the heads of families, Families, Great Families. I have tightly bound myself to the Nuel by business dealings.

"Don't you think, psychologist, observer of human culture, that among the Board of Operators who run the government of the eighty-three worlds there might be at least one as suspicious of my motives as you? Wouldn't it be sensible for one or two among them to wonder if I might not be doing more for the Nuel than merely facilitating their business activities within the UTW? Are they less observant than yourself?

"Come now, Chaheel. Exchange positions with me truly. How long did you think I could keep the intelligence agents of the UTW fooled? They are not stupid, as your own people of the family Si know. I had to do something to put their minds at ease.

"Now, as a psychologist, what method would you suggest? How might I relax them utterly?"

"By concocting a plan," Chaheel said slowly, reluctantly, "that would make them believe you were working for the interests of humanity."

"I live in a universe of amoebas," Loo-Macklin murmured to himself. Then, to his guest, "You see it now. It was not meant to be easily seen. Of course that's what I did.

"This mysterious 'additive' that Lindsay told you about was truly created by my own chemists. The testing on it was done by a tiny staff working directly under my supervision and instructions. It was then turned over to Nuel bioengineers working for a firm I control, to make certain of its harmlessness. I will give you the name of that family firm if you wish, so you can check for yourself." He laughed. "If the Si functionaries guarding its privacy will admit you, that is.

"The Board of Operators is convinced that within fifty years they're going to face a race of pliable, drugged Nuel who'll do exactly as they're told."

"Fifty years, human scale," mumbled Chaheel. "Do you think that will hold back the Board of Operators' more warlike members long enough for you to deliver on your promises to the Council of Eight Families?"

"I don't know. I'm doing all I can. Push too hard and the entire effort will be uncovered. Patience is all that will make my efforts on behalf of the Families work. The Si, at least, understand that."

"I'd heard, but not believed, that they had finally made you an honorary family member. Such an honor is unprecedented."

"So I was told," said Loo-Macklin.

Chaheel Riens tried to unknot his thoughts. "Truly would

you give me the name of the firm among the families which is aware of and has tested this supposedly subverting additive?"

"Truly, Chaheel."

"But could you not somehow. . . ."

Loo-Macklin cut him off impatiently. "You forget the *lehl,* psychologist. It sits where it was placed, monitoring my thoughts, protecting the interests of the Nuel."

"Then this whole elaborate structure you've put in place, the entire plan to insert this additive in our food supplies, is simply a deception, a means to ensure the human government of your loyalty to them while in truth you are helping the Families?"

Loo-Macklin nodded, a gesture Chaheel recognized easily. "It should never have come out. That damn technician stumbled across it and then had the brains, and the guts, to get in touch with you."

"What would you have done if I had conveyed this knowledge to my superiors?"

"That could've meant trouble. Of course, the leaders of the Great Families are entirely aware of what I've been doing." He chuckled. "They would have been very upset by your actions.

"Since you are not privy to the decisions of the Great Family Heads, you are as unaware of the plan as most of your kind. The less who know of it, the better, even among the Nuel. You have your own dissatisfied, your own mentally unstable. Your own Thomas Lindsays."

Chaheel was too confused to think straight. He'd come to this place with the avowed intention of killing this man and then dying in a rain of fire. Now he was about to be shooed on his way, leaving behind a greater ally than the Nuel had ever had, along with much of his self-respect.

"Why should I believe you? How do we know that this

additive you are going to put in our offspring's food, ostensibly to fool your own intelligence people, will not recombine at some later stage of growth to cause all the harm you say it cannot?''

"You should hear yourself." Loo-Macklin was still amused. "I told you that your own biologists checked it out." He touched a hidden floor switch. Another metal cylinder rose out of the floor. It was more massive than the simple drink dispenser. Chaheel recognized the shine of an impervious eutectic alloy.

The man ran his fingertips over one side of the safe and a single information storage chip slid out. He handed it to the psychologist. It was blank, of course, the information contained inside stored along lines of light.

"Here are the names and codes for some of your less widely publicized but most brilliant scientific research families. Contact them. This chip will serve as your entry. You'll be able to study the test procedures and results for yourself, thus saving yourself the embarrassment of going before some high Family official and insulting me to a friend."

"I suppose," Chaheel's bulging eyes both focused on the transparent chip, "I suppose I owe you an apology, Kee-yes vain Lewmaklin."

"Nonsense." The human touched him in a comradely fashion, trying to reassure him. "Your instincts were good. Based on what you knew, or rather what you didn't know, you acted like a true scion of a Great Family."

"I could have killed you before you had the chance to tell me all this. When I entered and we exchanged body fluids, for example."

"Perhaps." Loo-Macklin shrugged, indifferent to death as ever. "Physically you are stronger than I, yes. But I'm quite strong for a human. Quite strong. You would have had to

223

finish me quickly. My own protection machines," and he gestured widely, encompassing the entire immense room, "would have had time to come to my assistance. Would've been a waste of a sharp mind, psychologist."

"But one that you would have been prepared to live with. Why let me come here in person and let me risk my life, when you could have informationed me thus on the mainland?"

"Because I felt it would carry more conviction if I told you in person," was the reply. "Considering your dedication and all the trouble you'd gone too, I thought I owed you that much. Besides," he flexed massive arms, "life grows stale for me. Small risks are really not risks at all, but spice."

Chaheel thought of something else. "What of the technician, Thomas Lindsay?"

"As soon as I was informed of what he'd done, I had him disposed of. Fortunately, you were the only one he'd gotten to. He could have ruined everything. No chance of that now. You might keep in mind the fact that his death was required to protect Nuel interests."

"I understand," whispered the now thoroughly numbed psychologist.

"Now that that's all finished with," Loo-Macklin clapped his hands together, his expression cheerful once again, "can I persuade you to take food with me? I have an extensive food supply system which can conjure up the delicacies of many races, including your own. I would also enjoy showing you around my little home. There are a great many things within which I think you would find of interest. I have a collection of primitive art which is somewhat famous. It includes, you might be surprised to know, a modest section devoted to the Nuel."

"That's not pos . . . ," Chaheel started to say, then shut up.

For one as valued by the Great Families as this human, nothing was impossible.

"There are other entertainments also," Loo-Macklin added coaxingly.

"No . . . thank you no. Feeling am I most awkward and uncomfortable. I would like mostly to return to my work as quickly as possible."

"If that's the way you feel." The human appeared genuinely disappointed. "I wish I could convince you to come and work for me. I have many Nuel working for me on the worlds of the Families, but not many in the UTW. Not many can cope with the shape-prejudice which still lingers like a cancer among my people. I could use you, and you would learn much."

"No, no." Chaheel's cilia began backing him toward the door. He'd been fooled, badly fooled. That frightened him. This smiling, pleasant-voiced soulless human frightened him. Get away from him, his instincts screamed at him. Get out, get away, before he uses you the way he's used his own government.

What he said politely was, "I'd rather pursue my own research. That has always been my dream. I desire election to the Family of Academissionaries. I have hopes of eventually maturing to medical research."

"I understand," murmured Loo-Macklin sympathetically, "though I won't try to hide my disappointment. You're a bright helmzin," he added, using the word for highly intelligent adult. "But I defer to your own desires, which clearly differ from my own. I wish you farewell and good luck with your work." He gestured toward the distant door, seemingly miles away across the polished matrix floor.

"And should you ever actually have any questions involving human/Nuel commercial interactions and their psychological effects, please don't hesitate to contact any of my company supervisors if I'm not available myself. I'm quite busy these days.''

"Sure am I that you are.'' He hurried for the exit as rapidly as was decent.

And that's how he left Kees vaan Loo-Macklin, his mind adrift on a sea of confusion. Part of him admired the human and the intricacy of the plan he'd devised to fool his own intelligence service and government.

Fool, he admonished himself! You leapt to an assumption because it fit your private, preconceived notions. You should have checked out this Lindsay's information further before considering action, let alone murder.

Oh, he wouldn't take Lewmaklin's word, of course. He would take transport home, process the information chip the human had given him, check it with other sources. He would truly locate and talk with those Nuel who had worked on the development of the additive. Only then could he relax, safe in the knowledge that Kee-yes vain Lewmaklin was still a trusted ally of the Nuel and Chaheel Riens a paranoid idiot.

The marcar cramped him unmercifully as it sped back across the emerald sea. It was fortunate Lewmaklin had agreed to assist the Families. Any mind which could construct and then manipulate such an intricate framework of deception and lies would have made a terribly dangerous enemy.

Yes, Chaheel was frightened of him, and his fear did not embarrass him.

The Commander of the transport ship who was in truth a military officer incognito inside the UTW greeted the psychologist as he boarded the shuttle which was to take him into orbit. From there the ship would depart the UTW. Chaheel Riens was going home.

The Commander's eyes, however, were nearly devoid of color. Chaheel knew instantly that something serious was troubling the commander.

Naturally the Commander was troubled, he reminded himself. They knew that if he returned at all they would be greeting a murderer and a fugitive. The officers would be glued to their screens, frantically scanning orbital space around Evenwaith for the signs of pursuit they expected to arrive at any moment. He hastened to reassure the officer opposite him.

"All is at rest, Commander. I was in the wrong. There is no plot to poison our children. Our own government is aware of it. It is only minor functionaries like ourselves who have been kept ignorant of the details of this fine working, to protect it from accidental disclosure. They trust us not, truly.

"I did not have to kill the human Lewmaklin. The *lehl* remains within him. Both implant and host continue to function efficiently on family business."

"Truly," murmured the Commander. He seemed distracted. "That is excellent news indeed." He moved to a communicator, absently called off the alert.

Chaheel frowned. "Did you not understand? There is no plot to poison our young. The additive that is to go into their food is harmless. It degrades within the bloodstream. All is part of a wider plot to fool the humans into believing that Lewmaklin is working for them." He held out the information chip the man had given him.

"Here is proof. Names and locations of our own scientists who have worked on this project. I would think you would be excited, Commander, by such news."

"I am greatly relieved," the Commander admitted, trying to muster some enthusiasm.

"Then why do you look so virelsham?"

227

"We have a new puzzle."

"It cannot confuse or depress me as much as the one just unraveled," Chaheel assured him.

"I am certain it cannot, but it is a puzzle just the same and your opinion is urgently solicited. Come." He motioned with a tentacle tip and they started up the corridor.

In the same conference chamber where not so very long ago Chaheel had announced his intention to slay Loo-Mácklin waited a cluster of silent officers.

The Commander indicated Chaheel's cupouch, slid greasily into his own.

"Several days ago we picked up a transmission that originated from this Lewmaklin's personal residence, the one you have just returned from. We were monitoring all transmissions from that place because that was your destination and we hoped we might learn something useful to you. The residence conceals an extremely large and powerful deepspace broadcast array."

Chaheel thought back to the array of seemingly decorative, gleaming towers which rose like a metal forest from the island. As he suspected, Lewmaklin did not indulge in frivolous decor.

"The beam employed by this system is of a new, formerly unknown type, apparently designed to cover great distances without the aid of the usual booster stations. Our chief communications officer was scanning when he happened to encounter an ultrafast series of numbers being blasted out via this method. Fortunately he had them recorded before they escaped completely.

"It took us until yesterday, shiptime, to decode the mathematical sequence. I will play the gleaning back for you now." He made a gesture.

At the far end of the oval depression around which the

cupouchs and their occupants were grouped another officer touched controls. The already dim room darkened further and the hollow in the floor lit up.

Chaheel saw the squat shape of Loo-Macklin standing in the same grand room where he himself had stood the previous evening. The human turned to face a visual pickup. His expression was solemn. A storm-tossed ocean was visible through the transparent wall behind him.

"Hail tomothee, Falexia. Everything goes as planned. It will not be longer now until the final phase of our dealing can be brought to fruition, an end toward which we have worked for so long. The projections for success are still good. I look forward as always to meeting you in person.

"I am in position to manage all details of the business from my end. All final concerns have been obviated. Until we have the honor of a successful meeting, Falexia, I faretheewell."

It was not a long transmission.

Chaheel had just finished a graphic lesson in the folly of jumping to wrong conclusions. The message left him curious, but untroubled.

"Save for the somewhat stilted language, which may be due to improper decoding—" an officer across the oval stiffened slightly—"and the unfamiliar forms of greeting, I see nothing to be concerned with here. He is clearly in converse with some commercial opposite, finalizing the details of some large transaction.

"Lewmaklin's business interests are among the most extensive known. Is it surprising that he should utilize a new variety of tightbeam communication for such purposes? The heads of certain Families employ similar methods for security purposes."

"I question nothing you point out." Despite this confession the Commander still appeared uneasy.

"Then why retain you the aspect of a crespik deadbone?" Chaheel wanted to know.

"Three days following, evening yesterday local planetary time, and apparently in response to the message you have just viewed, we intercepted another transmission. Incoming, this time. It is only because we continued to monitor the special beam frequency that we were able to trap it."

The depression in the center of the floor flickered to life once more, only this time the image was distorted and violent with static.

While engineers worked to clear it, the Commander continued to talk. "The method of broadcast actually differs slightly from that used by Lewmaklin. Despite the aid of computers, our decoding efforts were not completely successful. As you see, it is highly difficult to unscramble.

"I believe that this is an instantaneous response to the broadcast you just saw."

Chaheel did some rapid calculating. He was neither physicist nor communications expert, but even he knew that within a volume of space several parsecs across, subspace communications took a matter of minutes. Transmission across greater distances required proportionately more time.

If the Commander was correct and this garbled communication was truly instantaneous, then that could mean that Lewmaklin's outgoing message took a day and a half to reach its destination, instead of minutes. And another day and a half for the reply to reach Evenwaith. That implied conversation over distances so great that. . . .

"Truly," whispered the Commander as he saw astonishment come over the psychologist, "the scale involved is nothing less than incredible. To mention not the power requirements necessary to boost such a signal."

"Surely Lewmaklin doesn't have access to such energy sources?" Chaheel ventured.

"Perhaps not," murmured the Commander. "Perhaps it took his transmission three days to reach its destination and the reply only minutes to return."

"That's quite impossible," said Chaheel.

"So say you. So say my own communications and engineering staffs. Yet I wonder. Many important developments have emerged from this human's laboratories. They have produced this mysterious additive which you insist is harmless to us yet effective enough to fool the UTW's own scientists. Might they not also invent a new and unique method of long-range communication?"

"Is that what you think has happened?"

"No. No, I do not. I think Lewmaklin has purchased the technology necessary to build it."

"Purchased it? But no known people. . . ."

Again the Commander cut him off, discarding all semblance of politeness. The image on the screen was clearing. It resolved into a thing.

The creature was huge. At least, Chaheel had an impression of considerable size. There was nothing in the field of view to give scale to the being.

It stood against a metal wall which generated its own light, a harsh bronze glow. The being was a quadruped, clad in thin golden scales like a fish. A curving row of tiny black eyes ran in a line across the center of the massive, rotound body. A pair of long arms reached out from either side and ended in hands which were interlocked beneath the row of onyx-colored eyes.

Overlapping scales fringed a wide mouth. When the orifice moved a strange whistling sound emerged from hidden depths and short, pointed teeth became visible. The black eyes remained solid, showing no visible pupils. There were no other visible external organs.

When the creature altered its stance, which it did with ceremonial frequency, it moved on a single revolving limb which was somehow fastened to its ventral side. It appeared that the creature was spinning, balancing on a cushioned ball covered with thicker, darker scales.

"Distance and slightly different methodology of transmission made it rough on our decoders," the Commander reminded Chaheel. "All we have been able to do thus far is produce a clear picture and sound. As to the language, if it is one, we are still ignorant.

"The being is of no known type. It is not one allied to us, to the humans, the Athabascans or any other civilized race. The light-emitting wall the alien stands in front of is as unique as its probable builder."

Chaheel considered a moment, said, "Lewmaklin has apparently contacted a new sentient race and is keeping the discovery private until he concludes some no doubt highly profitable business with it. Perhaps he is doing this because they are technologically advanced but commercially unsophisticated. I would not put it past him to cheat an entire race if he thought he could get away with it."

On screen the strange creature continued to dance and whistle, the sounds rising and falling in intensity. After awhile the performance concluded and the screen went to black. Dim light returned to the conference room.

"I see not your reason for concern," muttered Chaheel, afraid of what might be coming. "Lewmaklin is a devious individual. His private commercial transactions are not a matter of concern to the Families."

"They are when they involve an entirely new and apparently

more efficient method of deepspace communication," the Commander argued. "The military applications should be obvious even to a non-warrior such as yourself. I can assure you that the war-family of the Marouf is extremely interested in this."

They would be, Chaheel grumbled to himself. He had almost resigned himself to the expected request.

So tired am I of all this, he thought. He longed for the mental cleanliness of pure academia, for a chance to study history set in time and rock, whose surprises are almost always pleasant.

But it was not to be.

"You wish me to continue my surveillance of this Lewmaklin so that I might discover the location of these whistlers and thereby make it possible for the Families to have access to this new transmission methodology, is that it, Commander?"

He looked greatly uncomfortable. "The Marouf have requested it. I merely pass along the directive."

Chaheel thought of boldly confronting Loo-Macklin and simply asking for the technology. That wouldn't work, he knew. The human aided the Nuel, but kept his business and politics separate. This was a business decision some Family heads had forced on the Marouf, he was certain.

But he could do nothing about it except get it over with. A refusal would make unhindered research impossible.

"Ship's staff concurs in the decision," the Commander added.

"Boil the ship's staff!" *I am getting old*, Chaheel thought. *I should fight this*. But he knew it would be better to comply, and probably easier.

"I will strike a bargain with the Marouf, Commander. I will remain on this miserable world and do my best to learn the location of these whistling aliens with the long reach. I will do this for one year only. If at the end of that time I have not succeeded in learning anything, I will be permitted to return to my private studies.''

"I believe the Marouf will agree to that,'' the Commander murmured, most unhappy at the position he'd been placed in.

"I have been offered the chance to work for this Lewmaklin. I will accept. That will put me in a position to probe. I should like a copy of this,'' and he gestured with a tentacle toward the floor screen, ''in solid form, so that I may study it also.''

"Anything you wish, psychologist.''

"Anything but my freedom. Anything but the chance to go home. The Families demand much.'' The officer said nothing. There was nothing to say.

"Very well then. It is settled. I will work to soothe the anxious minds of the Marouf, a paranoid Family if ever there was one. There are a few observations I left incomplete. This will give me time to tidy them up.

"But woe to the Marouf, Commander, if certain members of the Si should learn of this, for they have made of this Lewmaklin one of their own, and they don't enjoy anyone spying on a member of their family unless he's a relative. . . .

XIII

Chaheel Riens did not see Loo-Macklin when he returned to Evenwaith. Undoubtedly the great man was too busy. But word of his open offer to the Nuel psychologist had been placed in record, and Chaheel was immediately offered a choice of positions.

He selected an important one, in a department in the metropolis of Cluria which was responsible for monitoring trade details between the UTW and the worlds of the Families. As an alien well-versed in human psychology, his advice was welcomed by his human colleagues.

Somewhat to his surprise, though he should have anticipated it, he also encountered other Nuel who'd been hired to serve Loo-Macklin's enterprises in similar capacities. There were enough of them in Cluria to have formed a tight little community of their own. Chaheel did not try to hide his pleasure at finding members of his own kind to visit with. Constant human company depressed him.

Rather more of a surprise was the discovery that Loo-Macklin had provided many facilities for his Nuel employees and that they mingled quite freely with their human associates. Chaheel had been so involved in his own studies that the lessening of tension between other Nuel and the humans they worked with had escaped his notice.

One Nuel, an elderly female named Purel Manz, had been working for Loo-Macklin's family interests for nearly fifteen years.

"I was one of the first," she told Chaheel. "It was hard and lonely in the beginning, but I persevered. The pay was very remarkable.

"Over the years I have watched some of the human's prejudice toward us fade, and I in turn have lost much of my shape-paranoia. Even before the arrival of fellow Nuel such as yourself the insults had ceased to trouble me. You grow inured."

"Even though such execrations have not disappeared from human society entirely?"

"By no means, young one." She was being funny. Chaheel was nearly her age. Maternal humor, the psychologist mused. "But truly has the volume lessened. There are times when I think the Orischians, for example, now loathe us more than the humans."

"Of course," Chaheel reminded her, "the lessening of tension has taken place primarily among humans who have regular contact with us or who are accustomed to our presence here in large metropolitan centers."

"I suppose that's so," she said. "You still hear of violent incidents taking place on outlying worlds. Restavon, Terra and Evenwaith are the only places where we have been truly accepted.'' Her voice dropped to a guttural whisper. ''That will matter no longer when we assume control of their government. '

Chaheel expressed surprise. ''So you know about that.''

''I am senior functionary here,'' she informed him pridefully. ''It would be impossible for me to function properly without knowing the true intentions of the Families.''

Her aura of professionalism faded and she asked with sudden interest, ''I understand you have actually met Kee-yes vain Lewmaklin himself.''

''Twice.'' He was a touch put off by the admiration in her voice. ''Once quite recently when he offered me my present position here. That was barely a year ago.'' Have I been in this place another entire year, he mused? The home-longing bit at his soul once again.

''The other time was many years ago on one of our own worlds. I was instructed to monitor him while he witnessed a Birthing.''

Purel Manz was shocked. ''That is difficult for me to believe. Did it not come from so respected an individual as yourself, I should not believe it.''

''It's true. I found it hard to accept at the time myself. Permission was granted him.''

''Well, he is such an important person,'' she murmured. You've no idea how important, Purel Manz, he thought. ''I suppose exceptions must be made.'' But the shock still showed in the contractions of her eyelids.

''Tell me,'' Chaheel asked her, ''how many others on the Nuel staff here know that their commercial work is only part of a greater plan to infiltrate and subvert human government and commerce?''

''Only my personal assistant. The rest believe only that they participate in interworld commerce which is of itself beneficial to the worlds of the Families. Most tolerate the drawbacks of working on a UTW planet in return for the remuneration, which benefits their immediate families and which is considerable. Lewmaklin pays his employees well.

"And as I told you, it has become much easier here these past few years, much more tolerant than it was for those of us who had to be first. It will be a gentle take-over when it finally comes. Humans are not so bad after all, when they can be disabused of some of their more primitive, deeply ingrained prejudices."

"You almost sound as though you're becoming fond of the race," Chaheel suggested.

"When you work with certain individuals, no matter what their shape or attitudes, for as long as twelve years, it is hard not to form some sort of attachment. Occasionally the feeling is reciprocated.

"Nevertheless," her multicrinkled skirt rippled as she shifted her position, "we serve first the Families. No personal feelings can be allowed to interfere with the greater purpose which places us here."

"No, but such emotion has weight. That's part of my job here," he lied faultlessly, "to keep watch on your feelings and attitudes."

"On behalf of the Families," she asked him, "or on behalf of our mutual employer?"

"You should know the answer to that," he replied without giving her an answer. Let her stay a little uncertain, a tiny bit in the dark.

"How I envy you for having actually met him. For a mere human he seems truly to be the most remarkable individual."

"Tired I am of hearing that," said Chaheel exasperatedly. "He is not more than a single successful sentient. There is nothing unique about him. He has merely shown himself to be unusually adept at commerce.''

Full of large lies today, aren't you, psychologist? Angry at himself, he elected to kill the idle bantering and get to the reason for this little meeting. He reached into a top pocket and removed a solido reproduction which had been cast from the information received a year ago on the Nuel monitor ship orbiting Evenwaith.

"Tell me," he asked her, handing it over, "in all your workings for Lewmaklin's businesses, have you ever encountered an alien or representation of an alien that looked anything like this?"

She studied the casting briefly, said with assurance as she handed it back to him, "No. Never. Peculiar-looking creature. Where is it from?"

"I don't know. He returned the solido to the empty pocket. One of the *el* busily remodeling his attire promptly sewed it shut.

"Is it important?" –

"Not really," he assured her. "Just something of personal interest."

They discussed items of no importance which would be of interest only to another Nuel. Then Chaheel left Purel Manz and returned to his station.

Another year passed. Another year on an alien world, another year of home-longing.

Though he would not have said Loo-Macklin was becoming an obsession with him, he had as corollary to his formal assignment begun studying the human's early history, researching his rise in human society and the development of his commercial empire all the way up to the present.

Most of the material available for general review was

excruciatingly boring. He supposed an economic historian would have found it all fascinating, but for him there was nothing of interest in the long lists of figures and recordings of mergers and take-overs. Credit-shuffling gave him no insight into the workings of the man's mind.

Then he stumbled across a peculiar entry in the section of company history which dealt with Loo-Macklin's extensive and historic interests in mining. He paid a little more attention to the words rolling up on the screen. It was all in human script, of course, which Chaheel could now read more fluidly than most humans.

One of Loo-Macklin's exploration vessels, the *Pasthinking*, had discovered massive deposits of cobalt and related minerals on the distant world of a star designated NRGC 128. While the crew was mapping the location of the deposits the ship's automatic monitoring system had picked up a subspace transmission. The frequency of the transmission was noted.

Chaheel leaned forward, made his own note of the frequency. That was the end of the entry.

In his own quarters that night he ran the notation through his private unit. Translated into Nuel terms, the frequency became one he recognized instantly: it was the same that Loo-Macklin had employed for his mysterious conversation with the unknown alien some two years earlier.

Breakthrough. Maybe, he cautioned himself. He now was in possession of a subspace communications frequency. That was all. Frequency plus suspicion did not equal revelation. That would require additional digging.

Months passed before his probing at the company computers yielded a cross-reference for the frequency designation. It was a minuscule entry, one impossible to locate without knowledge of the precise frequency itself.

Anxiously, Chaheel keyed the necessary code information into the computer. It responded efficiently.

Subsequent to the completion of mineralogical survey of NRGC 28-4, contact had been made by the exploration vessel *Pasthinking* with a new sentient race. Initial development classification Class One. No information available on type of government, no information available on population, no information available on number of worlds inhabited by, no information, no information. . . .

At the end of a long file whose entries were universally marked with the designation "no information" were figures giving the coordinates of signal together with estimation of coordinates for origination of broadcast. Somewhere toward the galactic center, Chaheel noted. That was rather more nonspecific than he'd hoped for.

The only solid information the officers and crew of the *Pasthinking* had been able to obtain was the name of the new race, which called itself the Tremovan. Survey followed of NRGC 128-5 and 28-6, whereupon the ship moved on to the star designated in the catalog as NRGC 1046 . . . and moved on, and moved on.

That was the sum of the entry. Coordinates for the beam, estimated coordinates for its source, phonetic rendering of an alien name, and a great deal of dull geology.

Tremovan. Chaheel thought again of the golden-scaled, multiocular alien of Loo-Macklin's conversation. Did this new name and unknown creature match up? Likely, but still not a certainty. There were no remarks in the report of the *Pasthinking* to indicate there was anything remarkable about the strength of the subspace communications beam they'd intercepted. Had the officers of the Nuel monitor ship floating somewhere on the other side of Evenwaith miscalculated its strength? And did that mean he'd spent over two years on this dreadful world for nothing?

He checked, and as expected found no reference in any human scientific journal to a people called the Tremovan. As he'd told the Commander of the monitor ship, it was the right of any discoverer like Loo-Macklin to keep knowledge private for purposes of commerce.

And yet . . . and yet, it had been many years now since the *Pasthinking* had made its contact. Over twenty. A long time to keep knowledge of a new species from the rest of society. What commercial advantages did Loo-Macklin hope to gain by maintaining such secrecy? The scientific community, at least, was entitled to such information. Overdue to receive it, in fact.

He re-checked the literature. The Tremovan might as well not exist. Two years ago, he might have seen Loo-Macklin conversing with one of them. Come to think of it, how long had Kee-yes vain Lewmaklin been cooperating with the Nuel? Certainly not twenty years. Yet he'd never mentioned them to his Nuel associates. Of course, if it was only a matter of private business, a commercial secret of no importance to the Plan of the Families, there was no need to say anything.

But. . . twenty years of secrecy. If indeed the Tremovan and the golden-scaled alien were one and the same.

And if they were, did it mean anything? Chaheel's mind churned. Here was a human whose dealings with the Nuel were unsuspected by his own kind. The depth of such dealings was known only to a few high officials within the Families.

Could an individual like Lewmaklin, who had negotiated and carried out in utter secrecy complex plans made with an alien people, forge a smiliar pact with a third race and keep it secret both from his own kind and from the Nuel? Or worse, might these Tremovan be known to the inner circles of UTW government? Was there something quietly, smoothly developing there that could pose a danger not only to the Plan but to the worlds of the Families?

Nonsense, Chaheel told himself. His thoughts were turning to mush. And yet he dare not let go of this thing until he'd searched it through.

Suppose he reported his suspicions to the Families and none of them turned out to have a basis in fact. His career would not be ruined, but his professional competency would be forever in question. The Si, certainly, would suspect no ill of Lewmaklin and would question everything Chaheel might say. Without *facts,* he was in a hopeless position.

Of course, there was one way to resolve everything, clear away the network of secrecy and concealment. He could request an audience with Lewmaklin and ask him straight out.

Pardon me, Kee-yes, but these mysterious Tremovan . . . who are they, what about your dealings with them these past twenty years, and just how do they fit into your workings for the Families?

Such questions might get him some interesting answers. They might also get him dead. There was still the *lehl,* living in the back of the human's brain. But in the years he'd spent observing Kee-yes vain Lewmaklin Chaheel had come to believe nothing was beyond the human's abilities. He did not see how a *lehl*'s programming could be subverted, but he no longer had the confidence in it his superiors seemed to have.

Lewmaklin had always been cordial to Chaheel, but the psychologist didn't delude himself for a minute into thinking such surface friendship would carry him very far. He knew the man respected his abilities. That was at least partly why Chaheel had been given his choice of positions within Loo-Macklin's commercial empire. But Chaheel knew that if

Lewmaklin thought some plan of his was endangered by the psychologist's actions, he would have his alien employee eliminated.

Chaheel needed something, some proof of the human's intentions if not his actual plans. It had occurred to him that there was a way to push the issue. Dangerous, maybe lethal. It might not work at all. But it was something, and he would not have to confront Loo-Macklin in person.

He'd worked out the details very carefully before he began. First he tendered his resignation, giving as an excuse the fact that he was tired of working on Evenwaith and that his home-longing for the worlds of the Families had swollen to the bursting point. All true. So far.

Calmly he made his reservation on one of the commercial liners that now plied the routes between the UTW and the Family worlds. He packed his belongings and chips, took leave of his friends including a few human coworkers, and prepared to abandon forever his association with Loo-Macklin's company.

On the morning of his departure he detoured to the central computer terminal in the tube office where he'd worked for two years and filed several requests for information about golden-scaled quadrupedal aliens discovered by the exploration ship *Pasthinking* some twenty years ago. He also requested information on any dealings these people, the Tremovan (still a guess on his part) might have had in the subsequent decades with Kees vaan Loo-Macklin, any of his associates or related businesses, or the Board of Operators.

The computer replied exactly as Chaheel Riens expected. No such race discovered, insufficient information for further processing, questions not relative to stored information, and so on. Elaborate methods of disclaimer and negativity.

He did not for a second expect any of his questions to

provoke a reply . . . . from the computer. What he expected as he hurried from the terminal toward the spaceport was that his open inquiries would trigger some kind of alarm circuit within the network and that this would provoke a response of the non-informational variety.

He was rushing for the spaceport as fast as he was able in hopes of avoiding the consequences of that response. If no reaction was forthcoming he would be safe, and wrong. If he was correct he could be in real peril. It was a most difficult situation to be in.

At the port he mingled as best he could with the interracial crowd. In spite of the fact that his attention and senses were directed elsewhere he could not help but notice that not nearly as many humans shied well away from him as had on his initial arrival.

Slowly and as though nothing were going to happen he made his way toward the loading ramp leading to his ship shuttle. Three ships to depart parking orbit within the hour: one direct to Malporant, the Nuel world nearest the UTW. One for Dumarl, a minor industrial-agricultural world in the opposite direction and thence to points inward. One for several small colony planets between Evenwaith and Malporant.

His reservation was for the ship to Malporant direct and he started up that loading ramp. At the top of the ramp, as at the top of the other two, was a conveyor which split in three directions. Only the center was for off-planet shuttle. Chaheel paused and casually extricated a monocular from one pocket. He used it to scan the crowd but that melange of beings and colors did not interest him.

His attention was caught by a cluster of large humans at the far end of the central conveyor strip. They were clad like their supposed fellow travelers, but they were not going on board. They stood there and chatted and waited. Occasionally one would glance down the conveyor. Chaheel saw no sign of sight-enhancing devices. No need for them, no doubt. Not here, in port, with only one entrance per ship.

He saw no sign of weapons but there was no doubt in his mind that each of the large humans, male and female alike, was appropriately armed.

He crossed over to one of the return conveyors, ignoring the puzzled and occasionally hostile stares his action drew. At the split he shifted to the loading ramp on the far right.

When they discovered he was not on the shuttle for the ship to Malporant they would likely check for his presence on the smaller vessel heading for the colonies in between. It might take underoperatives a while to think to check on a vessel headed in the opposite direction, deep into the heart of the UTW. Loo-Macklin could not supervise everything personally, could not be everywhere at once.

Chaheel was traveling under an assumed name. There were enough Nuel moving about the UTW now to confuse his human hosts. They would assume, if and when they finally tracked him down, that he would take passage from Dumarl to Restavon and then back out to the worlds of the Families. He could not hide on as provincial a world as Dumarl.

But Chaheel had no intention of trying to conceal himself on Dumarl until he could reach Restavon. He had no intention of setting cilia on another world unless it was controlled by the Families. To ensure that, he had committed all the personal prestige and reputation that had accrued to him over the past years.

If he had guessed wrongly in this, despite the evidence which had presented itself to him at the spaceport, then Loo-Macklin would not have to worry about his interference any longer. Chaheel's own family would see to that.

If he had guessed correctly . . . he almost wished for something to prove him wrong.

A light-year out from Evenwaith in transit to Dumarl, something extraordinary happened. Though it was an unusual thing to do, the Captain of the liner on which Chaheel was traveling was compelled to order a drop from supralight drive back into normal space.

A Nuel transport vessel materialized alongside the coasting liner while passengers gathered at observation ports to stare and wonder at the unique interruption of their journey. Human ships had tangled with Nuel craft many times in the past, but such incidents always took place in disputed sections of space, around worlds or suns claimed by both governments. An attack this deep in recognized UTW territory was unprecedented. Therefore it likely was not an attack, although none among the travelers could think of another explanation. So they watched and waited and drank and shot up and did whatever else they could think of to calm jangled nerves.

A small shuttle detached itself from the Nuel ship and drifted across to the UTW liner. Soon the word was passed around and the passengers relaxed. There was some mechanical difficulty aboard the Nuel craft. One ship always helps another in the endless ocean of interstellar space. The problem was that a ship in trouble was rarely anywhere near another unless they happened to be traveling in tandem.

What an extraordinary stroke of good luck for the slimeskins, the liner passengers thought, that our ship happened to be so close to theirs when they encountered trouble. Wonder what they're doing in this part of UTW space anyway?

Despite the unwritten code the Captain of the UTW vessel had hesitated before ordering the drop from supralight. Perhaps Loo-Macklin's people had already contacted him and he wondered at the timing of the Nuel ship's problem. He argued with his subofficers, but not stopping for another ship in distress could provoke more trouble than stopping, it was pointed out to him. Reluctantly he gave the order to drop speed.

Human engineers helped the Nuel make some minor repairs to their craft which were less than vital. It was more a matter of missing material than actual damage.

The whole business, of course, was engineered simply to provide an excuse for docking with the UTW liner in order to get Chaheel off. The humans could not prove that the damage to the Nuel ship had been cleverly faked.

From the manner in which the human Captain looked askance at Chaheel's departure, the psychologist assumed that Loo-Macklin's forces had moved faster than he'd believed possible. It was fortunate he'd chosen to cast caution aside and direct this little drama to take place. He could envision the small private army already gathering to greet him at the Dumarl spaceport.

Now they would greet a ship devoid of the passenger they planned to welcome. Loo-Macklin's people planned with commendable speed, but an experienced psychologist could plan faster.

The Captain remonstrated with the Nuel Commander, who replied to every argument and expletive with commendable restraint. Yes, I realize this is unusual. Of course you can lodge a formal protest. No, the family member in question is not being taken off your ship by force, as you can plainly see. No, there are no hidden reasons for this action. Merely coincidence that upon stopping to assist us, we happened to encounter a fellow citizen whose journey we can expedite, and thank you very much, Captain. You have been most cooperative.

There was not much the Captain could do except rave to any who would listen. His own subofficers wondered what all the fuss was over. The Nuel had paid for his passage. If he preferred to interrupt his journey to go off with his own people, why object? The ship was a cleaner place without the slimeskin oozing about anyway.

Besides which the Nuel who came on board the liner were armed. Lightly, it was true, but the human crew was not armed at all. And even if they had been, the Captain could hardly precipitate a violent incident on behalf of an alien passenger who wished to depart of his own free will. So he fumed and broadcast a report toward Dumarl as he watched the Nuel ship wink out of normal space, taking the individual he'd been directed to keep watch on with it.

So it was that Chaheel was finally able to relax in the familiar confines of a family ship. He congratulated himself at having confounded Loo-Macklin's hirelings. The man was not omnipotent, after all. The family starship was driving at high speed for the nearby empty region that lay between UTW and Family dominated space. Interception by a private UTW vessel was now impossible. Interception by a military craft, should Loo-Macklin be able to arrange such a thing, would be impossible within minutes.

The Commander of the vessel was new to Chaheel, and looked very young. Or perhaps I have aged more rapidly than I like to believe, the psychologist mused. She sounded upset and confused. Well, that much was understandable, Chaheel knew.

"I was ordered to intercept the ship you were traveling on and take you off. I was empowered to use force as well as farce if necessary to accomplish it. I would very much like to know why this little shadow-play was so important."

"It is not necessary that you understand and perhaps better

for you if you do not," Chaheel said. He was not in the mood to debate possibilities with this youth. "The information I carry can be disbursed only to representatives of the Council itself."

The Commander seemed to accept that. "It was a lot of trouble and could have precipitated a potentially damaging incident."

"The human vessel was purely commercial," Chaheel reminded her. "There was no possibility of an armed confrontation, as you saw."

"There can be violence without arms."

"It happened too quickly for the humans to react, even had they been so inclined. Can you imagine a group of unarmed humans rioting on behalf of a slimeskin, and one leaving voluntarily at that?"

"The human Captain was very distressed and appeared ready to fight," the Commander argued.

"I'm sure he was, but not by himself. The man was loyal, but starship Captains are not fools. Are they, Commander?"

"I have no more questions," said the Commander with sudden alacrity. "Should you require anything, please let me know."

"Truly, I will do so. Thank you very much, Commander. You and your crew have performed admirably."

The Commander acknowledged the compliment with a gesture of eyes and tentacles and left Chaheel to his thoughts.

They were busy, and pleased. Loo-Macklin had finally made a mistake. By acting quickly Chaheel had not given the humans time to plan. They'd been forced to react with comparable speed and in so reacting had provided Chaheel with the proof he'd been unable to find.

He'd been unable to prove that the mysterious Tremovan

and the golden-scaled alien Loo-Macklin had conversed with were one and the same. More important, he'd been unable to find out why Loo-Macklin had kept knowledge of the Tremovan a personal secret for some twenty years.

In trying to forcibly stop Chaheel, Loo-Macklin's operatives had thereby given him proof that there were more than reasons of commerce for keeping the Tremovan hidden. What those reasons were the psychologist could still only guess at.

But now Loo-Macklin would know that the Council of the Families, if not his own government, was aware of the existence of the Tremovan and his ties to them. It was going to be interesting to see how the human would react.

His questioning of the central computer in Cluria had set off all kinds of alarms. That implied that there was something worth becoming alarmed about.

Loo-Macklin could keep his silence still, of course, and wait to see what happened. What Chaheel intended should happen is that representatives of the Si should question the man under a truth machine. Between that and the *lehl* they would learn what twenty years of secrecy concealed. If it was merely business, why then, that was fine.

If it was something else and Loo-Macklin somehow plotted against the Nuel, then he would achieve his martyrdom earlier than he planned.

Loo-Macklin, or Loo-Macklin's subordinates, had tried to have Chaheel Riens killed, or at least to prevent him from leaving the UTW. To Chaheel that was confirmation enough that something nasty was going on.

He slumped into the warm mudbed, quite pleased with himself and only just realizing how tired he was. Right or wrong, at least he was going to have an answer. And perhaps the war department would gain its much-desired new deepspace transmission beam.

He fell into a deep sleep which was not as undisturbed as he might have wished.

XIV

The reaction to his information was not exactly what he'd expected. If he didn't know that the reply came from a personal representative of the Council of Eight he might have suspected that the individual was somehow in Loo-Macklin's service.

They were resting in a comfortable room which the university repository on Jurunquag had provided for its distinguished psychologist guest. Outside it was dark and wet, a lovely day. Inside, the bright sunshine of disbelief seemed to be burning Chaheel's eyes.

"The Council simply doesn't believe that there is anything sinister behind these revelations and suspicions of yours, Chaheel Riens." The representative seemed bored and anxious to get away from the dour, moody scientist she'd been ordered to report on. She was a handsome female with eyes alive with iridescent green flecks and the flashes of purple light from her flesh were more frequent than most.

Though not mating season, Chaheel found her attractive. He would have been more than just professionally interested in her save for two preventatives: his hormone level would allow nothing beyond visual admiration and she was obviously uninterested in him.

Her attitude was making her rapidly less desirable anyway, even though she was only reporting the opinions of others.

"But don't they see the connection?"

"They see no connection," the representative replied coolly. "Lewmaklin the human remains a vital element in the overall Plan to subvert and control the sphere of worlds dominated by humankind. Perhaps, I was told, the most crucial element. No indication has he given us, truly, that there is any reason for us to doubt his sincerity.

"What you have given us," she went on, forestalling Chaheel's incipient protest, "is a tale founded on personal suspicions, an unhealthy position for a scientist to put himself in. It is known that you personally dislike and mistrust the man."

Chaheel's lids snapped half together. "Are you saying to me that I have been the subject of observation?"

"The Si are a prominent family because they have spent ten thousand years exemplifying the meaning of caution. Yes, you have been watched, Chaheel Riens."

"And exactly what have my watchers decided?"

"That you are no less brilliant than ever, but that you have allowed your obsession with this particular human to cloud your judgments where he is involved. Your obsession has made you valuable because it has compelled you to work hard. Now, however, it has affected your professionalism."

"Truly think they this?"

"Truly. Can you deny it?"

"I am obsessed by nothing and no one. Certainly not a mere human. This Lewmaklin is, as you say, vital to the future plans of the Families. He is an interesting specimen. I would hardly call my interest an obsession, and while I truly suspect the human's motives, because I cannot puzzle out his motivations, I do not hold personal dislike for him."

"That is not the opinion of others." She seemed to soften slightly. "I am not privy to the details of the case, of course.

"We digress. The facts are these, as I am aware of them. Twenty years ago one of this human's exploration vessels contacts an alien race of new type. Two years ago the Commander of your support vessel intercepts and descrambles a communication between an alien and this Lewmaklin. The communication takes place on an unused frequency and via a beam also of new type.

"One: we have no proof the aliens of twenty years ago and those the human talked with two years ago are the same. Two: as long as the *lehl* functions, and periodic checks indicate it is healthy and intact, we have no reason to suspect Lewmaklin's intentions. We have only your word that his minions attempted to harm or restrain you."

"If the Council doubts my word . . ." he began furiously.

"Not your word, truly," she said calmingly, "but your motivation. Much as you doubt this Lewmaklin's motivations. It is not enough, psychologist. Do you not see that?"

"Of sight speaking," Chaheel said tiredly, "doesn't anyone see that if Lewmaklin is running a lucrative and secret trade with these Tremovan—for I *am* convinced they are the golden-scaled aliens of the intercepted communication—that there would be some evidence of ship movement in the region of space marked by the communications beam? And that the human's business empire would show evidence of such trade

255

in the form of large shipments of rare ores or new technology, or something? There is no hint that twenty years of secret commerce with a new race has been taking place!''

"Such trade could be small, difficult to detect signs of, and still quite valuable,'' she argued. "Some trade in rare gems, for example, or in the tiny components of advanced intelligence machines. You would have to destroy expensive and bulky equipment to discover the latter.''

"In twenty years even gems or componentry would make itself known to the marketplace,'' Chaheel shot back.

"Perhaps,'' the representative suggested with infuriating indifference, "he is stockpiling them for saturation release at some still future time.''

"For twenty years? You do not understand this human. No one does. Not even I, who have studied him for years. That is not the manner in which he operates. He does not waste anything, least of all time. Certainly not twenty years.''

"Certain economists would regard such a stockpiling not as a waste of time but as a shrewd business move,'' she told him confidently.

"Is it important enough to try and intercept me to prevent me from telling you all this?''

"Again, we have only your insistence that the humans were attempting to do so. You say that you observed a group of suspicious-looking humans waiting to assault you prior to your departure from Evenwaith. You say that because of this the Captain of the starship on which you were traveling resisted your departure.

"Those humans, even if they were the type you believe, could have been waiting for someone else. They might have been Clurian police watching for a fleeing Evenwaith criminal. As to your starship Captain's reaction, it is only logical that he would be upset to have a booked passenger removed in midspace from his vessel. Particularly if that passenger was a member of an alien and sensitive race."

"Rationalization!" Chaheel was surprised at the violence of his outburst. He was beginning to despair. "None of you sees what this human is up to. None of you want to see. He has made blind cave crawlers of you all!"

"Rationalization," replied the government representative, unperturbed by the psychologist's outburst, "is an excellent defining of your own theories. You have built implication of betrayal out of your own personal suspicions and deductions. Proof you have naught of. I begin to believe," she added grimly, "that you are indeed obsessed with this human. Unhealthy are you, psychologist."

All the resistance, the will to argue, went out of him.

"You don't know of him, what he's capable of. No one does."

"Even admitting truth to all that you have declaimed," she said placatingly, "what would that leave us with? You admit you've no idea what he 'supposedly' works with these Tremovan."

"No," said Chaheel exhaustedly, "I do not."

"He provided you with a position close to his base of operations," she went on, "openly and without concern for what you might discover. You had access to sensitive information. Are those the actions of one with much to hide?"

"He had no reason to suspect that I suspected his intentions," Chaheel replied. "I expressed such misgivings once and he thoroughly disarmed me of them. Besides, by offering me a position near him, he could have his people keep an eye on me."

"You say he disarmed your suspicions. Now you say they returned."

"We must find out what business he has with these

Tremovan! Twenty years, representative. Twenty years of secrecy.''

She rose on her cilia and prepared to depart. "Truly, Chaheel Riens, I would expect less hysteria from one of your learning and experience. Think a moment. Who has given us more reason to doubt his intentions? Lewmaklin . . . or yourself? You have worked long and hard for the Families, Chaheel Riens. Too long and too hard, perhaps. Too much time spent away from home, too much time living among bipeds. Time perhaps to be concerned about yourself and not aliens whose loyalty has been proven many times over.''

She left him, scuttling out through the diaphragm entryway.

Chaheel rested there, surrounded by all the comforts of a family world yet coldly terrified.

It was clear now, oh yes, quite truly clear. They didn't *want* to think that Lewmaklin might be up to something. Didn't *want* to believe the possibility that their valuable ally might be somewhat less loyal than he appeared to be.

As for myself, I am not obsessed. My decisions are reached on the basis of calm examination of the evidence. Admittedly much is based on personal experience, but that is what a psychologist must draw upon when hard facts are lacking. We interpret the subjective as well as the objective. If they insist on ignoring my findings. . . .

Lewmaklin, Lewmaklin. The name haunted . . . no, no, it did not haunt him! Was the representative right? Should he forget all about Kee-yes vain Lewmaklin, forget about secret intentions and deceptions?

He could not do that, any more than he could wipe his mind clean of all thoughts. Lewmaklin had wormed his way so deeply into Nuel society that he now had as many friends among the families as among his own kind.

Very well then, he thought, making a sudden decision. If

the Council is not interested in my opinions then perhaps the Board of Operators on Terra may be. For it was evident that the human government was as ignorant of Lewmaklin's association with these Tremovan as were the Nuel. And if men and Tremovan were locked together in some ploy, then possibly the death of one suspicious psychologist might alert one or two among the Si to probing a little deeper into the records he would carefully leave behind. He prepared himself for a return to the eighty-three worlds of the UTW. . . .

Loo-Macklin walked into the massive bedroom and studied the figure napping on the canopied bed. The circular canopy was an imaginarium, a specially coated metallic cloth sensitive to the thoughts of anyone resting beneath it. It was activated by dreams as well as by conscious imaginings.

At the moment it was filled with stars, unreal constellations, the clusters too close to one another for astronomical veracity. He watched them for awhile, then moved close to the bed and whispered to the supple woman recumbent upon it.

"Tambu. Tambu, wake up."

The woman stirred sleepily, rolled over and stretched. Her tone was languorous. "Ah, lord and master of the big mouth. What is on your mind?"

He turned away from her. "I am about to embark on important work."

She made a face. She believed that in knowing him she had softened him somewhat. That in coming to understand him a little she had made him more human. Not that they'd grown close. The true Him remained always hidden from her and she could not pry it open. But for her, at least, the marriage consummated in jest on Terra had become real. He might be distant, but he was kind.

She was about to learn how little she knew him.

"You woke me up to tell me that?"

"That and one other thing, Tambu. We are separating."

Her inviting smile vanished. She seemed to age a dozen years in the space of a moment. The last star cluster flickered out overhead, leaving the marvelous canopy again only a sheet of silvery metal cloth, cold and empty. Cold and empty as the man hovering near her.

She sat up, propping herself with her hands and swinging her long legs over the side of the bed. "That's not funny, Kees."

"It's not meant to amuse you."

"You're lying to me. Testing me for some reason. You're always testing people, Kees."

"Not you, Tambu. Not this time, anyway."

"Then what the hell are you talking about?"

"We are separating. To go our different ways, proceed individually with our lives."

She shook her head slowly. "I don't. . . what have I done?"

"You've done nothing . . . overtly. This is necessary." His expression was grim. "You're gaining control over me, Tambu. Long ago I vowed I would never, ever permit that. Would never let another being gain the slightest control over my life."

"I've left you alone," she argued. "I never questioned where you went or what you did, even when you were gone months at a time. I've followed your lead in everything because I saw instantly how important it was to you. How have I exerted the slightest control over you? I don't understand."

He continued looking away from her, though whether to spare himself or her she could not tell. "Tambu, I believe I may be falling in love with you."

"Damn." She sat there silently, beneath the unfocused canopy. A desire had come true, a feeble wish neared fulfillment. This grand, unknowable, empty man had warmed to her at last. Because of that it seemed she might lose him.

"Is that so terrible that you can't cope with it? Can't you survive with love as well as without it, Kees?"

He made a curt, angry gesture with one hand, slicing the air. "Love is the most powerful kind of control. I will not permit it, anymore than I would any other form of control."

"Kees, it's not weak to love another."

Now he turned to stare down at her, anguish mixing with determination in those penetrating blue eyes. "It is for me. Why do you think I've avoided children? Because that much love, that much control would ruin me forever."

Her fingers moved aimlessly, entwining, relaxing. "I know that tone of voice. There's nothing I can say to change your mind, is there?"

"No. I'm ... sorry. This is my fault. I ought not to have done this to you."

Her smile was crooked. "Done this to me? You flatter yourself. *I* did this to me. I accepted you, not the other way around. You were a challenge, Kees. I thought I saw something else, something more in you where others see only ruthlessness and ugliness. I guess I was wrong. Or else I failed. Either way, it seems that I'm destined to lose."

"I'll see that you're amply provided for for the rest of your life." This was making him more uncomfortable than he'd believed possible. End it now, he told himself.

She laughed at him. To his very considerable surprise, he discovered that it hurt.

"The marriage seemed advisable at the time," he went on. "Certain important outside elements found it mollifying. And I was curious myself, never having tried it before. I did not expect ... did not expect myself to be so threatened. It frightens me."

"Kees, Kees." She sighed tiredly. "Do you think that makes you unique?"

"That is part of the trouble, Tambu. I *am* unique." He stated it flatly, without pride. "I will not risk all that I have done."

"Of course you won't. Since I can't change your mind, I will abide by your wishes, Kees. Because you see, regardless of how you feel about me, I've come to love you."

He started to comment, decided not to and strode from the room. He did not look back.

Two weeks later the word arrived that Tambu Tabuhan Loo-Macklin had died on Terra, in her new crag house, of a carefully measured overdose of narcophene. Loo-Macklin accepted the information quietly and said nothing further about it to anyone, including Basright, though that sensitive old man noticed a slight slumping of his master's shoulders from that day on.

He's no normal man, the aged assistant thought. He's not Nuel either. He's made himself something else, something that partakes of both races and yet of something more than that. He's a prisoner, a prisoner of himself, and I don't know what he's done it for, or what it is.

But he had a feeling he was soon to find out.

On Twelfth Day Eighth Month Loo-Macklin entertained a visitor. The man who was wheeled into the audience chamber overlooking the ocean was wasted away beyond reach of medication, withered beyond hope of transplant redemption. He breathed only with the assistance of a respirator which forced air into his exhausted lungs. His eyes were glazed and dry.

He dismissed his two nurses and was left alone with Loo-Macklin. They chatted for a while, interrupted only by the rasping, hacking bouts which shook a once vital body.

Then the ancient visitor bid Loo-Macklin come near with a

wave of one crooked, weak finger. Loo-Macklin politely bent over the bed, admiring the tenacity of purpose which had brought this man across the gulf between the worlds simply so that his curiosity might be satisfied.

"A long time have I watched you, Kees vaan Loo-Macklin. One last thing would I ask you."

"If I'm able to answer I will, Counselor Momblent."

"Come closer." Loo-Macklin bent over the thin body and listened intently. He nodded, considered a moment, then whispered a reply.

"Louder. My hearing is not what it used to be, along with the rest of me."

So Loo-Macklin spoke more clearly into the Counselor's ear. Momblent strained to make sense of the words. Then a smile spread across his parchment face and he began to cackle delightedly. The cackle became a cough and the nurses had to be summoned in haste.

Counselor Momblent died six hours later, only partway back to the city. But he died happy.

Making contact was hard. The problem was that Chaheel Riens had no intention of unburdening himself to anyone lower than a personal representative of the Board, if not an actual Boardmember. The Board of Operators was the supreme programmer, the highest human level of UTW government. Trying to gain an audience with one of them was like trying to meet with a member of the Council of Eight, or a Family Matriarch.

He could not settle for anyone of lesser status for fear that an underling might be part of Loo-Macklin's extensive network of personal contacts. Surely the word was out to keep watch for a particular Nuel scientist, though in a sense Chaheel was protected by Loo-Macklin's own high opinion of him. He would think that Chaheel was too intelligent to come back into the UTW. Only a complete idiot would do a fool thing like that.

At least enough Nuel now moved freely through the eighty-three worlds so that Chaheel's mere presence was not cause for comment. His thoughts and remarks might give him away, but not his shape.

Prior to departing for the UTW Chaheel had undergone a change of eye-color. Additional surgery had removed the characteristic wisdom-folds from his abdominal skirt. Loo-Macklin's minions would be searching for a psychologist named Chaheel Riens. With luck they would never look twice at a minor family functionary named Mazael Afar, on loan to the Board of Operators Research Foundation from the Varueq family.

Surgery and fabrication had to be carried out in secret. So powerful was Loo-Macklin's influence among the families that Chaheel didn't doubt they would forcibly restrain him if they knew of his plans.

It was his first trip to Terra, also called Earth, also Gaea, mother world of humanity. It was a measure of how deeply the Nuel had penetrated human society and how extensively shape-prejudice had been overcome that Chaheel was even permitted to travel there.

He was certainly not the first Nuel to visit that blue planet. Clearly the Plan was moving ahead nicely. Praise and glory to the Families . . . and to their allies, like one Kees vaan Loo-Macklin.

Subsequent to arrival Chaheel made certain he was not being followed or watched. Then he initiated inquiries. Who was accessible, whom might he talk with?

Eventually he was able to arrange a meeting with a Programmer of eighth status. Though hardly a member of the

Board of Operators, it was still something of a coup for Chaheel to have secured a meeting with someone so high in the computer hierarchy.

He insisted that the meeting take place in the man's home and not a government office. Oxford Swift found the request, not to mention the insistence, peculiar, but then what else but perversity could you expect from a Nuel? Already he regretted agreeing to the meeting.

His home was a rambling falsewood structure which ambled along the south bank of the Orinoco. Similar residences were strung like beads along both sides of the mighty river, carefully stained to blend into the thick vegetation.

Chaheel arrived by marcar early in the morning. The meeting was to take place before Swift was required at his office. It gave the man an excuse to cut the interview off early should the alien's presence prove disagreeable.

"Greetings, uh, Mazael Afar." The human did not extend a greeting hand to the creature which flowed down the ramp leading into a curved room overlooking the river. "It's nice to meet you," he lied. "I've worked with the Nuel on one or two other occasions, though never before in person.

"I understand you have some questions you want to ask me that involve your projected work for the department?"

Chaheel replied by removing a small instrument from a pocket. The man eyed it curiously as Chaheel turned in a slow circle. Insofar as he could tell this residence was not being monitored. The conversation could proceed without fear of detection.

"My name," he said as he slipped the device back into his pocket, "is not Mazael Afar but Chaheel Riens. I'm a psychologist, not an economic programmer."

Oxford Swift digested this silently. He was of middle age, with long black hair tied back in a single fall. Thin puce suspenders held up blue and white trousers. His wife glanced curiously into the room from the food preparation area, vanished hastily when Chaheel turned a single huge eye on her.

"I expect you have an explanation for this subterfuge," Swift murmured. He thought about the little ceremony with the strange device. "Let's go out on the porch. It's a nice place to chat."

At least this individual is perceptive, Chaheel thought. Perhaps I have made a lucky choice.

"My reasons are of the utmost importance," he told the man. "I was informed that you were more honest than most." The man made a little gesture with his head which Chaheel knew to signify modesty.

"What I have to tell you is possibly vital to both my own people and to mankind. I will tell you truly that my government ignores my pleas. I am hoping that your own will prove more receptive."

"Why come to me?" Swift wanted to know. "Surely not because I have the reputation of being an honest man?"

"Partially that, and because of your position. You have access, albeit limited, to the highest level of UTW government. That is more than I could hope to gain in the short time I believe may remain to us."

"You're afraid of something."

"Yes, truly. I fear the intentions of a man named Kee-yes...," he struggled with the syllables, "Kees vaan Loo-Macklin."

"Loo-Macklin." Swift did not have to think long. "The one who opened commerce with the worlds of the Families?" Chaheel indicated assent. "That's a man many people are probably afraid of. I take it your reasons are more than petty."

"I will tell them to you." He eyed the opposite bank of the river and its string of half-concealed expensive homes uneasily. "Is there still a safer place where we might talk?"

"Come downstairs." Swift looked toward the kitchen. "We're going into the den, honey. Be a few minutes."

The woman looked out of the area. "I have to be at the airport in a couple of hours, but I've time to fix you something if you want it." She hesitated, forced herself to face Chaheel. "Can I prepare anything for you, sir?"

"Thank you, I have already eaten this morning." He allowed for her obvious ignorance. To the Nuel the majority of human food, consisting largely of dead animal parts, was inedible.

They descended a staircase. It required all Chaheel's courage and skill to negotiate the descent. Cilia were not adapted to steps.

Downstairs was barely above river level. A large glass window shaded by the porch they'd been standing on earlier opened onto a screened-in swimming area. Without waiting for an invitation, Chaheel divested himself of his attire and slid gratefully through the arched entrance into the warm water. After a moment's uncertainty, Swift copied him.

Chaheel did not worry about parasites. As for other water-dwellers, he was sure the man had the area screened in for a reason, and stayed carefully within the protected area. Outside, a few piranhas watched his gray bulk hungrily.

"What sort of information is so important that you have to hide it from your own people, Chaheel Riens?" the man asked him.

The psychologist considered how to begin, staring curiously at the human. He'd never seen one in water before. They moved awkwardly but did not sink as he suspected they might. Now that his chance had arrived he was unsure how to proceed. He'd been unable to convince his own kind. How could he convince these bipeds?

This particular human, this Oxford Swift, seemed receptive enough. If he failed with him he would have to try another human, perhaps in a different branch of the government.

Might as well begin, truly, he told himself, and see what happens. "It began, Oxford Swift, some years ago. At that time I was. . . ."

He was interrupted before he could say anything of importance by a noise from above. Both man and Nuel turned in the water to look toward the stairs. The man's wife was standing there, looking disheveled and concerned.

Flanking her and rapidly filing into the den were a considerable number of heavily armed humans. They wore legal uniforms. To Chaheel's surprise they wore complexion armor in addition to their weapons. The thin mylar flashed in the dim light of the den.

Too late, forever too late, he told himself in despair. Loo-Macklin had discovered his return to the UTW, penetrated his carefully concocted disguisings, and tracked him down.

I shall be escorted to some quiet section of wild jungle where I will meet an accidental and carefully engineered death, Chaheel told himself grimly. It should not be too hard to cover up. Nuel psychologist traveling under alias meets unfortunate termination in the wilds of Terra. Or perhaps they would simply report Mazael Afar's death.

After awhile the Science Registry of his home world would wonder what had happened to the brilliant psychologist Chaheel Riens. They would list him as missing. And of course he would be difficult to trace. He'd seen to that himself. I do hope Loo-Macklin appreciates how easy I've made this for him, he thought bitterly.

One eye swiveled to study the metal net barring access to the open river. He was a better swimmer than any human and not burdened by weapons or armor. If he could get over the net. . . .

Alas, the Nuel are not constructed for climbing any more than they are for jumping. He could probably pull himself over the metal mesh, but not quickly enough.

Actually, the only real surprise was that he'd managed to get this far without being discovered. He noted the look of puzzlement and mild fear on the face of his human host. Have a thought for this poor human who might have helped you, he ordered himself.

"They are here for me," he told Oxford Swift.

The leader of the clustered invaders stepped into the water's edge, stared at him. "Are you the psychologist Chaheel Riens?"

"You know that I am as truly as I know the reason for your presence here."

The man seemed surprised.

"I had been expecting you, in fact," Chaheel continued. Now Oxford Swift's momentary fear had given way to bewilderment.

"They just broke in," his wife said from atop the stairs. "I tried to tell them you were in conference, darling, but they just pushed past me."

Oxford Swift was beginning to recover some of his aplomb. He was an eighth-status citizen, after all.

"This is outrageous, whoever you are. Unless you have a warrant for entry I suggest you take your pack of armed monkeys and. . . ."

The officer in charge frowned but held his temper. "My armed monkeys and I are operating on an Interworld Government Priority class Over-A. Until this morning I didn't even know there *was* such a thing, sir.'' He looked back and up at the unhappy Ms. Swift.

"I apologize for all this, ma'am, but you'll know the reason for it soon enough.'' He looked back toward Swift. "You too, sir.'' He turned a puzzled look on Chaheel, who bobbed easily in the water.

"I'm glad that we found you, visitor, but how did you know to expect us?''

"Don't play word-games with me, human,'' snorted Chaheel. "I am a student long-time of your culture, in case they did not tell you that. It's obvious that even though you wear the trappings of officialdom you are here at the direction of Kee-yes vain . . . Kees vaan Loo-Macklin. You are to see that I have an accident before I can unburden myself of certain information. Truly.''

"I don't know what the hell you're raving about, slimeskin,'' said the obviously upset officer. "All I know is that Caracas Intelligence received word you might be in this area. We've been scouring the whole Orinoco Basin trying to locate you. Apparently someone remembered processing your communications with Mr. Swift here,'' he gestured toward the human, who had left the water and was dressing himself, "and so we came straight away to check out the possibility you might be with him.

"We're to escort you to Caracas immediately where you're to be put on a suborbital transport for São Paulo. There's some kind of emergency brewing down there.''

Now it was Chaheel's turn to suffer bewilderment. "You mean you are truly not here by order of Loo-Macklin? You are not to kill me?''

"Hell, no. I don't even know the guy you're babbling about.''

"São Paulo is headquarters for the Board of Operators."

"Our orders have that seal," the officer admitted, "but didn't come from them. The request for your presence was put out by the Nuel Ambassador to Terra."

The officer paused as one of his subordinates whispered to him. He nodded once, looked toward Swift.

"I think you'd better come along too, sir."

"Me?" The Programmer took a step backward. "I haven't done anything. I haven't even been told anything." He looked askance at his alien visitor. Chaheel felt sorry for him. "He came here saying he had some information he wanted to give me. You broke in on us before. . . ."

"Please calm down, sir. It's only procedure. Nothing's going to happen to you."

"But I have work to attend to today, and tomorrow my presence will be required at. . . ."

"They don't tell guys like me much, sir," said the officer, "but from some of the word coming down, there are people high up in the government who think there may not *be* a tomorrow."

Chaheel noted that they brought along the man's mate, too. Outside the house was a small, if decorously dispersed, army. Someone was badly worried about something.

Down the river and then by marcar tube to Caracas. From there via superfast suborbital aircraft to the capital city of São Paulo. Chaheel's mind was spinning as fast as the turbines in the aircraft's engines.

The Nuel Ambassador wanted him, not Loo-Macklin, not the Terran government, not the Board of Operators. If Loo-Macklin was not involved in this business somehow then what did the Ambassador want with Chaheel Riens? And why bring along two ordinary, innocent humans? On the chance they might have heard something? Heard *what*? What was going on?

271

His thoughts were still unsorted when the aircraft touched down on the broad landing plain outside the megalopolis of São Paulo. Ground transport whisked them at dangerous speed into the heart of the immense city. The Board of Operators functioned here, overseeing the decisions of the Master Computer which made critical civic decisions for every one of the eighty-three worlds.

Machine and attendants were housed in a gigantic pyramidal structure overlooking the distant Mato Grosso. By satellite relay the Master Computer was tied to two dozen other massive computing installations scattered across the surface of Terra. The capacity of the two dozen exceeded that of the Master Computer. Their job was to work in unison to compose the questions which were to be put to the Board of Operators.

Somewhere inside the bowels of that tower of knowledge worked the thirty men and women, operating in shifts of ten, who composed the Board of Operators. They were chosen by competitive testing every two years and held their positions for four-year terms. They were the decision makers, or so the population thought of them. Actually they were no more than nurses, or perhaps glorified mechanics, attending to the needs of the Master Computer. But even in this day and age there were those who grew uncomfortable at the thought of having their lives run by a machine, however capable. So responsibility was attributed to the Board, which accepted it as simply another duty.

Chaheel began to grow excited. There were possibilities here. Never mind poor, confused Oxford Swift. Here he might have the chance to corner and unburden himself to a truly important human, perhaps even one of the thirty Operators themselves. If the opportunity presented itself he would certainly seize it, no matter how his armed escort might react.

The pyramid rose three hundred and twenty stories into the subtropical sky. Its crown vanished into the clouds that swirled in off the Atlantic. They entered via a back service entrance so as not to disturb the usual crowds at the main entryways with the sight of armed men.

High speed elevators lifted them to rarified heights. At the two hundred and eightieth floor they slowed and stopped, exiting into an endless room dominated by half a dozen multi-story-high viewscreens. Currently each was filled with complex plottings and mathematical readouts. Humans in multi-hued uniforms wandered busily through the auditorium. There was an air of expectancy as well as confusion among them.

The armed party, which had been shedding personnel step by step, was met by a high officer. He exchanged military gestures with the officer in charge and they conversed for a few minutes. The man and woman were shunted politely but firmly off to one side.

"What's going to happen to us?" Oxford Swift was yelling. "I have to be at work . . . I want to see my attorney! I'm an eighth status . . . !"

No one paid him the least attention. Chaheel still felt sympathy for the biped. He'd been unwittingly drawn into something he did not understand. Well, he had company.

Suddenly, his skirt jouncing impressively as he oozed forward and his exquisite silver and purple tunic being woven by no less than a dozen *el* working at such speed that he appeared to be covered by steadily changing pictures, there was Piark Triquelmuraz, Ambassador to Terra and special envoy to the Board of Operators of the eighty-three worlds of the UTW.

He was overbearingly large, no taller than Chaheel but much wider. The Nuel had a tendency to grow out instead of

273

up. Their cartilagenous internal supports could not handle great height, but did very well with distributed weight. His cilia were invisible beneath the many folds of his abdominal skirt and green-flecked eyes both focused appraisingly on Chaheel.

Two assistants accompanied him; one a Nuel subambassador, the other a human. "Chaheel Riens," Piark huffed importantly.

"First father ambassador," replied Chaheel, executing the greeting one reserves for a much-honored elder. "I would know why I am brought here, truly?"

"Shortly you shall. We have been searching for you for some time, ever since you unexpectedly fled the worlds of the Families. Fortunately, there are not even today all that many of us working within the UTW and most of us are located on the large industrial worlds. Your alias did not slow us, but your surgical alterations did. Providential that you were so near, yet that doubtless cost us time. I did not think to look for you under my skirt."

"I had reason to be there," Chaheel replied tersely. "No reason longer to conceal my purpose. I expect you know of it already?"

"You came here to apprise the human government of possible collusion between Kee-yes vain Lewmaklin the industrialist and an alien race known as the Tremovan."

"I could not have better said it myself, first father ambassador."

"You see, psychologist, though your accusations were disregarded when you made them, they were not completely forgotten. They were properly filed and stored. When the present situation began to develop there were those entrusted with such esoteric information who went asearching for explanations for it. Your report was among the vast volume of material scanned.

"Reluctant conclusions were arrived at. Given our present circumstances, I am instructed to offer you at least a conditional apology plus reinstatement of all honors and privileges ... and to solicit your advice, which we are badly in need of."

"You mean there *is* an alien race called the Tremovan?" Chaheel struggled to readjust his thoughts. He'd come here expecting death, not vindication. "One that Kees vaan Loo-Macklin truly is involved with in other than commercial endeavor?"

"Still we have no proof of the latter," the Ambassador informed him anxiously. "We have proof of nothing save what exists incontrovertibly. That, and your wild tale which is all that correlates with what is happening."

"What *is* happening?" Chaheel demanded to know.

"Come with me." He turned and led Chaheel across the floor of the great room. Of the Swifts there was no sign. The psychologist hoped nothing had happened to them. Little people swept up in great affairs are easily damaged.

A circular depression in the floor was lined with glowing, buzzing consoles. At least two dozen technicians manned the battery of instrumentation. The Ambassador's human assistant leaned over and spoke to one of the techs. The woman nodded, her bony fingers dancing over controls.

Instantly one of the huge viewscreens lost its array of symbols and abstract graphics. In their place showed the darkness of deep space, occasionally interrupted by lines of interference. Lights moved against the darkness. Chaheel suspected that they were ships because the starfield behind them remained constant. The picture varied from fair to barely viewable.

A small craft of unfamiliar design hove into view. Its silhouette was unique. Tiny objects swirled insect-like around it, their purpose unimaginable. They could be cleaning it, or they could form part of the drive system.

A soft yellow-bronze glow emanated from their surfaces.

The Ambassador saw the start of recognition from Chaheel, quickly murmured something to his human assistant who in turn removed a remote communications unit from his waistband and began speaking into it. The assistant's eyes were on Chaheel.

"Something familiar?" the Ambassador whispered, his voice carefully neutral.

"Perhaps. A minor technological device." Chaheel indicated the screen. "I may have seen photic metal like that somewhere before."

"It is involved with the Tremovan?" the Ambassador pressed him.

"Possibly. Possibly very likely. The emission hue is familiar, truly." The vessel moved out of pickup range and once more Chaheel saw only moving lights against the starfield. "There is more than one ship? A secret trade exchange, perhaps, between these Tremovan and Kees vaan Loo-Macklin?"

"Quite an exchange would it be," said the Nuel sub-ambassador, speaking for the first time. She indicated the viewscreen. "Coming there are five hundred of them."

Chaheel thought back to the half-forgotten image of the quadrupedal, golden-scaled alien. "Five hundred Tremovan?"

"No," murmured the Ambassador. He was staring with both eyes at the poor image on the viewscreen. "Five hundred starships. ..."

XV

There was a long pause before the Ambassador continued dryly, "We think it safe to assume that a force of that size is intent on something rather more serious than the opening of general trade. Until your long-buried tale was resurrected there was unrelenting panic both among the Board of Operators here on Terra and among the Council of Eight. That has been reduced to merely relenting panic."

"I am still only offering a guess," Chaheel reminded him. "Commander Quazlet of my former monitoring ship should be here to give his opinion.

"Commander Quazlet," the Ambassador informed the psychologist, "has been dead for two years. So have most of the crew of his ship. Truly, we had little hope of finding you alive either."

"Accident?" Chaheel wondered.

"So it seemed at the time. You are our sole link with a

possibly vital discovery. Tremovan, you called them?" He gestured with a tentacle-tip toward the screen.

"If that's indeed who they are. Recognition of a certain kind of metal is hardly the same as recognition of species."

"And this transmission that you and Quazlet puzzled over was between this human Lewmaklin and one of these Tremovan creatures?"

"So it is called. Furthermore, I have reason to believe that Loo-Macklin has been in contact with these people for more than twenty years."

That shook the Ambassador. He knew only of the intercepted transmission of two years ago. "What gives you reason to believe that, Chaheel Riens?"

So the psychologist related what he knew of the quiet contact between Loo-Macklin's exploration ship and an unknown intelligent race living toward the galactic center.

"Since then I have spent much personal effort attempting to convince those in power that this extraordinarily secretive connection deserves deeper investigation. None would listen to me, none wanted to believe."

The Ambassador was still staring at the towering viewscreen. "I believe you, Chaheel Riens."

"Where are they?" Chaheel grimly studied the cluster of slowly moving lights that indicated the presence of ships.

"Quite a ways from both the eighty-three worlds and the worlds of the Families. We were most fortunate that a human research vessel studying variable stars happened to be near enough to detect unusually strong long-range transmissions."

"I could quote you the frequency for those transmissions," Chaheel murmured. "That would be final proof."

"Then by all means truly do so, psychologist."

Once Chaheel had conveyed the necessary information to the human assistant, who went scurrying off toward the room's nerve center, the Ambassador continued to enlighten Chaheel.

"Transmissions went under mask shortly after they were detected, though surely not in response to such detection. I am sure they were not under mask earlier because whoever is in command of those vessels saw no reason to maintain silence while still so far from the nearest human or Nuel world."

"Speaking of destinations," wondered Chaheel, "toward whose sphere of influence do they run?" He had one eye on the screen and the other on the Ambassador.

"As close as can be determined at such a great distance, they are heading for a point somewhere midtween. That research ship which first detected them has been shadowing them as best as possible. It is not a military craft, but the sensitive detection equipment it normally employs is proving of great use to us."

"There is still time then for either the UTW or Family fleets to mass to counter this threat," Chaheel pointed out. "I see reason only for determination, not panic."

"You see not the entire problem." The Ambassador was anything but confident. "All we have on our side is time, thanks mainly to this fortuitous early interception. Unfortunately, according to the research vessel serving as our eyes and tentacle-tips, the five hundred or so vessels now ascertainable on our screens precede by several days' travel time a much larger force whose strength our brave scientists estimate at some four thousand vessels."

Chaheel tried to imagine a force of interworld ships that large. Though he was a social psychologist, not a military man, the sheer quantity of material and energy involved was intimidating.

"And," the Ambassador added glumly, "for all we can tell

there may be more coming behind those. The instruments on the research ship can probe only so far. Joint military command has decided those scientists cannot be risked for a deeper probe. They constitute our only point of contact with the aliens."

"A sensible decision, at last," Chaheel muttered. "It is time to. . . ." He hesitated and his second eye swung around to focus on the Ambassador. "Pardon, first father ambassador. But you said 'joint military command'?"

"Truly naturally," was the reply. "The only possible way an invading force of such size could be countered is with the full armed might of both the UTW and the worlds of the Families."

He escorted Chaheel to another part of the cavernous chamber and showed him humans and Nuel standing intermixed before another large screen. Bipeds and ciliates conversed busily, some with the aid of interpreters, a few without.

"The plotted approach indicates this alien armada is slightly more inclined to enter the UTW first," he explained. "Hence command has been established here. Members of all military families have been arriving on Terra for days. Ships are being called in from all the family worlds.

"The combined fleets will assemble near a colony world named Larkin which lies somewhat northinner to Masermun, the family world nearest the alien s path. From there the joint force will move out to an intercept point in free space." He paused, added, "We know nothing of these Tremovan's weapons or capabilities beyond the fact they have a unique communications system and the ability to muster a large force. Whatever the odds we shall fight, of course."

"You say we know nothing of the Tremovan's military capabilities," Chaheel said evenly. "That may be so, but there is one human who might have such information."

"Ah." The Ambassador expressed himself wistfully. "The Kee-yes vain Lewmaklin of whom you have spoken. There may be members of the families who sleep through the obvious, but once awakened they can move quickly enough.

"First detection of the aliens was made by the human scientific vessel some three weeks ago. We have spent most of that time trying to locate this Lewmaklin, ever since your profoundly ignored information was rediscovered and recredited.

"He is nowhere to be found. For such a powerful individual to vanish so quickly and utterly bespeaks much fear . . . or careful preplanning. Even his closest aides, who have been interrogated on truth machines, have no idea as to his whereabouts."

Chaheel was thinking furiously. "He rose out of the human underworld many years ago. Is it possible he has run to cover there again?"

"No. Once the nature and magnitude of the emergency was made clear to those humans who dominate that peculiar social structure, they began searching for him just as intensely as the legal authorities. They have no knowledge of his present location either. There was one rumor which had him taking ship to Restavon from Evenwaith with only two close assistants, but the humans have turned Restavon inside out without finding a slimetrail of him."

Chaheel considered this as he turned away from the noisy cluster of milling military personnel, human and Nuel alike, and then gestured with a couple of tentacles back toward the towering screen which still showed the silently advancing cluster of lights.

"I should venture to predict that he is now somewhere between there and here, assuming he has not reached his allies already. There is no telling what important information on human and truly also on family fleet strength and deployment he has already provided to these Tremovan."

"But he is not a military man," the Ambassador objected. "Surely he cannot. . . ."

"Naïveté peers from beneath your skirt, first father." Chaheel's quiet frustration finally overwhelmed his instinctive politeness to one of superior family standing. If they had listened to him in the first place. . . .

"This human has spent most of his long life insinuating his tentacles into every imaginable business and aspect of commerce not only in the human sphere of influence but in that controlled by the Families as well. I would venture to predict that a check of commerce records would reveal that among other dealings companies controlled or directed by him have supplied ship frames to the military as well as armaments, engines, navigation equipment and everything else." He pointed toward the milling human soldiers.

"Likely he possesses as much knowledge of the military as any of those uniformed individuals working with our people, and quite possibly more."

"Then we can do nothing about him," said the Ambassador with admirable resolve. "There are ships out looking for him, but space is very large and a single small vessel can go, if it so wishes, anywhere it desires without the rest of the galaxy noticing its passage. We shall have to confront these Tremovan as best we can. This Lewmaklin will have transmitted all useful information to his alien friends by this time anyway.

"Should by some chance of fortune he be found, however, we will at least have the satisfaction of dealing with him in person. Perhaps the humans can be convinced to turn him over to us. Our plans for him would be more suited to his treachery, his death more intimate." He put all four tentacles around the psychologist.

"Whether we are successful or not the Families and the

humans as well owe you apologies and a debt. Will you remain here to advise us? I will not restrain you if you wish to leave.''

''I've already told you everything I know,'' Chaheel replied, ''about these Tremovan. About Kees vaan Loo-Macklin I can tell you a good deal more, but he seems not so important now.''

''We still do not know for certain if the aliens crewing the approaching vessels are these mysterious Tremovan,'' the subambassador pointed out, ''anymore than we are certain they are warships bent on mischief.''

Both Chaheel and the Ambassador regarded the younger Nuel with compassion. . . .

Two days later the storm descended, and from a totally unexpected source. The Board of Operators had been consulting overtime with the Master Computer on a detailed plan of information dissemination. With the callup of reserves and the vast movement of ships the general population was becoming aware something more than the usual maneuvers was going on, and it would be important to prevent panic. The Families were experiencing similar problems, though not as great. The Nuel were less inclined to mindless reactions.

It was neither military nor civilian sources which released the information to the public, however. Instead, a transmission roared through the ether overriding the general signal employed by the media services of the UTW. It was picked up and rebroadcast by the Nuel back to their own worlds.

Chaheel was wandering through the Operations Center in the Board of Operators building when the subambassador slid close to him and beckoned him anxiously toward a screen. It was a commercial monitor, half an inch thick and far smaller than the gigantic displays which dominated the many-storied chamber. A few technicians had left their positions to gather in front of it. Most of them were human, though a single Orischian stood politely behind the rest, craning its three-foot neck for an over-the-top view.

Around the little screen soldiers and programmers swarmed too and fro, unaware that all their efforts were in the process of being rendered superfluous.

"Where's the Ambassador?" Chaheel asked the sub-ambassador.

"In conference with several members of the Board of Operators and with the first father and first mother recently arrived from Segren-al-faw." He turned an eye on the knot of technicians. "According to one of these bipeds something peculiar is happening."

One of the techs overheard. He spoke a little Nuel and did his best to explain.

"There's been an interruption in normal news information services." He sounded as puzzled as he looked, Chaheel thought. "I didn't think the military and the government planned to release the information about the Tremovan assault for a couple of days yet."

"They have not," the subambassador assured him. He turned an eye on the screen.

A human stood before a globe twice his height. It was a three-dimensional map of this section of the galaxy. He wore simple white coveralls. Chaheel didn't recognize him but apparently several of the humans did. He heard one woman mention the well-known broadcaster's name several times.

". . . extraordinary occurrences," the human was saying. "All are advised to remain calm. There is no reason to panic. We bring you now the realtime feed from Soltech Research Vessel *Tarsis* on station somewhere in space between Restavon and the Galactic Center."

One of the technicians fiddled with the monitor's controls. "Feed's going direct to Restavon," he explained, "then being sent by relay to Terra and the other worlds."

"I thought the *Tarsis* was supposed to keep quiet about all this and let the government handle the formal release," commented another.

"Somebody's going to catch hell," said a third with confidence.

Suddenly the broadcaster and his globe vanished and there was a distorted, fuzzy face visible on the screen. Chaheel let out an inarticulate gurgle. The subambassador and one or two of the humans turned to stare at him, but most kept their attention on the screen.

"Greetings," said the face. It was smiling. Of the billions who must be watching the broadcast, only one knew how false or real that smile was likely to be, and he wasn't human.

"My name is Kees vaan Loo-Macklin. I'm speaking to you realtime delay from the bridge of the Solar Technological Institute's research vessel *Tarsis*."

"Frank, put this on all the screens," another technician mumbled softly. Another man nodded, touched controls. Suddenly the big screens dropped their columns of figures and their complex graphics and that enigmatic face dominated the entire chamber.

Everyone stopped what they were doing to stare at that multiple portrait.

"Behind me," said the steady, measured voice which Chaheel knew so well, "is a viewscreen." He moved to his left. Human technicians came into view, scattered around a miniature of the massive screens which filled the Operators' chamber.

"On that screen in graphic representation is the war fleet of a race none of you has heard of but are soon to be familiar with. They are called the Tremovan. There are approximately four thousand eight hundred and twenty warships in this armada of which the breakdown by type is as follows: fast pursuit vessels, three hundred forty. Heavier medium duty craft with landing capacity, four hundred eighty-six. Light high speed. . . .''

Off to his right Chaheel overheard a Nuel officer whispering in crude terranglo to his human counterpart. ''Are you recording all this, Wan-lee?'' The diminutive human made a sign of assent, turned to check with several coworkers.

Loo-Macklin droned on until he'd finished reading his list, then turned full-faced to the pickup again, blocking out the screen behind him.

''Some twenty years ago,'' he began, ''an exploration vessel employed by one of my companies accidentally made contact with a ship of the Tremovan.'' There was a bright, violet flash and the image on the screen shook and blurred out for a moment. There was only white. The humans railed at their instruments but the reason for the interruption lay elsewhere.

''Excuse that, please,'' said Loo-Macklin, no longer smiling. ''That was caused by a blast from one of the lead Tremovan ships. They've been aware of the *Tarsis'* presence among them but until now had no reason to worry about it. I'll make the reasons for their unconcern clear, if I'm given enough time.''

Light flared in the background again but this time the image held steady. ''As I was saying, all this began some time ago. Further contact revealed that the Tremovan occupy an impressive number of worlds toward Shapely Center. They are a powerful and technologically advanced race and have been expanding for hundreds of years, gobbling up all smaller systems and peoples within their circumfluence.

"They are, however, also extremely conservative and quite reluctant to go to war with any peoples they cannot mass an overwhelming strength of firepower against.

"Those of you within range of my voice will recall, and this may seem odd to my younger listeners, that twenty years ago this portion of the galaxy was combat ground for two other powerful peoples. Circumstance set a virulent mankind and its allied races such as the Orischians and the Athabascans against the worlds dominated by the Families of the Nuel. There was constant fighting, albeit usually on a small scale, between these two burgeoning spheres of influence. Such conflict diverted strength and energy away from expansion in science and other fields.

"My private studies of the Nuel mass mentality indicated that their racial shape-paranoia had made them adept and resourceful politically as well as technologically. It was clear to me how the Tremovan would proceed once they also became aware of these facts. They would ally themselves with the Nuel against humanity and the United Technologic Worlds. Racial antagonism would blind the opportunistic Nuel to the real intent of the Tremovan, who would eventually swallow up the worlds of the Families as well as the UTW.

"The converse was also possible: that the Tremovan would join with mankind against the Nuel." Another explosion shook the image. It went blankwhite again. When the picture finally recovered it was no longer clear and sharp. Loo-Macklin hauled himself into pickup range from the deck where he'd been thrown. The view wavered and broke unpredictably, giving the industrialist a surreal look. His voice was strained when he resumed speaking, whether from tension or injury the watchers could not tell, and he spoke faster.

"It was evident that should I present my knowledge of the Tremovan to either government, human or Nuel, both would scramble to be the first to ally with this new race against a traditional enemy." There were mutterings of dissent from both human and Nuel onlookers.

"Computer crisis mathematics clearly indicated that if either race was to retain any chance of keeping its independence, they would have to combine forces against the Tremovan. Given the Tremovan's adeptness at diplomacy and what I knew of those humans and Nuel then in power, I knew that any contact would kill that chance for independence through cooperation as surely as I'd squash an ant.

"I therefore constructed a dangerous scenario, but the only one which I believed had any chance of success. I have been playing out that scenario for twenty years of my life.

"I warned the Tremovan of the dangers they faced in an attempted takeover of either the UTW or the worlds of the Families. Both were on a constant war footing, impossible to surprise. I persuaded them to allow me enough time to weaken both sides from within, to make them less ready to fight. Perhaps a race like mankind or Nuel would not have agreed to that, but as I said, the Tremovan are excessively cautious. Their successes have reinforced that caution.

"I then promised the Families that in return for commercial considerations and eventual political power I would help them to subvert mankind, reducing the Board of Operators to impotence. I convinced the Board that I was working closely with the Nuel only in order to gain admittance to their Birthing-related industries so that I might slowly poison the minds of their young.

"While thus keeping both sides from engaging in nothing

more damaging than minor incidents, my true purpose was slowly being achieved. Both races were learning to live peacefully with one another, in expectation of eventual conquest of course, but peacefully nonetheless.

"Without realizing it, the past twenty years have seen a passing of the older, more inflexible and antagonistic rulers of both sides. A certain amount of trust has blossomed between human and Nuel, so much so that even as I speak a joint human-Nuel military network is being formed at the Board of Operators building in São Paulo, on Terra. A network which is preparing to direct joint UTW-Family forces against the incoming Tremovan armada.

"I am hoping, praying, and willing to bet," Loo-Macklin continued as another explosion turned the image to jelly, "that given the highly conservative nature of the Tremovan, who have come intending to strike a surprise alliance with one race or the other, that finding a joint force of near equal strength waiting for them, they will immediately turn around and begin the long retreat back toward their own empire. They will expand in other directions and await a more propitious time to grab for this section of space.

"No such chance will occur, however. Having been presented with this threat, the Human-Nuel alliance should only grow stronger." The slight smile widened. "I assure you all that compared to the differences between human and Nuel those between the Tremovan and any other sentient being are shocking and extreme."

He moved aside. The viewscreen behind him had a section missing, damaged during one of the recent near misses, but it still functioned, still displayed the massed vessels of the Tremovan armada.

"There is the threat. I managed to stall the Tremovan for more than twenty years. Their impatience finally outgrew their caution, but it's too late for them now. Reason has come to this part of the galaxy, and it will not be easily duped.

"Unfortunately," he added, "the Tremovan have intercepted and are decoding this message even as I send it. At such close range it is of course impossible to hide a long-range communication even by use of tightbeam. They know how and by whom they have been tricked. The *Tarsis,* however, is no ordinary research vessel and I am hopeful that with a little luck and careful maneuvering it will be possible for us to make. . . ."

There was another bright flare accompanied by a roar of static. The screen went to white briefly, and then, for the first time, to black. You could hear a man breathe at the other end of the immense chamber.

A technician seated in the depression that marked Central Control said into the silence, a silence so deep even those on the upper catwalks could hear him clearly, "Transmission interruption. Signal not restored."

The officer he was addressing himself to nodded. Slowly, activity resumed in the newly christened war room. Nuel and human officers debated with grim determination as graphics on towering screens depicted the almost completed gathering of the joint UTW-Family forces.

Chaheel heard the subambassador murmuring. "A remarkable individual, even for a human being. I was told he'd been made an honorary member of the Si Family. Truly remarkable, think you not?" He got no response, reached out a tentacle and prodded a sensitive spot below Chaheel's mouth. "Think you not?"

"I suppose that's as good a word for what he was as anything," the psychologist responded noncommittally.

"How he fooled us all, human and Nuel alike," the

assistant ambassador murmured, not without admiration. "What was that he was saying about a plan to poison our offspring?"

"A false plan designed to fool human intelligence services, as he said. It involved food additives."

"Spirals within spirals, plans within plans." The sub-ambassador kept one eye focused on the nearest viewscreen as he spoke. "All these years when it was thought he was working on behalf of the Families, and when the humans believed he was working for them, he was in truth risking himself on behalf of both races. Not Nuel to conquer man nor man to conquer Nuel, but so that we might conquer our fears of one another in order to be able to face a greater threat from outside."

The psychologist remained strangely silent. *He is overcome by the loss of one with whom he has been so closely associated for so long*, the subambassador thought compassionately. *Though he was suspicious of this Lewmaklin's motives, one does not devote so much of one's life to studying an individual solely out of fear.*

Does one?

"It also explains," he continued, "why the *lehl* implant has not harmed its host. The *lehl* knew even when certain men or Nuel did not that its host was truly doing nothing against the best interests of the Nuel." His voice turned reverent.

"And truly has he given his own life by revealing these intricate plannings of his to us in such a way that we cannot but believe them. Will I regret forever upon my children that I was never to meet him and that so great a sentient should perish without being able to receive the acclaim due him for his efforts on our behalf."

"Oh truly," said Chaheel so softly the subambassador did

not hear him. Oddly enough he found himself thinking about the human Oxford Swift and his mate. He hoped they had been decently treated and released. What must they be thinking now, if they had been returned to their riverine home? What must he think of Chaheel Riens and his hysterical, accusatory opinions concerning one Kees vaan Loo-Macklin?

The Nuel Ambassador was gliding toward them. "You all saw, you all heard?"

They both made signs of assent.

"I have more news. This Solar Technological Institute ship, the *Tarsis*, departed Restavon several months ago. Before vanishing into deep space it made a short stop at Evenwaith. I think you both truly can guess the name of the passenger it picked up there.

"That is why we were unable to locate Lewmaklin. He has been on this *Tarsis* for some time. He planned everything from the beginning and everything has worked for him." He hesitated, made a multi-tentacular sign of distress. "Everything except his hopes for escape, that is.

"I only wish I had some way of expressing to him the gratitude of the Families. Not only has he enabled us to save ourselves from these marauding and voracious Tremovan, he managed to do it in such a way as to allow us to save ourselves from ourselves. The hate that existed between Nuel and human was ten times more dangerous to our survival than any alien invaders.

"What a kind, benign, self-sacrificing individual this Kee-yes vain Lewmaklin must have been!" He glanced concernedly at the psychologist nearby.

"Why, Chaheel Riens, you look ill!"

XVI

Anxious days followed Loo-Macklin's final broadcast. Chaheel spent his hours roving about the vast structure that was the center of UTW government, marveling at the use of metal where the Nuel would have used organic polymers, enjoying the views of the city, luxuriating in the special quarters which had been prepared for the use of very important Nuel visitors. He was constantly seen in the company of the Nuel Ambassador himself, and so no one commented on his presence in sensitive places or questioned his right to be there.

Somewhere below the hundredth floor was buried the immense computational heart of the United Technic Worlds, the final, inorganic arbiter of all government arguments and decisions. Working in conjunction with it were the much smaller but far more numerous semiorganic computers which helped the intricate networks of families govern the Nuel worlds. Together they mapped strategy and considered options.

Despite Loo-Macklin's revelations, the Tremovan armada continued its steady plunge toward the civilized worlds.

Chaheel was in the vaulted command chamber on the day when both massed fleets were to come within short detection range of one another. Then maneuvering would begin in earnest. The ships would be unable to see each other, even with the aid of powerful telescopes. Even at sublight speed, where physics dictates such fighting must take place, ships remained impossibly far apart until actual combat was joined.

"Truly will we know what our future is to be before this day is over." The Ambassador squatted, staring up at the main viewscreen, which occupied an entire wall and was three stories high.

Currently it showed two clusters of slowly shifting lights: white for the approaching Tremovan and mixed red and green for the united human-Nuel forces.

"Detection, mark," a technician's voice boomed over a speaker. The lights moved, changing position only ponderously on the screen but in reality at unnatural speed. There was a pause.

"Positioning," repeated the human voice. "Phase one," echoed the gurgling voice of a Nuel technician. A longer pause followed. The observers on the floor below the screens stared and waited.

"Still positioning," announced the two voices . . . and then, jubilantly in both languages, "Turning. Enemy forces are turning. Slow wheel through four degrees one half arc of space. They are definitely turning!"

The shift was not immediately perceptible on the huge screen. Parsecs away out in a vast open area of space where suns were thin, out between two arms of the galaxy, the huge Tremovan fleet had begun to turn away from the massed forces confronting it. Several hours passed before the announcers were able to declare it with finality.

"Observers and officers," the twin voices said, "enemy fleet is retiring toward Shapely Center. Exact course unpredictable. It appears they are taking evasive action. Velocity of retreat precludes pursuit."

There was some heated arguing to punctuate the wild cheers and shouts that filled the chamber. Despite the poor chances of overtaking the retreating enemy there were those among both human and Nuel staffs who argued for following, in order to administer a drubbing the Tremovan would not forget.

Fortunately, cooler heads prevailed. It was pointed out that while the conservative Tremovan apparently were not ready for a fight with a powerful and prepared opponent, if attacked they would have no choice *but* to fight. Thus far not a single sentient had died, not a missile or particle beam had been unleashed in anger. No, the Tremovan might elect not to attack, but they would most certainly defend. The outcome of such a battle could not be predicted. A standoff would result in a victory for the Tremovan, for they knew the location of the UTW-Family worlds while human and Nuel remained ignorant of their enemy's home.

In brief, the Master Computer finally declared portentously to the hawks of both races, better not to push your luck.

Chaheel saw the Nuel Ambassador conversing with a member of the Board of Operators, the latter recognizable by his haughty air and gilded coveralls. After a while the first father rejoined Chaheel and the subambassador.

"It has been decided that truly will the joint fleets remain at station until we are absolutely sure these Tremovan are not attempting some intricate circumferencing maneuver. As soon as the linked computation systems of both governments agree, the main forces will be withdrawn. A group of monitoring warships will remain in position and construction will begin immediately on a complex network of automatic surveillance stations. These Tremovan could not surprise us this time. We shall make truly certain they can never do so in the future.''

It had been a momentous day, one of those rare days that appear in bold type in the history books, a day for men and women to speak of fondly in their dotage.

"Verses untold will be composed to celebrate this occasion," said the subambassador. "The Si in particular will gain much in reverence, for this Lewmaklin is claimed as one of their own.''

For the wrong reason, Chaheel wanted to say, then decided it would be tactless.

"Birthings will be dedicated to this moment," agreed the Ambassador. "This is a Day of Names.

"Now work will begin to expand and improve the fleets. Human and Nuel knowledge will be combined to produce the most powerful spacecraft the nothingness has yet experienced. If we have to confront these Tremovan a second time we will be the ones in the position of confident superiority.''

They were strolling toward the exit, intent on an evening meal (Chaheel finding himself famished . . . he'd forgotten to eat) when a human woman came running past them. Her eyes were wild with excitement and she was shouting.

"He's alive!''

She stopped in the middle of the room before anyone; high officer, politician, programmer, human or Nuel thought to question her credentials. Her uniform was not military or operator. But it didn't matter. All that mattered was the message she brought.

"He's alive!''

Word spread rapidly around the vast war room. Finally someone thought to check for confirmation. A communications tech high up on the second catwalk pulled out his earpiece and yelled joyfully down toward the floor.

"It's true. He's alive." He threw the sensitive aural pickup high into the air, not caring what any superior might say. "Kees vaan Loo-Macklin lives!"

An explosion of exhilaration suffused the room with a mental glow the likes of which Chaheel had never felt before. Human and Nuel participated in the celebration with equal enthusiasm. As a trained psychologist he was doomed never to enjoy such outbursts because his brain was too occupied with recording and examining them.

Details of this minor resurrection filtered throughout the chamber as fast as communications was able to decipher them. The special engines which had been built into the *Tarsis* hadn't been quite special enough, or else the Tremovan pursuit craft had been a trifle faster than anticipated. It had been subject to attack (which everyone had seen evidence of during Loo-Macklin's broadcast) and pursuit (which they had not).

The *Tarsis* had managed to evade complete destruction, however, dodging and hiding until the Tremovan encountered the massing Human-Nuel fleet. At that point all alien craft had turned back, including those seeking the *Tarsis*.

By that time the research ship was a near-derelict, pitted and hulled by repeated near-misses, able to crawl through space only at sublight velocities. Under normal circumstances it would have drifted helplessly out of the galactic disk. Circumstances in that section of space were anything but normal by that time, though, not with thousands of warships filling a tiny corner of the firmament.

A Nuel vessel taking up position at its assigned coordinates near the upper curve of the outermost warsphere had fixed on the *Tarsis*' feeble request for help. More than half its crew had been killed. Most, including Loo-Macklin, who'd lost an arm and was near death from loss of blood when rescue finally arrived, had been wounded.

The Nuel surgeons had worked on him for hours, with the assistance via transcom of human surgeons elsewhere in the fleet. Stitching, repairing, and replacement of missing parts which had been shot away required the most delicate work. The Nuel were better at that than their human counterparts.

A prosthetic arm replaced the old one. Blood was analyzed and duplicated (the Nuel are especially facile with fluids). Skin was relaid.

It took a fleet decision to finally make the news known. No officer would take the risk of announcing Loo-Macklin's survival until it was assured.

Both on a personal as well as professional level, Chaheel found the events which followed to be of particular interest. Gratitude, the gratitude of many races, rained down on the man who had deceived the governments of both in order to save them on.

The main body of the conjoined fleet returned to bases, dispersed to active reserve status. An impressive wall of security monitor stations was erected along the edge of the galactic arm facing the stars from whence the Tremovan had emerged.

As it is wont to, the general citizenry soon forgot its proximate Armageddon and returned to living and dying and the plethora of ordinary activities which fill life in between. Business quickly resumed its rapid pace, as did the underworld.

Nuel and human commerce quadrupled in an impressively short time. The informal alliance forced on both governments by the Tremovan threat was now cemented permanently with taxes and tariffs, notices and exchanges, government officials and the gloriously hollow pronouncements of bureaucrats.

The first step in the actual merging of government functions took place when the Family Board of Ten was created. Chosen to sit on this prestigious panel of decision-makers were five Nuel, four humans and one Orischian.

For the post of Arbiter, who would have an eleventh and tie-breaking vote, a human was selected. He tried to refuse the position. Interracial acclaim forced him to accept. The nomination, after all, had been unanimously approved by both the Master Computer, functioning under the aegis of the Board of Operators, and the Nuel Council of Eight.

Months slid by, time infected with a droll normalcy. Nothing was heard of the Tremovan though the watch was maintained vigorously by tireless robotic eyes and ears. Commerce flourished in the heady atmosphere of interworld peace. Nuel and mankind drew ever tighter together.

Despite his protests, Kees vaan Loo-Macklin, one-time bullywot and apprentice vaper, was chosen to a second five-year term as Arbiter. When at last at the healthy but advanced age of eighty-seven he refused to stand for yet another term, his retirement from public life was noted by celebration, the bestowing of great honors, and much acclaim. They would have made his birthday a holiday, save that no one knew when it was, the proposed honoree included.

Chaheel Riens had retired to a mildly rarified position within the Nuel Academy of Mental Sciences. He had reached Nuel late middle-age when he put in his request to see the Great Man. Somewhat to his surprise, it was granted. But then, he thought, Loo-Macklin should have plenty of free time on his tentacles these days.

He had not changed his home. An entire moon had once been offered him for a residence, but he'd chosen to remain on his little island off the coast of Evenwaith's southern continent.

The sea has not changed at all either, Chaheel thought as the marcar whisked him across the marching breakers. At least some things are constant.

The island's security system was somewhat less in evidence than it had been those many years earlier when he'd first visited the sanctuary. He doubted it was less efficient for being less visible. The island still lived, in the sense that traffic in both directions was busy and constant. Although he had "retired" from public life, Loo-Macklin's commercial interests were basically intact and still had to be seen to.

Even the meeting room was basically the same: the furnishings, the sweeping window that overlooked the ocean, the well-polished wood mosaic floor.

Then he was facing Kees vaan Loo-Macklin once again. He was not shocked by the human's appearance. After all, he'd been a familiar figure on the media screens of both the UTW and the worlds of the Families for nearly half a century now.

The massive upper torso seemed to have shrunk slightly. The muscled arms were thinner and the flesh beneath the clothing perceptibly looser. Still, the man moved about energetically, if a little slower than years ago. The artificial skin covering the metal fingers of his artificial left hand and arm reflected slightly more light than the other arm. That was the only thing to hint that his arm was beryllium up to the shoulder.

Loo-Macklin extended a hand to exchange fluids and Chaheel responded. Beyond the signs of surface wasting, the man looked to be in excellent health. His hair was more than half gray now. Another ten years would see it all turned only slightly brighter than a Nuel's skin.

"Do you remember," Chaheel Riens said quietly, "when I last stood before you in this same room, Kees vaan Loo-Macklin?"

"I would think that of the whole race of the Nuel, you at least have the right to call me by my familiar name alone, Chaheel Riens. That was quite some time ago."

"Do you remember it, Kees?"

"Of course I remember." The human's voice had not shrunk in tandem with the body. It remained as sharp and distinctive as ever, as did those half-closed turquoise eyes. Sleepy, always he feigns sleep and disinterest, Chaheel thought.

Loo-Macklin smiled slightly. "As I recall, you had come here to kill me. You left feeling differently about me."

"Truly." Chaheel slid toward the window-wall, squatted and regarded the constant movement of the ocean. "So many webs and deceits had you enveloped yourself with that truth was hidden from both the families and your own kind. And from myself also, of course."

"All those elaborate fabrications were needed, Chaheel. I explained why many years ago. You saw why it was necessary, at the same time as everyone else."

"Did I? Sometimes I wonder."

"As a psychologist it should be more obvious to you than anyone else. Our two races are now bound together in peace and by the strings of mutual alliance in order to counter any threat from outside the UTW or the Family Worlds."

"Truly are they tightly tied together. Many years I've spent considering why."

Another man might have grown exasperated with the psychologist's obstinate refusal to accept the obvious. Not Loo-Macklin.

"Do you deny that the alliance has been of benefit to both peoples?"

Alan Dean Foster

"No. Nor can anyone deny it has been a boon in particular to a single individual named Kees vaan Loo-Macklin."

"Why should I deny it? War is bad for business, despite what a few primitives of both our races might think."

"Oh, business, yes, truly!" Chaheel gurgled with bitter delight. "You have spent several terms as the Arbiter of the Council of Ten, overseeing the course of government for both races. Through this you have been able to cement your position as not only the most powerful and wealthy single entity in this part of the galaxy, but the most respected and honored as well.

"It strikes me more strongly than most because our family oriented government differs from those of human history, Kees. Differed, I suppose I must say. We have never been ruled by the equivalent of what you call emperors and dictators."

"I'm no dictator," insisted Loo-Macklin. "I've never exercised nor demanded absolute power."

"Naturally, insists the egg, not. That would be bad for your public image. For your perceived altruism. The term is perhaps invalid: the reality is not. You have as much power as you choose to exercise."

"Not any more. I retired, gave up the post of Arbiter years ago."

Chaheel enjoyed the throw rug's struggles with his cilia. The material was designed to respond to the weight of human feet and cushion them accordingly. It was having difficulty with the Nuel's hundreds of supporting appendages. He pressed down savagely.

"Reality, Kees. I am something of a student of reality. You say you have no more power, yet I know for a fact that Karamantz, the Nuel first mother who is the current Arbiter,

302

owes her office to the influence of your commercial interests."

"I have no control over Karam. She's a fine administrator. One of your own kind. She makes her own decisions."

"And occasionally calls on you for 'advice'," added Chaheel sarcastically.

Loo-Macklin moved to his desk, sat down behind it and folded his hands across his lower abdomen. He had not developed an abdominal skirt, as some older humans did. Such extra flesh was not a mark of beauty among homo sapiens.

"I'd be wasting my experience and shirking my duty to both races if I selfishly turned down requests for advice. I have a lot of accumulated knowledge to share."

"Oh the proportions of the farce!" Chaheel muttered in Nuel, turning in an irritated circle. End this, Kees. Have yourself declared Emperor of the human-Nuel alliance and dispose of the sham! Think not to fool me, I've watched you for too long. The government makes many decisions you have no say in, because you choose not to. It does nothing you do not approve of. Why hide behind this veil of false modesty? It fits not your character."

"It pleases me," the industrialist said in response to the psychologist's accusing outburst, "to keep out of the public eye."

"Truly? Tell me, Kees, what if I were to take my conclusions, my sociographics and computer results, to the board responsible for monitoring government activities? To the moralists and lovers of freedom?"

"Wouldn't make any difference," Loo-Macklin replied calmly. "Even if they believed you and you roused them to action, they couldn't do anything. You might find a few allies among other social scientists, but the inhabitants of over a hundred worlds have come to think of me as sort of a father

303

figure. I have a hundred and sixty billion friends, Chaheel. I don't think your theoretical course of action would bring you anything but grief.''

"You're still nothing but a professional vaper, a killer," said Chaheel. "You're acknowledged a legal, but that's superficial. That doesn't change what you are inside. You've killed whenever necessary to protect your interests. Now you've murdered the freedom of two races."

"My, the grandiose gesture. It fits not your character," he said mockingly. "On the contrary, human and Nuel have greater freedom now than ever. The freedom to move between the worlds of their neighbors without trailing fear behind them or pushing prejudice before them."

"Tell me, Kees vaan Loo-Macklin, does that mean anything to you? Does that matter, or is it just an incidental by-product of your personal ambitions? It's power and control you've always sought. If you could have accomplished your ends by having human and Nuel war against one another, would you not have incited such a war? The Tremovan forced you to impose peace. It became necessary for 'business,' not necessarily desirable."

"It's true that I did consider the results of war at one time. As you point out, though, it was important to encourage peace and alliance." Something strange, Chaheel thought. Something strange in that always enigmatic smile-expression of his. Missing something important am I?

"This honor you accept, this posture as savior of both races, is all sham. I had your psychological profile correct from the beginning, from that day when you witnessed the Birthing."

"I always thought you did, Chaheel. Worried about you from that same day. 'There,' I recall telling myself, 'is one mighty dangerous and smart Nuel.' ''

"Tell me," said the psychologist, "what would you have done if someone had believed my story of suspicious transactions between you and the Tremovan, had acted on it years before you were ready to betray them and thus force the alliance?"

"Ah, the Tremovan," the industrialist/killer laughed softly. A genuine laugh, I believe, Chaheel thought. Over the years he had become acutely sensitive to human mannerisms.

"Yes. You betrayed them as you threatened to betray us. Three races at one time or another betrayed. The character of our savior!"

"I can't say for certain what I would have done, Chaheel. Had you killed, I suppose."

"I thought as much."

"Nothing personal. I like you, Chaheel Riens."

"I am not flattered. None of your murders are personal. You may have emotions, but they do not involve themselves in those slaughterings you deem necessary."

"Why recriminate based on events passed? Everything worked out as planned. I would truly have missed you. You were the pin around which a great deal pivoted, Chaheel Riens. I needed you alive and suspicious. It was the timing which was important. I wanted your story believed, at the proper moment."

Chaheel's thoughts stumbled, forced him to backpedal mentally. "You . . . you wanted my story believed? Then that means that you wanted. . . ."

"You to have the information. Truly. You remember the voluble computer programmer who first piqued your interest, the one who so kindly supplied you with the proof of your suspicions about me? The one who told you about the additive plot?"

Chaheel Riens searched his memory. "Thomas Lindsay.

305

But there was no additive plot. You had him killed to protect your plan to deceive the human government on the Families behalf."

"Yes, but he was no renegade from my company. He was sent to seek you out and give you that information."

"And still you had him killed."

"It was necessary to maintain the fiction."

"But that means that you wanted me to come to you and try to kill you."

Loo-Macklin nodded. "Then it was necessary that you return to your ship, uncertain of my true motives but persuaded that I was still working on the Families' behalf. Then the message your Commander intercepted arrived and you were compelled to return to Evenwaith and take a position where you could keep watch on me."

"You had the Commander and the others killed."

Loo-Macklin said nothing.

"The information on the Tremovan which I 'discovered'?"

"You have discovered many things, Chaheel Riens. You are persistent."

"All arranged, all planned by you. For why?'

"Isn't that obvious? So that when the Tremovan fleet was detected, your previously ignored accusations and suspicions would lend validity to their presence."

"That means you had to know well in advance when the Tremoven were going to attack. But at the time . . ."

He stopped. Kees vaan Loo-Macklin was laughing. Chaheel had never seen him laugh before and he was fascinated and appalled all at once. No one else had ever seen Loo-Macklin laugh long and hard either. No one ever would again.

"Always the Tremovan! I thought you would have it by now, Chaheel. Your instincts were always correct, always! It was your range which let you down."

"I do not understand, Kees."

"You will. I promise you. I owe you that much. I've used you for too many years. '

He turned and touched several contacts in sequence. A whirring noise filled the huge room as somewhere large motors came to life. Chaheel tensed.

Across the room to his left a panel was sliding upward into the wall. Behind it stood a large, globular body some twelve feet tall. Its golden scales glistened in the light that poured in through the window-wall and multiple black eyes gleamed like cabachons of malevolent onyx. It stepped out into the room, the weight of it clicking against the polished wood floor at the terminus of the carpet.

Chaheel Riens started to back away from that towering, threatening shape. Then something caught his eye and he hesitated. The Tremovan had stopped. It balanced on the floor, utterly motionless, turning neither right nor left and showing no sign of life.

He looked with one eye toward the desk, keeping the other on the massive alien form in case he'd guessed wrongly. Loo-Macklin was still smiling at him.

"Yes, it's a mechanical simulacrum. You've forgotten, a lot of people have forgotten, that both as legal and illegal I was deeply involved with the business of entertainment. It was the foundation of my legal fortune. I'm still heavily tied to the interworld entertainment industry, with interests in nearly every subfield.

"My engineers have become very sophisticated. Nuel bioengineering added a completely new aspect to the business." He gestured at the Tremovan. "This imposing fellow was built by my people thinking it was intended for one of the many amusement parks I operate throughout the eighty-three worlds."

"But surely you didn't plan to kill...." Chaheel cut himself off. How many people had actually seen a Tremovan? There were reports, many reports, but....

I'm the only one, he thought dazedly. I, and those officers on my monitoring ship.

No wonder he had them all killed.

"Then there was no Tremovan ship, no transmission between you and them?"

"Of course not, Chaheel. I was talking to my toy here, sequestered far out in free space where he couldn't be easily traced." He touched contacts and the huge alien form promptly tipped over and executed a headstand. It remained in that position while Chaheel Riens gaped at it.

"What if all these elaborate falsehoods had failed to provoke me properly?" he finally asked, feeling not like an experienced scientist but like a laboratory animal. "What if I'd failed to return to Evenwaith to study your actions, for example, and had returned home instead?"

Loo-Macklin shrugged. "I had backups in mind, other ways and means. But I was counting on your personal drive and intelligence, your intense curiosity, not to mention your suspicions about me and my motives, to drive you to seek further. You didn't disappoint me, Chaheel Riens. The success of the human-Nuel alliance is partly due to your efforts, even if you didn't know what you were doing."

"Used. You have used me truly, Loo-Macklin. My whole life has been toyed with in your service."

"Consider the end results, though. Your part in all this will be made known some day. Your family will be proud of your accomplishments, of the important events of history you played a part in. Even if you were something less than an active participant in planning those accomplishments.

"I used the Nuel. I used my own race. Why shouldn't I use a single brilliant psychologist?"

"Confirmation," Chaheel was muttering. "You needed someone to give confirmation." He switched both eyes to the human. "This Tremovan-thing is false. What of the Tremovan armada?"

"Oh, that," Loo-Macklin said easily. His fingers touched other controls.

The alien resumed its feet and backed up into its cubbyhole. The panel slid down, concealing it once again. Nearby, a screen lowered from the ceiling, came to life. It was vibrant with stars against which distant flecks of bright light moved slowly, traveling from right to left. The outlines of tiny ships slowly became discernible.

"With a little imagination it's not hard to build an alien," he explained. "If you can do that, why not an entire fleet of aliens? When you're talking about detection over distances that are in parsec multiples, it's possible to fool a lot of people in a lot of ways.

"Put a small but hot engine in a multiplier envelope of opaque mylarmer and to long-range detection equipment it will give the appearance of a ship. Expensive, but workable. Four thousand and several odd are much more expensive, equally workable.

"The components were manufactured in separate plants on different worlds. Final assembly took place out in space, by a small crew of very loyal engineers."

"I didn't think you trusted anyone."

"I had holds of one sort or another on every one of them. It's not necessary to voice threats when the subject is already aware of them. That sort of thing's for illegals fond of dramatics."

Chaheel let one eye favor the panel which concealed the Tremovan simulacrum. "So the whole business was truly faked. Fleet and threat as well as the original transmission. There never was a Tremovan attack. There was no reason for human and Nuel fleets to mobilize together."

"Indeed there was," Loo-Macklin shot back. "Unless you can get the military personnel of two groups working together, it doesn't matter how many treaties and professions of friendship two governments concoct." At a touch, the "fleet" of lights vanished from the screen, which promptly slid back up into the ceiling.

"All this sprang from your imagination, then?"

"Every bit of it." The industrialist did not seem particularly proud of having created and carried off the greatest fraud in human history. "Every bit, except for one thing."

"What's that?" Chaheel Riens did not care much anymore.

"There *is* a race called the Tremovan. My ship made the discovery of Tremovan frequencies. Their worlds do lie generally toward Shapely Center. They are completely and utterly dedicated to warring upon their neighbors.

"The difference is that they're not nearly as powerful, yet, as my simulated fleet made them out to be. They're not a danger to either human or Nuel, yet. But they can and likely will become powerful enough to pose such a danger. That's why it was important to establish a UTW-Family alliance *now.* Now both races will be ready to deal with the Tremovan when they break out of the Center. There will be no war with the Tremovan for some time. When there is, the alliance will be capable of dealing with it."

Chaheel was desperately trying to keep up, to keep truth and falsehood separated. "But when contact is finally made, the Tremovan will be treated as enemies because of this supposed earlier attack, when in fact they've made no such attack.''

"The computer analysis is clear, Chaheel. The Tremovan are incurably warlike. It was necessary to prepare human and Nuel for a war that's inevitable. There could be no peace. But they are not suicidal. If defeated, they can be absorbed into the community of civilized worlds. Commerce will break down their love of combat. But they will have to be defeated first.

"In order to assure success, it may be necessary for the alliance to attack them first. The Board of Operators and the Council of Eight would never have ordered a pre-emptive attack. The new Council of Ten will be less hesitant, since they have already been 'attacked.' ''

"Of course, they can always turn to you if their consciences trouble them."

Loo-Macklin did not bother to try to deny that. "It will be better for the Tremovan, just as the alliance I created by duplicity benefits both mankind and Nuel."

"It will also truly be better for Kees vaan Loo-Macklin's personal interests. So you will place the Tremovan, who are not even aware of what you've already done to them, under your domination as well. They'll never know how it happened to them, nor why."

Loo-Macklin said nothing.

"Tell me something, man," wondered Chaheel aloud. "When your *Tarsis* was found drifting and helpless after having been pursued by the nonexistent Tremovan fleet, half your crew was found dead or badly wounded." He gestured with a tentacle. "You yourself had lost an arm."

"My crew thought the attack, the fleet, was all quite real. I couldn't trust the secret to them as well as to the engineers who

311

assembled the false Tremovan ships. They had to act as if the attack was in earnest. I made provisions for a private warship, suitably disguised, to attack us. The explosions everyone saw while I was delivering my warning were real."

"And how many of your own, trusting people did die?"

"No more than was necessary."

"And your arm?"

"I was in a heavily shielded part of the *Tarsis*. The attacking warship had a schematic and did their best to avoid damaging that section. Verisimilitude was vital. I had one of my own people shoot me several times, carefully, while I was sufficiently narcotized to drown most of the pain. My wounds were as real as those received by the rest of the crew." He looked thoughtful. "An old man did that, on my orders. He died soon afterwards. Of natural causes. His name was Nairn Basright and he was the closest thing to a friend I ever had. Funny. I once offered him the friendship I denied everyone else, and he declined it." His thoughts returned from the place where they'd been lingering. He flexed his left hand.

"The artificial one works well enough. I don't really miss the original."

"Monster. I truly should have slain you when I had the chance. I could do so now."

"I think not, Chaheel Riens. We are both older and slower and you could not get to me in time now as you might have those many years ago. It's true I've been responsible for the deaths of many people. I killed my first man when I was twenty-two. I neither enjoyed nor disliked it. It was simply something which had to be done. There have been many deaths since, none of which I enjoyed, nor disliked. All were necessary."

"One such death to serve personal interests is too many," Chaheel said, rejecting the argument. He moved close, not to kill but to try and learn. "Why, Kees vaan Loo-Macklin? Not to save humankind and Nuel from each other, surely."

For the first time, for the last, Chaheel Riens saw something no one else had seen before or ever would again. He saw Kees vaan Loo-Macklin, effective emperor of the worlds of the Families, of the eighty-three worlds of the UTW and perhaps soon of the Tremovan as well, confused and uncertain.

"I think I know why, but even I'm really not positive. What motivates a man, truly? Greed? I care little for money, only for the convenience it bestows. Power? I told the truth when I said I never sought it. Ego? You will not believe me, but I have less ego than most men. Or Nuel.

"I've acted and reacted as I have all my life because something has driven me to do so. I remember when I was very young most of all. I did not have what you would call a..." he hesitated, "...a pleasant childhood. I was abandoned by a parent who was not ignorant. That I could have accepted. But she was intelligent, and wealthy. I was simply...an encumbrance on her life style. An object in the way, to be disposed of.

"Subsequent to that I was shunted from place to place. My physical appearance was abhorrent to most people. You should sympathize with that." Chaheel said nothing, merely listened intently.

"What remains with me, what drove me from my earliest conscious years, was no quest for power, nor for revenge. Those are strong feelings, Chaheel Riens. I lost the ability to feel true emotions before I was seven. It was an emptiness inside me, a feeling of utter helplessness, of having nothing to say about my own destiny. I was treated like an object. So I turned myself into an object. My reactions were purely instinctive, physical.

"I resolved to do two things: to survive, and to ensure that no one, *no one*, could ever control my life again except myself.''

He went silent. It was quiet in the vast chamber for a long time. When Chaheel Riens spoke again it was without the anger he'd felt on entering. This man, this emperor, this unbelievably powerful individual, deserved his pity, not his hate. He'd lived without family. To a Nuel, no greater crime can be perpetrated on the young.

No wonder Kees vaan Loo-Macklin had evolved as he had. But the psychologist was wrong about one thing. The man was not warped inside. He was simply numb.

''So you've spent your whole life,'' he said softly, ''spent the lives of others, manipulated individuals and worlds and entire races, to ensure that only you would be in control of your destiny. I sympathize truly, Kees. Most truly. But I do not, cannot approve what you have done.

''I am not even certain I believe what you say of these Tremovan's 'incurable' tendencies to war. Why should I? Why should anyone believe anything you say, knowing that whatever you do and say is ultimately because you are acting to protect yourself?

''Where will it cease, Kees? How long must you drag all of civilization along in your wake so that it will not make you feel helpless again? Must you control it in order to ensure that it cannot control you?''

Loo-Macklin's expression was twisted. ''I don't know, Chaheel Riens. I've tried to change what I am. I cannot. I don't know how. I am what my life has made of me. Wait until I die.''

''Is that supposed to mollify me? Not that that concerns you. What happens then? You are the glue that binds this still young alliance together, this new government you've imposed upon men and Nuel.''

"I'm sorry, but that doesn't concern me. I'll be finished with it. It will be left to those who live after me to keep it intact."

"No one else has the ability to do that, not to mention the will or the drive." Chaheel made a gesture of disgust. "It will all fall apart, this grand, awkward alliance of yours. There will ensue chaos, dissolution, war and worse."

"I don't think so, Chaheel. I think that what I've built for my own needs will hang together. I believe there are enough individuals of purpose and intelligence to manage it. You, for example."

The psychologist emitted a grunt of surprise.

"Yes, you. I'd like you to . . . I offered you a job once, a long time ago. It was not a real job. You performed services for me you were unaware of. This time I mean to make use of you honestly. I am capable of that, you know. You could be important to our new government."

" 'Our' government," the Nuel murmured sardonically.

"It will be that in truth as well as in name when I am dead. And you will outlive me by many years. Look at the offer dispassionately, Chaheel Riens. Look at it as a scientist. If you are convinced I have done wrong, here is your chance to correct me. The new alliance, the new peace, is it such a bad thing?"

And Chaheel had to admit that it was true. Peace was better than war, no matter the motivation behind its establishing. Commerce was prospering, Nuel and humans and Orischians and Athabascans and all the other sentient races who were part of the new alliance were safer and happier than they'd been since the beginning of interstellar contact between sensitives.

As for the Tremovan, who knew what they were really like or how they might react to real contact with the alliance? That was something for the future, a future which Kees vaan Loo-Macklin was preparing a hundred sixty billion beings for whether they liked it or not.

And yet . . . and yet . . . whatever he did, however grandly he lied and cheated and falsified to serve his own private demon, the end results always seemed to benefit the majority of intelligent peoples.

Loo-Macklin was coming around the desk toward him now, turquoise eyes wide open, demanding a response, a reply. He extended a massive hand dry with the wrinkles of age and smiled that peculiar, impenetrable smile.

"I stand openly before you, Chaheel Riens, accused by you of being a murderer of both men and Nuel, a traitor to two races, of using and manipulating individuals to serve only my own desires, of adjusting the future of all to sate my own selfish needs. I deny none of that. Will you therefore come and work for me? I have need of your good advice and your special intelligence. For you see, Chaheel Riens, you are much like me save for one thing. You are moral.

"Knowing all this, can you do anything *but* come to work alongside me?"

Liar most profound, Chaheel thought. User without compassion. Murderer of innocent multitudes.

Hail the savior?

"All that you say is truth, Kees vaan Loo-Macklin. You are the most monstrously evil, self-centered, cold and uncaring individual your race has likely ever produced." He extended a pair of glistening, slime-coated tentacles and exchanged liquid with the man.

"Naturally I will help you in any way I can."

To Everyone Who Loved
The Lord Of The Rings —
Welcome to Atlanton Earth!
THE CIRCLE OF LIGHT SERIES
by Niel Hancock

Enter the magical twilight world of Atlanton Earth, where the titanic struggle between two warring sisters, the Queens of Darkness and of Light, creates deadly enmities as well as deep loyalties, and evokes unexpected heroism among the beings who fight together against the evil that threatens to overrun them all. You will meet the mighty magician Greyfax Grimwald and his allies: Bear, Otter, and Broco the Dwarf, whose devotion to a common cause overcomes their individual differences and welds them into heroic fellowship.

The Starfishers Trilogy

___**SHADOWLINE**
by Glen Cook   *(E30-578, $2.95*
The first book in The Starfishers Trilogy starts with the ver
detta in space. They were the greatest fighting fleet in th
universe—battling betrayal and revenge, and the terribl
fate that awaited them on the edge of SHADOWLINE.

___**STARFISHERS**
by Glen Cook   *(E30-155, $2.95*
The second volume in this trilogy, *Starfishers* is scienc
fiction the way you like it. They were creatures of fusio
energy, ancient, huge, intelligent, drifting in herds on th
edge of the galaxy, producing their ambergris, the sub
stance, precious to man and the man-like Sangaree alike

___**STARS' END**
by Glen Cook   *(E30-156, $2.95*
The final book: The fortress on the edge of the galaxy wa
called Stars' End, a planet built for death—but by whom
It lay on the outermost arm of the Milky Way, silent
cloaked in mystery, self-contained and controlled...unti
...a sinister enemy approaches from the depths of th
galaxy, in hordes as large as a solar system. And its missio
is only to kill...

Books By
KARL EDWARD WAGNER

__**BLOODSTONE**   *(E30-629, $2.95)*
Half god, half mortal, Kane unearths a dreadful relic of an
ancient civilization that will give him dominion over the
world.

__**DEATH ANGEL'S SHADOW**   *(E30-749, $2.95, U.S.A.)*
                                              (E30-750, $3.75, Canada)
Three tales of Kane, a mystic swordsman, who conquered
the most brutal forces ever summoned against a single
man—until he entered the web of the vampire.

__**DARKNESS WEAVES**   *(E30-653, $2.95, U.S.A.)*
                                              (E30-668, $3.75, Canada)
Once Efrel was the beautiful consort of a king. Now she is a
hideous creature who lives only for revenge. She has allies
to aid her, but only Kane, the mystic swordsman can rally
her forces for battle. Only he can deliver the vengeance she
has devised in her knowledge of black magic and her power
to unleash the demons of the deep.

__**IN A LONELY PLACE**   *(E30-534, $2.95)*
A collection of the superb contemporary horror stories by
this well-known science fantasy and horror author. This is
the author's first new work in five years!

GREAT SCIENCE FICTION
From WARNER...